ALL THIS TIME

Also by these authors
FIVE FEET APART

ALL THIS TIME

Mikki Daughtry and Rachael Lippincott

SIMON & SCHUSTER BFYR

NEW YORK LONDON TORONTO SYDNEY NEW DELHI

SIMON & SCHUSTER BFYR

An imprint of Simon & Schuster Children's Publishing Division
1230 Avenue of the Americas, New York, New York 10020

SIMON & SCHUSTER BFYR is a trademark of Simon & Schuster, Inc.
For information about special discounts for bulk purchases, please contact Simon &
Schuster Special Sales at 1-866-506-1949 or business@simonandschuster.com.
The Simon & Schuster Speakers Bureau can bring authors to your live event.
For more information or to book an event, contact the Simon & Schuster
Speakers Bureau at 1-866-248-3049 or visit our website at www.simonspeakers.com.
Book design by Lizzy Bromley
The text for this book was set in Bell MT Std.
Manufactured in the United States of America
First Edition
2 4 6 8 10 9 7 5 3 1
Library of Congress Cataloging-in-Publication Data
Names: Daughtry, Mikki, author. | Lippincott, Rachael, author.
Title: All this time / Mikki Daughtry and Rachael Lippincott.
Description: First edition. | New York City : Simon & Schuster Books for Young Readers,
[2020] | Audience: Ages 12 Up. | Audience: Grades 7-9. | Summary: After a traumatic
accident, Kyle feels lost until he meets Marley, who seems like the girl of his dreams,
but as they grow closer he fears he is headed for another crash.
Identifiers: LCCN 2020012330 | ISBN 9781534466340 (hardcover) |
ISBN 9781534466364 (ebook)
Subjects: CYAC: Grief—Fiction. | Brain—Wounds and injuries—Fiction. | Friendship—
Fiction. | Dating (Social customs)—Fiction. | Single-parent families—Fiction. |
Mothers and sons—Fiction.
Classification: LCC PZ7.1.D335812 All 2020 | DDC [Fic]—dc23
LC record available at https://lccn.loc.gov/2020012330

For anyone who's ever had a Marley.
Never let her go.
—M. D.

For Mikki
—R. L.

ALL THIS TIME

1

The charm bracelet feels heavy in my palm. I've looked at it about a thousand times, but I check it again because I know it has to be perfect, able to fix whatever needs fixing. I considered daintier, more delicate bracelets like Kimberly usually wears, but something about this one spoke to me, its silver links solid and sturdy, just like our relationship . . . most of the time.

A few months ago, when I ordered the bracelet, it was supposed to be a present to celebrate our graduation, not an I'm-sorry-let's-make-up gift, but Kimberly's been quiet lately. Distant. Just like she always gets when we're fighting.

Even though, as far as I know, we *aren't* fighting, so I'm not even sure what this should be apologizing for.

I let out a long sigh and look up at my reflection in the hotel bathroom mirror, double-checking that the bathroom stalls are empty. My eyebrows knit together as I run my fingers through my unruly brown hair, trying to smooth it down in the way Kim likes. After a couple of failed attempts, my hair and I give up and I focus my attention on the bracelet one last time.

The sparkling silver charms rattle together as I inspect it, the noise mixing with the muffled sounds of my high school graduation party on the other side of the door. Maybe when she sees it, she'll finally tell me what's wrong.

Or, who knows. Maybe she'll just kiss me and tell me she loves me and the problem has nothing to do with me in the first place.

I lean closer to examine the six tiny charms, one for each year we've been together. I lucked out big-time when I found someone on Etsy to help me design them, since I have absolutely no artistic talent whatsoever. This is more than just a bracelet now. It's our life together.

My thumb gently traces the pieces of our history, a few of the charms winking at me as they catch the pendant lights.

A set of teal-and-white enamel cheerleading pom-poms, nearly identical to the pair Kimberly held as cheer captain the night I asked her to officially be my girlfriend.

A little gold champagne glass, tiny diamond bubbles tracing the rim, a reminder of my elaborate promposal a few months ago. I'd snuck a bottle of champagne from my mom's cabinet to surprise her. My mom grounded me for all eternity, but it was worth it just to see Kimberly's eyes light up when I popped the cork.

I pause on the most important charm, resting in the exact center of the bracelet. A silver diary, complete with a real clasp.

Back in middle school, we were studying in the kitchen at her house when she ran upstairs to go to the bathroom. I snuck her pink diary out of her backpack and wrote "I ❤ U" on the first three blank pages.

She cried when she found it, tears turning to accusations.

"You read all my secrets?" she shouted, pointing her finger at me with one hand and clutching the thing tight to her chest with the other.

"No," I said, and swiveled my stool toward her. "I just thought it'd be like . . . I don't know. Romantic."

And then she proceeded to launch herself at me. I let her wrestle me to the floor, because it was thrilling to have that beautiful face so close to mine, her annoyance finally dying down as our eyes locked.

"It was," she said, and then her lips tentatively met mine.

Our first kiss. My first kiss.

Carefully, I open the tiny charm and turn its delicate silver pages, three in total, spelling out "I ❤ U." We'll probably always have our little arguments, but we'll always love each other.

I smile at the empty links of the bracelet, just waiting to be filled with more life and more of the memories we'll build together. One for each year we'll spend at UCLA. And after that I'll get her a new one to fill too.

The bathroom door flies open, smacking loudly into the stopper poking out of the wall. I quickly drop the bracelet back into its velvet box, and the charms clatter together as a group of guys from the basketball team bound inside. There's a chorus of "Kyle, what's up, man?" and "Class of 2020, baby!" I grin at all of them and slide the box back into the pocket of my suit jacket. As I do, my fingertips graze the flask of Jack Daniel's tucked into my waistband, step one in my plan to convince my two best friends to ditch this school-sponsored graduation party to go to our spot at the pond and actually celebrate.

But first . . . I have to give her this bracelet. I head out the bathroom door, the short hallway giving way to the packed ballroom of this super-bougie hotel.

I step inside and pass under a sea of Ambrose High teal and white balloons, several of which have already broken free and are rolling along the high vaulted ceilings. In the center of the room are hundreds of streamers trailing from a huge banner reading CONGRATULATIONS, GRADUATES!

The noise moves over me in a wave, the excited WE MADE IT! energy pouring out of every corner. I get it. After this last year, I'm beyond ready to move on from here.

I make my way through a bunch of the most random clusters of people. One walk across that stage seems to have broken down all the shit that mattered so much this morning. What sport you played. What grades you got. Who did or *didn't* ask you to prom. Wondering why Mr. Louis had it out for you all semester.

Suddenly Lucy Williams, the class president, is flirting with Mike Dillon, the stoner who repeated the tenth grade twice, while the math decathlon captains are working together with two of my dudes from the offensive line to swipe beer from behind the bar.

Tonight we are all the same.

"Hey, Kyle." A hand plants a little too firmly on my bad shoulder. I try not to wince as I turn to see Matt Paulson, the nicest guy on the whole planet, which makes me feel like a dick for hating him. "Oh, sorry," he says when he registers the shoulder his hand landed on, and he quickly yanks it away. "Did you hear I'm heading to Boston College to play football in the fall?"

"Uh, yeah," I say, trying to swallow the familiar wave of jealousy that comes bubbling up. *It's not his fault*, I remind myself. "Congrats, man."

"Listen, if you hadn't led the team the way you did for the start of the season, I wouldn't have even been a blip on their radar. You were one hell of a quarterback. I wouldn't have gotten a football scholarship if it wasn't for everything you taught me," he says, unintentionally rubbing salt in a still-gaping wound. "But I'm sorry it happened—"

"It's all good," I interrupt him, then extend my hand so I don't seem like an ass. "Good luck next year." I release the handshake and turn on my heel to continue my search, my feet moving fast to put as much distance between us as possible. There's only one person I want to see right now.

I pause by the bar and crane my neck to scan the crowd for Kim, my eyes jumping from person to person with no success.

"Hors d'oeuvre?" a voice asks from next to me.

I look over to see a man holding out a tray of appetizers to me, lumpy shapes on a crisp white plate. He gives me an artificial smile that screams, *I can't wait to get off in two hours*.

I catch sight of the Owl Creek logo on his shirt, the only

restaurant remotely near here to be featured on the Food Network for their "hip and modern cuisine."

Apparently, even Gordon Ramsay had a meal there and couldn't find anything to complain about.

"Don't mind if I do," I say, flashing him a quick grin. I grab one, then pop the whole thing into my mouth before he shuffles off to continue his rounds.

Instant regret.

Is this shrimp? Rubber? Why the *hell* is it so chewy? And why does it taste like old ham?

Clearly, Gordon didn't get a taste of whatever lumpy meat this is.

I look both ways before quickly ducking to spit it out into the black cocktail napkin the server gave me, but a sudden flash from next to me makes me jump.

I toss up my nonshrimp hand, blinded, the black dots in my vision slowly fading and giving way to warm brown eyes and high cheekbones identical to mine. She's in her favorite white floral dress, and I can see her big grin peeking out from behind her phone.

"Mom, don't—" I start to say, but she taps the photo button again, and another ray of light mauls my eyeballs.

"You know, if you're going to take embarrassing photos of me, you can at least turn the flash off. You don't have to blind a guy."

"Oh, the girls on the 'gram will *love* this," she says, chuckling wickedly, her eyes narrowing as she taps away on her screen.

"Mom. Don't post that," I say as I lunge at her. I pull her into a half hug in an attempt to distract her while I try to wrestle the phone out of her grip. As I do, I see the shot, a look of horror on my face, eyes half-closed, rubber shrimp clinging to my tongue as it makes its way into the cocktail napkin.

There's no way in hell I'm letting the "girls on the 'gram" see this. Or *anyone*, for that matter.

Kim would never let me live it down.

Her grip loosens slightly as she leans into the hug, and I pry the phone away to delete the picture. "You can forget it, lady."

"Fine," she says, faking a scowl, the soft pink of her lipstick emphasizing her turned-down lips. "Break your old mother's heart. I can't have anything."

I laugh, planting a kiss on her cheek and sweeping her up into a real hug this time, careful to angle my body so she doesn't feel the flask tucked into my waistband. "You've got me, don't you?"

She lets out a dramatic sigh. "I guess you'll do." Her voice is muffled against the thick fabric of my suit jacket. "Hey," she says, pulling away and grinning. "Why are you on your own? You give her the bracelet yet?"

My heart pounds, just like it used to before a football game. "I'm waiting for the right moment," I say as I give the room a quick scan. "You seen her?"

"She was with Sam, by the terrace, a few minutes ago," she says, nodding to the right, toward the floor-to-ceiling windows separating us from the oversize-stone terrace that overlooks the hotel courtyard.

She reaches out to gently adjust the knot of my tie, a small smile tugging at the corner of her lips. It's a Windsor, not that I'm pretentious enough to know any other way to tie a tie, but she spent the morning of my seventh-grade formal learning the knot *just* so she could teach me how to do it. It was the first dance I went to with Kim.

Mom's been there through everything.

"You really think she'll like it?" I ask. I felt so sure when I ordered it, but now . . .

"Absolutely." She gently pats my face. Reassured, I give her the phone back. Total mistake.

She grabs it and quickly snaps two more pictures, still with a flash that is now popping behind my eyes. I attempt a glare, but the crow's-feet around her eyes wrinkle as she grins innocently at me, and my frown cracks right down the middle. Nothing will bother me tonight, not even my mom's incessant documentation of my life.

So I cheese it up, posing for one last photo, and once she's satisfied, I'm off to finally find Kim. I chuck the wadded-up cocktail napkin into a trash can as I make my way toward the terrace, where the sky is dark and ominous on the other side of the glass.

It usually doesn't take me long to find her.

She's always had this fire, this magnetism that pulls people into her orbit. At school, I usually have to wade through a crowd of people just to get to her, so I keep my eyes peeled for the largest group and a flash of that particular shade of blond that manages to hold whatever light is in the room.

It's been like that for as long as I can remember, the color the same as it was when we fought over the last swing on the playground in third grade.

I push into the crowd, and people part to let me through, smiles and high fives coming from every direction.

"Gonna miss those articles in the sports section next year, Lafferty," Mr. Butler, my journalism teacher, says, giving me a pat on the back as I pass by him. Another reminder of all that time sitting on the bench, writing about the games instead of actually playing in them.

Where *is* she?

The disco ball overhead sends out glimmers of sparkling light, making it hard to see much of anything. I'm about to pull out my phone and fire off a text when . . .

There.

Her blond hair peeks past Sam's broad shoulders as she shifts her weight ever so slightly to her left hip, her silk dress hugging her sides. She looks incredible tonight, long hair flowing around her shoulders, blue eyes bright and open, lips shiny with gloss.

But as I get closer, I see her face is serious, the familiar wrinkle in her forehead forming as she talks, like it always does when something is up. It's a look I saw a week ago at prom and this afternoon when we were taking graduation pictures, but whenever I ask, it all gets smoothed away with a wave of her hand.

I look from her to Sam, watching as he nervously runs his fingers through his dark hair.

And that's when I realize they must be talking about UCLA. The tension melts from my shoulders.

Kim and I have already committed, but Sam was wait-listed. Sam and I always dreamed of playing football together at UCLA, but after homecoming that was all over, thanks to me and my injury. I let the both of us down. After I was sidelined, Sam dropped so many passes and missed so many blocks, he was riding the bench almost as much as I was. When all of his football prospects dried up, his grades took a sharp dip right alongside his football career. So Kim's been helping him send in some essays and updated supplements that'll hopefully tip the scale in his favor.

Judging by the last few weeks, we'll definitely need him there. Not only is he the friend that's stuck with me through the mess of this last year, but he's the glue that holds our trio together. He's the voice of reason in all things, especially when Kim and I fight. He's the one who pulls us back together when things get rough.

If he gets in, we could still all *go* to UCLA together. Even if we aren't on the field anymore.

But from the look on Kim's face, it seems like that might not be happening.

I walk over, wrap an arm around Kimberly's waist, and lean in for a kiss. She returns it absentmindedly, her lips distracted.

"What's up? What's wrong?" I ask, looking from her to Sam and back again.

She leans in for another kiss, and her lips firmly meet mine this time, reassuring me, but she doesn't answer.

I'm about to ask again, but I just shake off the weirdness instead. Everyone's shaking off the old shit tonight, so we can too. Leave whatever this is behind for now. I came to celebrate with them, after all. I look both ways before unbuttoning my suit jacket to reveal the flask I smuggled in. "What do you say we go to the pond and—"

The words don't even leave my mouth before lightning flashes on the other side of the window, illuminating the entire sky with electricity. The glass shakes ever so slightly with the long roll of thunder, and my reflection wobbles in it, staring back at me, but Sam's and Kimberly's are staring at each other.

"Nah, man," he says, pointing to the sky. "I'm not looking to get fried alive tonight."

"Oh, come on," I say as fat drops of rain begin to loudly splatter against the window. "What'd you do with Sam? A little bad weather never stopped you before." I knock the back of my hand against his shoulder. "Remember the blizzard after we won state two years ago? I think *you* were the one insisting we go. I'm pretty sure I still have frostbite."

They don't say anything. The silence makes my skin prickle with an uneasy feeling.

"What?" I ask, trying to meet Kimberly's eyes. But she looks away at the streamers just over my shoulder instead. I'm beginning to think this isn't about Sam's application.

My hand slips from her waist as I pull away. "What aren't you guys telling me?"

"I . . . ," she starts to say, her voice trailing off. Sam looks away.

The rain on the other side of the glass comes down even harder now.

"Tell me," I say again as I slip my hand into hers, just like I have so many times. I look at her wrist and think of the bracelet in my jacket pocket, the pages of that small silver diary spelling out "I ♥ U."

But then I see her start to do that fidgety thing she does just before she tells me something I'm not going to like. I brace myself as she finally straightens and looks me dead in the eyes. The downpour of rain washes out every voice in the room but hers as the truth finally comes out.

"Kyle!" I hear Kim's voice call out from behind me as the drops loudly beat onto the metal roof of the front portico.

How could she?

It keeps repeating in my head as I make my way down the steps. I'm already handing my ticket to the valet when Kimberly comes running out after me. I ignore her.

"Wait, Kyle, please," she says, reaching for my arm.

The instant her fingers touch me, my instinct is to lean into her, but I pull away and grab my keys from the valet as I step out into the rain. "Don't bother. I got it."

She follows me, trying to give me an explanation that I don't want to fucking hear. If she really wanted to explain, she should have done it long before now instead of blindsiding me the *day* of our graduation.

"I should have told you, but I didn't want to hurt you—"

Lightning cracks across the sky again and a loud clap of thunder silences her before I even have to say anything. I spin around to look at her. Her dress is soaked completely through, and her hair is now hanging dull and limp around her face.

"Didn't want to hurt me?" I laugh. "By sneaking around behind my back? Sharing secrets with my best friend—"

"Sam's *my* best friend too."

"You *lied to my face*, Kimberly. For months." I unlock my car door and rip it open so hard it almost swings back. "Consider me hurt."

I get in the car and slam the door.

Berkeley. The word echoes around my head, every syllable a fresh stab of betrayal.

Berkeley. Berkeley.

She applied and she didn't even tell me. She sent in supplemental essays and updated transcripts, and *got in* months ago, and she just sat there pretending. Pretending while we picked out dorms and classes and talked about road trips home for breaks, knowing all along she was never going to go to UCLA.

She told Sam.

Why didn't she tell me?

I'm ready to get out of here, but she slides into the passenger side before I can pull the gearshift out of park. I pause for a moment, wanting to tell her to get out, but I can't bring myself to do it.

We have to figure this out. *The bracelet is still in my pocket.*

I put my foot down on the gas and we take off through the parking lot and out onto the main road, the wheels sliding on the wet ground as we turn.

"Kyle!" she says, clicking her seat belt into place. *"Slow down."*

I flick my windshield wipers on to the fastest setting, but it's still not fast enough for the sheets of rain pummeling the now-fogging glass.

"This makes no sense. We've been planning all year. You, me, Sam. *Our* plans." I reach up, swiping at the condensation to make a space big enough to see. My fingers hit the tiny disco ball slung around my rearview mirror, sending it swinging. It does make sense, though, in a Kimberly kind of way. I think of all the times she's changed her mind at the last minute, leaving me and Sam hanging. Like when she ditched our freshman-year formal to hang out with the varsity cheerleaders, or dropped us in the middle of a group final to work with the valedictorian instead. Moments I bury deep until we're fighting, like now. "You just decide, 'Screw it! I'll do what I want.' Just like you always do."

There's a clap of thunder, and the lightning that follows reflects off the glittering silver of the ball, scattering it all around the car.

"What *I* want? I *never* do what I want. If you just listen to me for five freaking seconds." She stops talking as we whiz past the street to my house, her head turning as it fades away. "You missed the turn!"

"I'm going to the pond," I say. I just keep thinking if I can get us there, I can salvage this night. I can salvage *this*.

"Stop. No, you're not. The pond will be an ocean right now. Just turn around."

"You've been thinking about this for a while, haven't you?" I ask, ignoring her. A tractor trailer barrels past us, sending a shower of water onto our windshield. I grip the steering wheel tighter, slowing down to steady the car. "You must have been. Kim, you could've just said you wanted to go to Berkeley, not UCLA. It's not like I have the football scholarship anymore. I don't care where we go, as long as we're togeth—"

"I don't want to be together!"

The words slap me right across the face. I jerk my eyes from the road to look at her, this girl I've loved since third grade. I don't even recognize her right now.

We've "broken up" plenty of times in the past, but not like this. Small, dramatic fights that are over the next day like a stomach virus. She's never said *that*.

"I mean . . ." She stops and her eyes turn away from me, widening. "Kyle!"

My head whips back to the front windshield just in time to see a blinking pair of yellow hazard lights in front of us. I hammer the brakes, and the car slides underneath us without slowing.

Suddenly I don't have any control over the direction we're going in.

I fight against it as I try to avoid a stalled car in the dead center of our lane, gripping the steering wheel tightly as I attempt to steer into the skid. The car miraculously regains traction just in time, and we swerve out of the way of the stopped car.

I pull onto the shoulder and carefully slow to a stop, my chest heaving.

That was *close*.

"I'm sorry." I take a long, steadying breath, looking over at Kimberly to see she is pale, shaken, the sharp curve of her collarbone intensifying and receding as she struggles to catch her breath.

She's okay.

But we aren't.

I don't want to be together.

"Are we . . . ?" I start to say, the words struggling to come out, fighting their way to the surface. "Are we breaking up?"

She turns her eyes to me, and I can see the tears lightening the blue of her irises. Normally, I would wipe the tears away and tell her everything will be okay.

But this time I need her to tell *me* that.

"I need you to listen to me," she says, her voice quivering.

I nod, the near accident wiping the anger away and replacing it with something even more intense.

Fear.

"I'm listening."

I tighten my jaw as she gathers her thoughts, my hand already reaching up to feel the charm bracelet inside my jacket while my heart thumps loudly in my chest just above it.

"I've only ever known myself as *Kyle's girlfriend,*" she finally says.

I stare at her, taken aback. What does that even mean?

She sighs, taking in my incredulous expression. She searches for the right words. "When you blew out your shoulder—"

"This isn't about my damn shoulder," I say, hitting the steering wheel with my palm. This is about *us.*

"It is," Kimberly says, matching my frustration. "It fucking *is.* You had so many dreams, and you were going to get them."

Her words catch me off guard, hitting their mark. I wince as a phantom pain radiates unexpectedly across my shoulder. I see the hulking lineman barreling right at me. The number 9 on his jersey as his hands wrap around my throwing arm, flinging me to the ground. Then . . . the sickening crunch of my bones and the tearing apart of my ligaments as his body slams into mine. Game-winning throws and college scholarships and a blue-and-yellow jersey with my name on the back. All of those things right at my fingertips. Gone with one play.

"I'm sorry," she says quickly, like she's seeing it too. "I can't imagine what it's like to have it all disappear, to have the scouts stop coming, the scholarships dry up—"

I clench my jaw and focus on the rain. Is she trying to hurt me more? "Why are we talking about this? It has nothing to do with you and me—"

"Kyle. Stop. *Listen.*" Her voice is firm and instantly silences me. "I loved you."

My insides turn to solid ice. *Loved.* Past tense.

Fuck.

"But when you couldn't play ball anymore, you changed. You became . . . I don't know," she says, searching for the word. "*Scared.* You were scared to take chances, scared to try anything else. And I became your enabler. Your crutch. You always had to have me there."

She has to be kidding me.

That's what she thinks of me? Seriously? That I'm scared and pathetic? That I can't do anything on my own?

Has she been with me all these months out of *pity*?

"I'm sorry you felt so burdened by me," I say, forcing myself to look back over at her as my hand instinctively reaches for my shoulder. "I'm sorry you had to miss a few parties. I'm sorry Janna and Carly went to the Bahamas while you felt obligated to sit by my bed and feed me soup because I couldn't lift my arm. But that's not on me. You could have walked away at any time—"

"Could I? Would you have let me?" she asks me, shaking her head. "Seeing each other every day at school, same classes, same routines, but not together? Every time we broke up, we never even made it a day." Would I have *let* her? What does *that* mean? We always got back together because *we* wanted to. Now . . . she's saying this?

"So, what? You just . . . pretended?"

"I didn't pretend. I just hung in there because I . . ."

Her voice trails off, but I already know exactly what she was going to say.

"Because you knew we wouldn't be going to the same college," I say, feeling like I'm going to be sick. "You'd be rid of me."

"No," she says, closing her eyes as she fights to get the words out. "I'm not trying to be *rid* of you. But—I do want to know what it's like to turn around and *not* see you there." Her voice cracks, but her spine straightens. She means this. She really means it. Her eyes hold mine, steady and sure. "I want to be me, just me, *without* you."

The words throw me off-balance, but I hold her gaze. We stare at each other, the rain still falling in sheets against the roof of my car. How long has she felt this way? How long has she not loved me?

"Kyle, come on," she continues, her voice soft. "Think about it. Don't you want to know who you are without me?"

I stare out at the headlights flickering in the storm. *Without her?*

We're *Kimberly and Kyle.* She's part of me, so I can't be me without her.

Her hand slides into mine, and her fingers gently tug against my skin as she tries to get me to look at her.

I can't bring myself to do it, though. I look at the steering wheel and the windshield wipers and the rearview mirror, before my eyes finally focus on the tiny disco ball.

I feel it in my bones that this is my last chance to make her see. To show her that my future wasn't just about football.

It was about us.

"I know who I am *with* you, Kim," I say as I reach into my jacket. I have to show her the charms, everything we have. The empty links will remind her of what is to come. "Before you make up your mind, please, just think about everything we've—"

The disco ball lights up, the tiny mirrors shooting photons of light around the car.

Then, impact.

My body is thrown forward. I feel the burn of my seat belt as it clenches around my chest, so tight it pushes the air right out of my lungs.

Everything registers slowly but in unison.

The car spinning.

The blare of a truck horn.

Headlights showering light across the windshield as we careen into an oncoming truck, a solid wall of metal that races toward us.

Time stops just long enough for me to look at Kimberly, her cheeks dotted with little freckles of refracted light, her eyes wide with horror. She opens her mouth to scream, but all I hear is twisting, shrieking metal.

Then darkness.

2

It hurts to breathe.

Everything is bright and out of focus, voices and faces coming in bursts of color and sound. I want to close my eyes, to sleep. But I'm in some sort of constant motion.

"Severe head trauma."

"Depressed cranial fracture."

White ceiling tiles blur. Machines beep. Gloved hands touch me.

"Kyle? *Kyle.* Look at me."

I zero in on the voice and see it's coming from a woman. Her red hair is tied into a rushed, messy ponytail, strands falling around a pair of intent blue eyes that quickly come into focus.

"Good. That's good. I'm Dr. Benefield. I'm a neurosurgeon," her mouth says, and I focus on the movement of her lips to try to grasp on to what she's talking about. "I'm going to take care of you, okay?"

There's a halo of light around her head, blazing, the red of her hair on fire. I stare at it as another voice calls out.

"Fractured femur and intrascapular lacerations . . ."

"Talks a lot, doesn't he?" she says, giving me a quick, confident wink.

Her blue eyes study my forehead as she begins to ask me about what kind of music I like. An overwhelming exhaustion tugs at me as I talk about the genius that is Childish Gambino, my words getting harder and harder to say.

I force everything else to go quiet except the doctor. Something about her calmness reassures me in all this chaos. The yelling voice, the beeping, the tearing sound of my clothes being ripped off me, fade. There's nothing but the ring of burning light encircling her hair. The smile on her face.

I start to smile back, but then I see . . .

Oh my God.

In her glasses, I see my reflection.

Blood is painted across my nose. A flap of my forehead lies open like an envelope, exposing the white bone underneath. *Cracked* white bone. My skull. Broken.

I start to panic, the sounds all pouring back as a wave of fear crashes into me. "Is that . . . ? Is—that's my . . . ?"

"You're okay," she says with a smile. I can't imagine how bone sticking out of my face is okay, but her expression remains as calm as ever. *Why* is she not freaking out at this? She reaches up toward my face, and it takes me a minute to realize she's touching my forehead, my jaw, my cheekbones.

"I can't—I don't feel that. Am I supposed to feel that?"

I think I see her smile falter for a fraction of a second, but then I'm sure I imagined it because she just continues on, her hands constantly moving.

I'm still trying not to freak the fuck out when the double doors into the emergency room slam open behind Dr. Benefield, and another gurney is wheeled in.

I start to close my eyes, the last of my energy pouring out of me, but then I see it. A shock of blond hair coated in a layer of blood.

No.

No, no, no. It all rushes back to me. The pouring rain. Our fight. The seat belt locking across my chest.

"Kimberly," I try to scream, but it comes out weak, my eyelids heavy. Everything is so damn heavy.

"Stay with me, Kyle," the doctor's voice says. "OR three. Now," she calls to the other voices in the room.

I fight to keep my eyes open, fight to keep them on Kimberly, but suddenly I'm moving, the fluorescent lights blinding me as they flash overhead, one after another, after another, faster and faster and faster. Flash flash flash flashflashflash . . .

No! I want to yell. *Go back!* But I don't have the strength to form the words and everything around me keeps moving.

I see a doctor carrying a child.

Flash.

An elderly woman getting oxygen.

Flash.

A girl reading a book. She looks up just as we round a corner. *Flash.*

Then Dr. Benefield, her white jacket whipping ahead of me, blurring and expanding into a glow that consumes the entire hallway, until there's nothing left but the blinding white light.

3

"Kyle."

Images swim before me.

A shattered disco ball.

Sheets of rain.

Kim's blond hair, matted and bloody.

Then pain. It radiates across my head, through my whole body. I grip the sheets until it recedes enough for me to make out a voice calling my name again, clearer now.

"Kyle?"

Mom.

I try to open my eyes, to focus on her face in front of me. I see her nose, her mouth, but her image is too bright. Blurry. Distorted. Like an overexposed photograph.

"Mom," I croak out, my throat as dry as sandpaper.

She takes my hand, squeezes.

I feel tired. So tired.

The doctor moves into my field of view. She shines a bright light into my eyes, asking me what I can and can't feel, then to follow her finger.

I can't—I don't feel that. Am I supposed to feel that?

And that's when the panic rushes back. The bloody, matted hair. The gurney. Kimberly.

"What happened—Kim—is she . . . ?"

She doesn't say anything, just focuses on something in her hands. A clipboard. A pen clicking. A note on her chart.

"Kyle, do you remember me? I'm Dr. Benefield. You've suffered a serious brain—" Her voice is cut off by the blare of a horn, the noise so loud I squeeze my eyes shut, desperate for it to stop.

When I try to open them, there is nothing but pain. Searing pain trying to swallow me whole. So I let it.

When I wake up again, I have no idea how long it's been, but everything is clearer. The white tile of the ceiling, the teal hospital walls, a TV in the corner, the flat-screen black.

There's an ache in my head, and I remember Dr. Benefield's words. I reach up to feel a bandage on my forehead, and the motion brings the unexpected tug of an IV on my arm. My eyes swing to the jumble of machines next to me and then down to the figure sitting at the edge of my bed.

"Sam," I manage to get out, and his head whips over to me. His eyes are red and bloodshot, his cheeks wet.

Instantly, dread bubbles through me.

Our entire lives, I've only seen Sam cry twice. Once when we were ten and he broke his arm falling off his bike, and then when his family's golden retriever, Otto, died three summers ago. But this doesn't feel like either of those times.

It feels worse.

"Sam?"

I can't ask the question and he doesn't answer. He just turns his bloodshot eyes out the window, and I see the tears falling faster now.

"Sam," I say again, desperately struggling to sit up with a body too weak to comply, until my arms give out and I fall back onto the bed. "Sam?"

But still he doesn't reply.

Kim's smiling face dances in front of my eyes, and I struggle to breathe, horror and guilt wrapping tightly around my lungs as a bolt of pain ricochets across my head.

She can't be . . .

I relive it all. Starting with Berkeley, the fight, and ending with her wide, panicked eyes in the glow of the headlights.

And as the truck makes impact, I feel my entire world shatter, the pain from my head building and building until my entire body explodes into a million pieces, pieces that won't ever be put back together.

4

I rest my bandaged head against the cool glass of the car window and watch as the droplets of rain catch the shining red of the brake lights in front of us as Mom drives. It's been two whole weeks and I still can't believe it.

I thought that losing her in the breakup was the worst pain I could ever feel, but this . . . I can't fix this. I can't take out a charm bracelet and make things right.

She's really gone. Buried at the local cemetery five days ago in a ceremony I was too busted up to attend.

When we get to the house, I stand there in the rain, clutching the cardboard box from the hospital to my chest. Inside are my dress shoes, the tattered remains of my suit, and the charm bracelet hidden somewhere in the mess, those unclaimed links that will never be filled.

The rain stops abruptly. I look up to see a black umbrella looming over me. My mom reaches to touch the rain-logged bandage around my head, but I gently brush her hand away. I don't want to be comforted or taken care of. It won't work anyway.

"I just need you to be okay," she whispers to me, her mouth barely moving.

Okay.

Like I could ever find a way back to okay. She gives me a concerned look, her eyes boring into mine as she takes the box from me and tucks it under her arm.

I need to be alone.

I steady myself with the crutches before I hobble toward the house and up onto the porch, my head foggy as I try not to put weight on my shattered femur, currently held together by a metal rod. She helps me through the front door, and I make the world's slowest beeline for the basement, wishing for a dose of whatever they gave me in the hospital to let me fade away to nothingness. My crutches thump noisily on the floor as I go, loud and steady, like a heartbeat.

"I thought maybe you'd stay up here," my mom calls after me. "I made up the couch. You won't have to worry about going up and down the—"

"I want to be in my own space," I say firmly. I pull open the door to the basement, the floor that's been my own since sophomore year, and noisily fight my way down the staircase, determined.

I hear her coming after me, and her hand wraps firmly around my arm just as my foot reaches the bottom step.

"Wait, honey . . . ," she starts to say, but it's too late.

I flick the light on and instantly see all the tiny holes where she used to be. Books missing off the shelf, her favorite blanket missing from the couch, even pictures missing from the wall.

"Where . . . ," I start to say as I push through the door to my bedroom and stumble inside. My hand reaches up to touch an empty nail where Kimberly's senior picture used to hang.

"Her parents came for the things she left here. I didn't expect them to—"

"They took everything," I say, feeling like I'm going to throw up. I missed her funeral. And now this?

I swing my head around, looking for anything they might have missed. But even the pink charger she always used to keep here is gone. Ripped out of the wall like a life-support plug.

Anger builds inside me, growing and growing, until all at once I deflate. They weren't the ones to take everything.

I was. From Kim.

I'm the one who drove us out there. I'm the one who made her feel like she had to hide what she actually wanted and now will never get.

"I'm sorry, honey," my mom says, reaching for me.

"Can I be alone, Mom?" I manage to croak out as I move away from her.

She opens her mouth to say something, but then hesitates and finally leaves. Her footsteps fade as she climbs the stairs, and the door above closes with a *click*.

I struggle across my room to a shelf in the corner, gold trophies and sparkling medals sitting next to a framed photograph, one of the only ones they didn't take. The two of us at the homecoming game, her pom-poms in the air, my number painted on her cheek, my arms wrapped around her waist.

Twenty minutes later my football career would be over. Two weeks later I was officially just Kyle Lafferty, the guy doing game write-ups for the school newspaper on the player who replaced him.

All I wanted for months was to go back to that moment. Back to before. Now, though, I'd live through that injury a hundred times over if I could just have Kim back.

BEEP, BEEP, BEEP.

I jump, and one of my crutches clatters to the floor. Frowning, I turn toward the source of the sound and find my alarm clock beeping loudly on my bedside table.

Limping across the room, I see the red numbers begin to flash over and over again, glaring and in time with the noise.

My hand freezes on the button, a memory washing over me. Mom out of town, Kim waking up beside me, her face scrunched up and sleepy.

"Who even uses an actual alarm clock anymore?" she grumbled, pulling the sheets up over her blond hair and wiggling closer to me while I shut it off, the morning run I was supposed to go on with Sam instantly forgotten as she curled into my arms.

I accidentally hit the wrong button, though, and fifteen minutes later the alarm was blaring again, loud and obnoxious. Kimberly bolted awake, completely upright, and launched the thing across the room. I remember how hard we laughed, the morning sun slowly rising outside my window, casting a warm glow onto her face.

I'd never seen anything so beautiful. I can almost see her—

BEEP, BEEP, BEEEEP.

I bend down and rip the plug from the outlet. The beeping stops abruptly, and Kimberly's face fades like a dream after waking. My chest tightens and I struggle to pull off my sweatshirt, my arms getting twisted as I fight it. I tug and tug, until the fabric finally gives way, a gasp escaping from my lips as I pull it off at last and toss it onto the back of my desk chair.

I look around the room at all of the corners that Kim used to fill, and realize that I didn't prepare for this part. I've been so focused on getting home. On the fact I was missing her funeral. On being strong enough to leave the hospital my girlfriend died in.

I never thought about after.

A week later I pull open the front door, the morning light shining too brightly on the wooden porch stairs. Nothing has really changed since I got home. The front path is still lined with the sweet-smelling flowers my mom planted, the driveway still filled with cracks, the white picket fence still desperate for a paint job.

Everything is the same. It's *me* that's different.

I adjust the crutches under my arms and push forward, hobbling down the street to complete my daily doctor-prescribed lap around the block. She said it could help clear my head, help get me back out into the world. Help my brain to heal. Unfortunately, it's a world that doesn't have a place for me anymore.

Before I know it, one block turns into two. And then three.

Soon I've crutched all the way into town, the streets around me strangely empty for a warm summer day. I'm exhausted. I reach into my pocket but realize I left behind my cell phone, which is probably for the best. It's only filled with ignored calls from Sam. Voice mails of him pleading for me to talk to him, to say something, to let him know I'm okay.

I'm not, though. So what am I supposed to say?

I stare at the window displays of the shops along Main Street. Striped T-shirts and propped-up books and bouquets of flowers. Every time I crane my neck to look inside, I feel myself searching. Looking for something. But it's something I know I'll never find on a dusty shelf or hidden in a corner. I have no idea why I've even walked here.

I wipe a bead of sweat from my forehead and find myself in front of Ed's Ice Cream, the vintage red-and-white sign swinging on its squeaky metal hooks in the faint summer breeze. Weakly, I collapse into one of the black metal outdoor chairs, my body exhausted from even this short walk, one of my crutches chafing the hell out of my armpits.

I stare longingly at the front door, the cool, air-conditioned room on the other side of the glass feeling so close but too far for my broken body to manage right this minute. I don't think I could take another step now if I tried.

Headline: WASHED-UP VARSITY FOOTBALL STAR BARELY MANAGES A MILE WALK.

The skin under my arm burns where a painful blister is starting to form, hot and irritated.

Just great. As if a head injury and a fucked leg weren't enough.

After a few minutes of scalding myself on the black metal chair, I pull myself back up and head inside. The bells on the door jingle noisily above me as I'm hit with a blast of cool AC, well worth the extra strain.

I order two scoops of chocolate on a cone and sit down automatically in the seat by the window. The ice cream melts in my mouth as I stare at the empty seat across from me. Sam, Kim, and I were usually always together, but going to Ed's for ice cream was something just for the two of us. On warm fall days after practice, or on a random half day of school, I'd make up some excuse to walk into town, surprising her with a cup of mint chip. She'd always snap a picture before her first bite and post it on Instagram.

I realize now that it feels like a real long time since we were last here. I wonder what I would see if I pulled up her Insta. When was the last mint chip?

I can't remember coming after my injury. Not even once. And I don't have a single good reason for it.

I stare at the empty chair across from me and feel a pang of guilt, her words from that night making me wince.

I pull my eyes away and my breath hitches when I catch sight of the girl working the counter. She's leaning over the giant freezer to get a customer a scoop of butter pecan, her blond hair in a messy bun. A painful sensation claws at my head, like the icy burn of brain freeze.

Kimberly.

I hold my breath, expecting to see those high cheekbones, that megawatt smile that makes everything feel right in the world, her blue eyes rolling as she asks me what the hell I'm staring at.

She raises her head to smile at the customer and . . . it's not her. Of course it's not her.

I quickly get up from my chair, tucking the crutches under my arms. The girl's brown eyes watch me from behind a pair of wire-rimmed glasses as I move to the door as quickly as I can.

"Have a great day!" she calls to me, bright and friendly. I manage a small smile, but the corners of my mouth strain from the effort. Even the simplest human interaction feels harder than running laps during practice. The reality of Kim being gone is a series of everyday heartbreaks. Moments and reminders that chip slowly away at me until there's nothing left.

I need a distraction.

I push back outside and restlessly head down the street.

I can't go home right now. To my room with the empty spot where her picture used to be. To my couch where we'd stay up late on Friday night, watching scary movies until the sun came up. To the cabinet, still stocked with two unopened bags of the Lay's barbecue chips she loves.

The gold doors of the historic movie theater on the corner of the block swing open as an older man shuffles inside. The vintage marquee's thick black letters call to me.

I crutch over to the ticket booth and buy a ticket to the next showing, not bothering to even ask what it is. It doesn't matter.

There are a dozen or so people in the theater, scattered all around, trying to beat the midday summer heat, but no one I recognize. I catch sight of a young couple giggling in the very back, their hands interlaced, and make it a point to sit as far away from them as possible.

Just a minute later, the lights dim and I stare blankly at the screen, watching the characters float in and out of their scenes while my mind does the exact opposite. It stays stubbornly on the throbbing pain in my leg, the sore skin under my arm, the fact that Kimberly isn't sitting next to me trying to guess the plot and ruin it.

A belly laugh from the guy in the middle of my row snaps me out of my attempt to stretch my leg, and I realize what an enormous waste of time this is.

What an enormous waste of time *everything* is.

Grabbing my crutches, I shift my weight out of the squeaking red chair and toss the practically full tub of popcorn in the trash on my way out.

By the time I get home, every part of my body is on fire, my T-shirt completely drenched with sweat.

I stand on the front porch, my hand on the doorknob, lungs heaving as I steady myself before I push inside.

From the entryway, I glance into the living room to see my mom getting up from the couch, concern tugging at the corners of her mouth and the crease in her brow. "I've been so worried about you—"

"I'm fine." I cut her off, meaning for my voice to sound certain, but it comes out all wrong, harsh and whiny.

The wooden floors creak as she comes over to me and holds up my cell phone. The screen lights up to show me a series of missed calls and texts. "You left without your phone. I had no way to call you, to find you if something happened."

I grab it from her and try to move past her to the door leading down to the basement, but as I sidestep, I come face-to-face with a picture on the wall. It's the two of us from the summer after my dad died, her arms wrapped around me as I give a toothless smile to the camera. Only this time I see something behind her smile. Something I now recognize. Loss.

I take a step back and give her a hug, smelling that familiar perfume she always wears.

When her arms wrap around me, the same arms that held me close that summer, I blink furiously to keep it together.

I pull away and hurry to my room, my breathing coming in uneven gasps, images from the ice cream shop and the movie theater and the moment before the crash all blurring together as the room tilts and I crawl into bed and pull the covers over my head.

Everything is the same except in the only way that matters.

But the world can keep going on if it wants to.

I won't.

5

"Kyle. Wake up."

It's Kimberly's voice. A shooting pain cuts across my forehead and sweat clings to my arms and back and legs. I reach quickly for the lamp and snap the light on. I scan the room to see a shadow disappear up the steps.

Frantically, I throw back the covers and limp as quickly as I can up the stairs to fling open the door. "Kimberly!" I call after her. "Kim."

I look around, but only silence answers me, the darkness echoing loudly in my ears.

I *heard* her. Felt the weight of her hand on my arm. She was here. I'm sure of it.

Just as sure as I am that that doesn't make any sense.

I hobble down the hall, gripping the wall for support as I

stumble into the living room and flick on the light to reveal . . .

Nothing.

The couch is empty. No one's here.

Like an idiot, I try the front door, twisting the knob right and left, but the lock is firmly in place. It's only then that I remember Kim never had a key.

I let out a shaky exhale and rest my head against the worn wood, my temples pounding from the sudden jolt out of bed, the adrenaline draining into defeat. I will my breathing to slow down, but when I turn to head back to bed, that hard-fought breath rushes out of me on a loud whoosh.

Kimberly.

She's sitting on the couch, a fuzzy white blanket draped around her shoulders. She pulls the blanket a little tighter, its blue butterfly pattern moving as if the little insects were alive. Kimberly. Right here in front of me.

It can't be real. I know it can't. I know that it can only mean my head is definitely more messed up than the doctors thought.

But I need it to be real.

I rush toward her so quickly that I trip on the rug in the entryway. I reach out to grab the wall before I topple over.

By the time I right myself, she's gone, leaving only couch cushions, bare and unoccupied.

I make my way to the chair, never taking my eyes from the sofa. I sit down and stare at that empty spot for the rest of the night, waiting for her to come back, my fingers curled around the armrests.

Every time I start to drift off, the fact that I actually *saw* her jolts me awake, like a full can of Red Bull.

I don't even realize the sun has risen until I hear my mom's footsteps coming down the stairs.

"Good morning, then," she says.

I blink and look up to see her in a pair of black pants and a dress shirt, her hair neatly brushed. I force myself to stand, my bad leg aching from sitting in the chair all night, tense and unmoving.

She leans against the banister and raises her eyebrows at me.

"Wanna explain?"

"I, uh," I start to say, stretching to buy myself some time to think of an excuse. "I couldn't sleep."

I can tell she doesn't buy it, but I slide past her, hobble to the basement door, and duck inside before she can pry any further.

Leaning back against the closed door, I let out a long exhale. For the first time since Kim's death, I have something to focus on.

I have to see her again.

For the next three nights after my mom climbs the stairs up to bed, I sit vigil in the living room chair, alert to every flicker of light or creak in the house. But no Kim. No white fuzzy blanket or blue butterflies.

I'm practically holding my eyes open by the time my mom's alarm goes off each morning, and I have to slink back downstairs before I get slammed by a sunrise edition of twenty questions.

By the fourth night my head is killing me and it's proving harder and harder to stay awake. I squint at the empty couch cushion, trying to fight the exhaustion. Kim did always like to keep me waiting. It's the only thing I hang on to. The only thing that keeps me going.

The clock in the entryway is barely ticking past midnight, so I prop my bad leg up on the coffee table in an attempt to get slightly more comfortable.

I doze off for what feels like a fraction of a second, and when I open my eyes, the vacant spot is filled once again.

By my mom.

"Wanna explain *now?*" she asks as she crosses her arms over her patterned navy-blue pajama shirt.

I know it shouldn't, but her question pisses me off.

Do I want to *explain* that I think I'm seeing the ghost of my dead girlfriend? Not really. I already start to feel a little ridiculous just thinking about vocalizing it.

I swallow hard on that bit of insanity and shake my head. Before she can pry any further, I get up and limp down the hall toward the basement.

"Kyle." Her feet gently pad after me, but I close the door just as she gets there. I'm not in the mood to be questioned about something I sure as hell can't even begin to explain to myself. I only know what I saw. At least I think I do.

I slide down onto the top step as I wait for her to go. My head rests against the wood and my eyes slowly begin to close, but a whisper pulls me back to consciousness, her voice coming from the other side of the door.

Mom.

"I lost your father like this," she says softly as I listen. "Watched him waste away."

I stand slowly, my hand reaching out to lie flat against the door as she keeps talking. Soft hallway light creeps under the door. "Oh, Kyle." She sounds so sad.

Sighing, I twist the handle. She's sitting on the floor, her back pressed against the wall, eyes closed. She *looks* so sad. Instantly I feel terrible.

"Your old bones okay?" I ask with a small smile. "Sitting on the floor like that?"

She looks up at me and rolls her eyes, clearly not amused by my jab. "Ha ha."

I reach down and pull her up, her hands wrapping gently around my forearm.

"Okay, you win. I'll go to bed . . . ," I say, nudging her toward the stairs. "If you will."

"I love you. You're going to be okay," she says as she studies my face, deciding, before finally giving my arm a squeeze and heading off in the direction of the stairs.

I pull the door closed behind me and sit silently at the top of the basement steps, holding my breath, waiting for what feels like an hour, until I'm certain she won't be straining to hear the creak of the door opening or my feet on the hardwood floor. I check my cell phone, and the screen lights up to show it's only 3:30 a.m., a few hours still left before the sun rises.

I creep quietly into the living room, ready to take my spot in the armchair, but a shape on the couch stops me dead in my tracks.

It's my mom, curled up into a ball, fast asleep. Her light snores are the only sound in the room. I take the quilt off the back of the couch and cover her with it, something about the image making all of this worse.

You're going to be okay.

The thought of her words makes my heart rate spike. Turning to head back downstairs to my room in defeat, I touch the bandage on my forehead, worried that what lies underneath is way more broken than the doctors initially thought. Worried that I'm *not* going to be okay.

Worried that I could've stayed up for a hundred nights and that spot on the couch would have been empty for every single one of them.

Because she was never there in the first place.

6

Days all start running together. Texts are left unread; food wrappers litter the floor. A week blurs into two, and then a month, and soon almost the entire summer drifts by, the sun slowly setting earlier just outside my small basement window.

I don't get out of bed in the morning. I don't do anything.

I just lie around, refusing all of Mom's attempts to get me out of my room. I'm not interested in torturing myself. I know what waits for me out there.

In the basement, on the other side of my bedroom door, are the French doors that lead to the backyard, the same doors Kimberly would use to sneak in after my mom fell asleep. I could go upstairs, but I would see the front lawn she used to cartwheel across in middle school or the kitchen where we made that monstrous-looking, but insanely delicious, chocolate cake for Sam's birthday.

But, mostly, I don't want to give my brain anything to twist and trick me with. I don't want to think I see *her*.

My mom's knocks on my door become more and more frequent, just like the clicking sound of her feet pacing outside my door as she pleads with me. "You're in there. I know you are." Today she tries the doorknob. Once. Twice. But I've locked it now.

I can feel her on the other side, willing me to let her in. Instead, I let daylight melt into evening once more. I fight to keep my eyes open as long as possible, because when I do sleep, my dreams are filled with images of sparkling disco balls, fluorescent hospital bulbs, a truck's headlights getting closer and closer.

At least when I'm awake, I can suspend myself in nothing.

I'm not sure how much time has passed, but however much it is, it doesn't matter.

"Get up. Right now."

I struggle to open my eyes and squint to see my mom standing over me, shaking me awake. I look past her to see my bedroom door against the wall, taken completely off the hinges, a gaping hole now leading to the rest of the basement. How did I sleep through that?

"You get out of bed and get yourself together," she says, throwing my blankets off of me. "We need to have a talk."

I groan and grab the blankets right back, pulling them up to burrow underneath them.

"About what?" I grumble as she sits down at the edge of my bed, her eyebrows forming a V.

Uh-oh.

Serious Mom.

I peer at her over the top of my covers, worried about what she's going to say.

"Kyle, it's almost September. Your friends are all starting to leave for college. Sam is enrolled in classes at the community college," she says, taking a deep breath. "So, UCLA."

I sit up and push my mess of hair out of my eyes, my fingertips grazing the raised scar on my forehead. She can't possibly think I'm actually going. "What about it?"

"I *know* UCLA was supposed to be you and Kimberly. I know how much that plan meant to you," she says, reaching out to grab my hand. "But you need to accept that the exact future you had planned isn't *possible* anymore."

My eyes find the UCLA pennant Kimberly bought me hanging on my wall, the blue and yellow taunting me. The future I had planned wouldn't have been possible anyway. Kimberly would've been packing her bags to start a new adventure at Berkeley.

Without me.

I feel the tiniest twinge of anger and then a familiar wave of guilt. Kim would give anything to be going anywhere. Just to *be* here.

"But that doesn't mean you don't have a future," she continues. "You're supposed to leave in a week and a half, and maybe that would be—"

"I'm going to defer," I say, making a decision. The only decision that will get Mom off my back, at least for a few more months. "For the first two quarters. It's too soon."

She doesn't have to know yet that I'm never setting foot on that campus.

She blinks. This was not at all what she expected. I can tell from the set of her shoulders she was ready for a fight, but this is logic she can't ignore, which is what I counted on. So she nods, satisfied, I guess, that I've made any sort of decision about my life.

"Fine. But if you do that, you need to make a new plan. If you defer UCLA, you can't just do . . ." Her voice trails off, and she motions to the pile of dirty clothes. The used dishes. The overflowing trash can. "*This*. You have to do *something*."

I look around the room. I haven't left it all summer and it shows, but I can't muster the energy to care.

"You're still alive," she says, squeezing my hand. "And you can't stop because she isn't. You need to keep living."

I let out a long exhale, running my fingers through my matted mop of hair. Just having this conversation is exhausting. I have no idea what living even looks like now.

"I don't even know where to begin," I say honestly. Maybe if she just tells me what she wants, that'll be enough.

"Sam wants to see you," she offers, holding up my phone. I have no idea how she even got it. "It's been months since you talked to him, and I know for a fact he's hurting too. You could start with that."

She tosses it to me, and it hits me square in the chest, my hands fumbling as they miss it. My reflexes are way out of practice. The screen lights up to reveal dozens of missed calls and texts, mostly from Sam, a few from guys I played football with through the years, though those tapered off ages ago.

Sam's the only one still trying.

I scroll slowly through his messages, watching as they go from hey man, how you doing? to dude, it's been almost two months since I've heard anything from you. call me. I'm worried about you.

I don't know how to look him in the face after everything that went down. How can he even *want* to see me? Hanging out together would just be another painful reminder that our trio isn't a trio anymore.

"You can't shut him out forever," my mom says, reading my mind. She pats my leg twice and stands.

"Now, call him and get up. Go to the grocery store. I'm not shopping or making food for you anymore," she says, heading for the door. "Maybe if you get hungry enough, you'll have to come out and join the living," she adds.

My stomach growls loudly in response.

Traitor.

I'm dripping sweat by the time I get to the Stop and Shop. My jeans cling to my legs, my skin used to the fuzzy insides of sweatpants. It took me close to an hour to get here, limping along the winding blacktop path that passes by my high school and the library, my leg suffering without the physical therapy appointments I've been avoiding.

Mom subtly left her spare key out on the counter, but there's no way I'm getting behind the wheel again.

I try to avoid looking at all the storefronts that remind me of Kim. The Chinese food restaurant where we'd always get take-out during finals week, Sam hogging all the lo mein. The coffee shop where Kim would get her seven-dollar latte with oat milk, insisting it was "better than the real thing." The corner hair salon where she'd get highlights while Sam and I watched football on our phones in the waiting area.

So I keep my eyes on my feet until the sliding doors of Stop and Shop open with a burst of cool air. I grab a cart to take some of the pressure off my leg and roam the aisles to pick up the essentials, munching from a huge bag of Funyuns I grabbed off a shelf as I walked in.

Milk, eggs, bread. I add in a few bags of pizza rolls because Mom didn't specify what exactly counted as a meal and I have a microwave in the basement for a reason.

And that reason is pizza rolls.

The sun is just starting to set as I walk home with my two bags, the sky turning orange and pink, slowly giving way to a deep blue. I must have been there a lot longer than I thought.

The sound of thunder fills my ears, loud and steady and rolling. For a second I flinch, suddenly back in the storm from that night, but then I look to the side to see the football stadium at Ambrose High aglow, the parking lot filled with cars.

Drums. Not thunder.

Cheers pour from the stands, nearly drowning out the steady drumbeat of the band. It's Friday night; one of the first football games of the year is in full swing. I find myself tucking the grocery bags under my arm and veering off the path, the lights and the cheers pulling me into the crowd and onto one of the cool metal benches.

I take a deep breath. Everything feeling . . . strangely right for the first time in a long time. The crowd around me. The teal-and-white uniforms on the field. Coach blowing the whistle that hangs around his neck.

Some of the current Ambrose High players laugh on the bench, shoving one another as they joke around. One gets up and does the spirit dance that Sam started incorporating into every huddle junior year, while another sneaks a few Pringles out of a drawstring bag at his feet as everyone else is distracted. That *so* reminds me of Sam.

When we were freshmen and distinctly second string, we would sneak snacks onto the field in our helmets, eating them when Coach was in the middle of calling a play. One game, I convinced Sam we should try to be a little healthier by bringing peanuts instead of Famous Amos cookies. Of course, that was the day Lucas McDowell, a senior benchwarmer, decided to rat us out at the end of the third quarter.

Coach made us run laps for every peanut left in the bag.

I nearly lost a lung that day. And then I had to listen to Sam bitch the whole time about how we would've been done twenty laps ago if we'd just stuck with cookies, because there wouldn't have *been* any cookies left in the bag by the end of the third quarter.

I smile to myself and watch as the game goes on. Before I know it, I get swept up in the crowd in the best kind of way, cheering when our team pulls out a first down on a carry up the middle by the running back, or when the other team misses an easy thirteen-yard field goal.

The cheerleaders' bright uniforms catch my eye. They're in formation on the track, right in front of the stands, their teal-and-white pom-poms moving precisely. When a girl with blond hair is launched into the air, I look away before my mind can try to mess with me.

I refocus my attention on the quarterback as he calls the play on the field. My eyes follow the players as they move into position. I spot a fullback standing out of place, leaving a gap wide enough for the defense to easily slip right through. *Oh no.* I want to shout to the quarterback to *look out*, but my voice is frozen.

The center hikes the ball. I grip the bleacher I'm sitting on as the offensive line breaks to run their play. The quarterback cocks his arm to launch a pass just as the defense blitzes. Red jerseys rush the offense, and hulky Number 9 finds the gap.

Everything seems to slow down. My chest is heavy with dread, but I can't tear my eyes away. It's too familiar. Way too familiar.

On the field, the fullback freezes, realizing his error. He leaps to protect his quarterback, but it's too late. Number 9's already there, nothing but air separating him from his target.

I lurch clumsily to my feet as the ball drops awkwardly from the quarterback's hand, his entire body crumpling under the weight of Number 9.

His scream reverberates around the stadium.

My shoulder twinges in sympathy as I see the fullback calling for help, his quarterback writhing on the ground, arm splayed behind him at a nauseating angle. Coach runs onto the field and rips the quarterback's helmet off to reveal messy brown hair and . . . *Oh my God.*

I'm staring at myself. That's *me* down there, arm twisted backward.

I almost vomit, barely managing to swallow the sour bile. *This isn't happening.*

The fullback drops to the grass. He yanks his helmet off. It's *Sam.* Sam missed the block.

I can see the panic on my best friend's face from here.

My bad leg trembles and buckles, no longer able to hold my weight. I collapse onto the bench, one of the worst moments of my life playing out right in front of my eyes. How is any of this happening? My brain is fucking with me again. It has to be. Just that thought starts to calm me.

It's not real. It's a hallucination. That's all.

"You're stronger than this, Kyle," a voice says from next to me.

I freeze, then slowly turn my head.

God, there she is. Kimberly, sitting on the bench beside me, eyes straight ahead, focused on the field, her skin as smooth as porcelain under the bright stadium lights. I blink furiously, waiting for her to disappear, but she doesn't.

"You're not here," I whisper.

"I haven't left," she says as she turns to look at me, the stadium lights illuminating the rest of her face. The entire right side of her head is cut up and bloody, her blond hair matted and red. She reaches out her hand to touch mine. And nothing stops her. I feel it. But no one else is reacting.

"You're not here." I rip away from her and jump to my feet, trying to put as much space as possible between us. "You're not here! *You're not fucking here.*"

"The fuck?" someone says, knocking me back into reality.

In one blink Kim is replaced by a curly-haired guy a few years younger than me, his face painted teal and white. "I'm here, dude," he says, sliding away from me as he looks me up and down. "You might need to be somewhere else, though."

Fuck.

What just happened? What is *wrong* with me?

I grab my defrosting groceries and get out of there as quickly as my busted leg will carry me.

My head is searing by the time I open the front door. I drop the groceries in the entryway and run straight to the bathroom.

Taking a deep breath, I grasp the edge of the sink, the marble cool underneath my palms.

"She isn't haunting you. It's all in your head, idiot," I say to my reflection.

I lean forward to stare at the scar, the long, jagged red line still inflamed and angry. I reach up, almost touching it, wanting to feel the healing skin underneath my hand, wondering what is still broken underneath it.

Which might be everything.

I let my hand fall, and my fingers find the counter again, gripping tighter. My gaze drops from the scar to meet my own reflected eyes, the pupils large and unsteady.

"Kyle?" a voice says from behind me, and I practically jump a mile.

I lean to the side and look past my reflection in the mirror to see my mom, still in her work clothes, her eyes tired but alert.

"Are you okay?"

When I don't deflect right away, she grabs hold of my hand, leading me down the hall and into the living room. She sits me down on the couch, and I finally blurt out the truth.

"I keep seeing Kimberly," I say as I brace myself for the look of pity to cross her face. "On this couch, and at the ice cream parlor, and *today* in the stands. I know it's not real—you don't have to tell me that. But, Mom . . . it feels *so* real. And I keep feeling like it's because it's my fault that—"

She squeezes my hand to stop my rambling, my words hanging heavy in the open air.

"Kyle, *none* of this is your fault," my mom assures me, her voice calm. Certain. "None of it. You're going to get better."

I don't believe her, but at least she's not looking at me like I'm insane or pathetic, which is a relief. Just telling her seems to help me get my breathing back under control.

"Do I even deserve to get better, though?" I ask. My voice cracks on the last syllable, and I swallow hard, fighting to pull myself together.

She takes my face in her hands, her thumbs softly tracing my cheeks. "You're going to be just fine. It takes *time* to heal. To move on. And not just physically," she says, then takes a deep breath. "When your dad died, it took everything in me to pull myself together so I could show up and be the best parent I could be for you."

My memories from then are so hazy and incomplete because I was just barely in kindergarten. I can't get my shit together now, but she did it all while taking care of a kid.

"How did you do it, Mom?" I ask her. "Kim said that night that I didn't know how to be myself without her, and I'm starting to think that she's right."

"I'm still doing it. One step at a time," she says. "Always forward. Never back. Just like you'll do." Her eyes grow serious. More serious than I've ever seen them. She reaches out and pulls me in for a hug. With her face buried in my neck, I can just barely make out her whisper. "You'll fight to come back."

Always forward. Never back.

I think about that as I unpack the groceries and smuggle the pizza rolls into my mini fridge in the basement. She said I'd fight my way back. But I've never had to fight alone. Through the shoulder injury, through pregame jitters, through tough classes at school, I always had Kim's support.

Kim told me that night that I could move forward without her. The thing she didn't tell me was how.

I pick up the photo of us from the homecoming game and sit down on my bed. Her smile glitters up at me.

My forward always had her in it. We had already signed up for classes at UCLA, my schedule mirroring hers, even though she was the only one with some idea for a major. But I thought there would be time to figure out the specifics for me. To figure out what *I* wanted, Kim alongside me the entire time.

I guess, if I think about it, I didn't have much of a plan for myself. More of a plan for *us*.

Even if I *could* picture it, there's no way I can move forward now, haunted by the ghost of my girlfriend.

Ex-girlfriend, I correct myself. And somehow that makes it worse. Like I don't have claim to the grief inside me. Just the blame. Even thinking of Kim haunting me makes me feel like a dick. She didn't want to be with me in life, so why would she spend her time following me now? I toss the photo of us down on my bed, realizing there's only one other possible answer for what happened tonight.

One that actually makes sense.

Maybe I'm just going crazy.

Maybe that's what I deserve.

7

"Well?" I ask Dr. Benefield first thing Monday morning. "Am I cracked?"

My mom scheduled the appointment to prove to me I'm not crazy.

She clicks her penlight off and slides it into the pocket of her white jacket as she shakes her head, giving me an amused smile. "No. You suffered a significant loss, and that could be manifesting in unexpected ways."

"Like being haunted by Kimberly?"

"Like . . . seeing what you *want* to see," she corrects, holding up her iPad to show me my brain scans from this morning. "Look." She flips back and forth between a healthy brain and my brain to make some point about how I'm "just fine." My mom cranes her neck to see the images, but I don't even bother to look.

"Our brains are magnificent machines," Dr. Benefield adds, closing the iPad. "They'll do whatever it takes to protect us from pain, whether that's physical or emotional. There's nothing wrong with yours that time won't heal. Okay?"

To *protect us from pain?* How is seeing my dead girlfriend protecting me from pain?

She looks at me until I comply with a nod, then pulls out a prescription pad and a pen and scribbles on a page before ripping it off and holding it out to me.

I take it from her, looking down at her handwriting. I expect to see a gibberish prescription name, but instead it says: *Chill out. It's not really happening.*

Great.

"Kyle," she says, and I look back up, meeting her no-nonsense gaze. "The visions you're having, they're not real, okay? They'll fade when you're ready. I promise. But for now, when they happen, you take out that prescription. Read it, remember it, believe it."

I nod, but her words don't reassure me. *Fade?* What happens when even this last trace of Kim fades? When I see her, I feel crazy, which sucks, but I also see *her.* And I'm not ready to lose that.

After we get back home, my mom heads to work. I pour myself a bowl of Lucky Charms and slide into a spot at the kitchen table. For a while it's just the sound of my noisy crunching, but then I swear I hear a muffled voice, the words difficult to make out. I pause, the spoon halfway to my mouth, my ears straining.

"Mom?" I call out, my voice echoing around the empty house. Did she forget something? I listen harder and realize the sound seems to come from below. My pocket.

When I pull my phone out, noise is crackling through the speaker. Oh man. Who did I butt dial?

". . . Sam," the voice says as I lift the phone to my ear, the words finally becoming clear enough to hear. I open my mouth to respond, but he keeps going. It's a voice mail. "I don't even know if you're going to hear this, but I gotta tell you, I'm scared. And before you laugh, asswipe, I'm serious. You're scaring us."

The voice mail cuts off and the screen lights up, showing the string of other unheard messages.

I stare at my phone in the palm of my hand. My thumb lingers over the green call button so long that the screen goes dark. I swallow hard, then shove the phone back into my pocket.

It isn't until after I've finished my cereal, cleaned off the couch in the basement, filled an entire trash bag with food wrappers, cleared out all the dishes and glasses from next to my bed, and done every conceivable chore I can think of that I have the balls to call him back.

The phone rings for so long I'm not even sure he'll pick up, rightfully pissed at me after my months of ignoring him.

But he's Sam, so even though I don't deserve it, he answers.

Sam drains his whiskey, then picks up the flask to peer at it, his face curious. I watch him, taking in the tired look around his dark eyes, the patchy five-o'clock shadow that I've literally never seen on his face.

Normally, I'd tease him about it, but he's been all one-word answers since he got here fifteen minutes ago, no matter what I say.

My conversational skills are clearly tanking hard after an entire summer alone.

"What, uh, made you decide to stick around here?" I ask, nodding to the blue-and-gray T-shirt he's wearing, from the local community college. I know he got into a few state schools, so I'm not sure what exactly changed his mind.

He raises one of his eyebrows at me, and I see something I've only rarely seen in our lifetime of being friends.

Mad Sam.

"Things haven't exactly been rainbows and sunshine for me, dude. One of my best friends died and the other dropped off the face of the earth," he says. After a beat, his expression softens. "I had no idea what was going on with you. I had to keep checking with your mom."

I take a long sip of the whiskey, my throat burning, but it helps the words come easier. "I'm sorry, Sam," I say.

And I am. But I owe it to him to be honest.

"I know I was a shitty friend, but I just . . . couldn't. I couldn't be around you. I couldn't be around *anybody*. Sometimes I think maybe I still can't."

I feel his eyes appraising me. "You look like shit," he says finally, gesturing to my wrinkled shirt, overgrown hair, weirdly curly beard.

I shrug, not particularly caring what I look like. Kimberly isn't here to see me. She was always the one who'd tell me that I looked like an animal if I wore sweats to school. That maybe there were clothes other than gym shorts. What does it matter now if I shave or brush my hair or wear a clean shirt? What did it matter then, if my ass was always going to end up here?

"Well." Sam sighs, and the last of his anger seems to roll off his shoulders. "I'm glad we didn't lose you, too, even if you do look like shit," he says as he tips the flask in his hand and pours more into his glass.

He grins and nods to the flask. "How'd this make it through customs?"

"Found it in the bags from the hospital," I say, nodding to the closet where my mom moved everything after disposing of my bloody and tattered suit. "Mom must've missed it."

I know I could take the out. Keep the conversation here on whiskey and bullshit. But his words are still in my ears. Something about them feels wrong.

"You're glad you didn't lose me, too," I repeat, shaking my head. "Sometimes I wish it had been me. Sometimes I feel like I'm waiting for her to walk right through that door." I look across the hallway to the couch, the empty gray cushion. "Waiting for things to go back to normal."

Sam's face gets serious, just like it used to when he'd start the chant in our football huddles before a big play. "Me too," he says, his voice firm. "That's why we can't forget her. We have to stick together because we're the only ones who will keep her memory alive. That's what Kim would've wanted."

What Kim wanted. I used to think I knew what that was better than anyone. But I didn't. Sam did.

I think about all the conversations that happened behind my

back. How he knew how she *really* felt. What she really wanted.

"How long did you know?" I ask him. "About Berkeley?"

He pauses, but instead of answering, he hangs his head. "I'm sorry. I should have told you."

"Yeah," I say simply. But I think of what Kim said in the car about breaking up. About her going to Berkeley. *Would you have let me?*

Did he think that too?

He watches me for a long moment, and when he realizes I'm not going to explode, he continues. "I know that night was bad, but she loved you. You have to remember that."

I let those words sink in, making my head swim more than the alcohol. The "loved" past tense is still just as jarring as it was that night. And it's too much to unpack right now.

Sam doesn't stay much longer. We move to safer territory, talking about his plans for this semester, the upcoming UCLA football games, even though I haven't had it in me to catch up on any preseason coverage.

And then, as he leaves, I promise to not be an asshole and text him more.

But after the door closes behind him, I find myself reopening it a few minutes later and stepping outside, a light chill in the late-summer air. It takes me a second to realize I'm walking to the pond, the half-finished whiskey flask in tow as I limp along the path to the park. I sit at the water's edge in the shade of one of the huge looming willows, looking out as the afternoon sun reflects off the surface of the water and sends twinkling light all across it.

Gently, the wind blows, tugging at my hair and bringing with it a voice. A whisper. The words are too soft to make out.

I look around, trying to find the source, but this time I'm not surprised when I'm met with nothing—just the green grass around the pond, the trees lining the shore, and a feeling I can't shake. What Sam said keeps running circles in my mind, like laps after a confiscated bag of peanuts.

I'm not worried about forgetting her. I never could. But how the hell am I supposed to know what she'd want me to do? How she'd want me to be without her?

The voice fades with the breeze, and I run my hands through my hair, wondering how I can possibly stand on my own when I feel so damn unsteady.

8

I stare at my reflection in the bathroom mirror, tucking the hem of my white button-down securely into my pants as I give myself a final once-over.

My hair is still a mess, long and overgrown, but the patchy beard of the last three months is gone, and the new aftershave I bought before graduation has finally been put to use. The scar on my forehead has faded, and the redness is now a soft, far-less-noticeable pink.

I wouldn't say I look good, but I do look like I'm trying.

Plus, I don't want to go see Kimberly looking like I've "never heard of something called a shower."

I smile to myself, remembering the athletic banquet at the end of junior year. I showed up straight from a touch football game with Sam. She roasted me with that before we even set foot inside, then pulled out a comb from her purse to slick down my hair in a way that only she could somehow manage.

It's always like this, some memory rooting me to the spot, stopping me in my tracks.

But Sam was right last week. I have to go and see her. I can't let her think I would forget her.

Sighing, I head out of the bathroom door and into my bedroom, determination turning into uncertainty as my hand hesitates over a bouquet of irises, the purple petals shockingly bright for such a heavy day.

Am I really ready for this?

I think back through the weeks since Mom decided to take my door off its hinges. I guess I feel stronger in some ways. I'm actually going to my PT appointments. Replying to Sam's texts instead of ignoring them. Not having a freak-out every time I see Kim in empty chairs and across the room and in places she couldn't possibly be.

But today I'm *actually* going to see her. Going to the cemetery and standing in front of a gravestone with her name on it and trying my very best to figure out what exactly she'd want me to do.

And now that the moment is here, I'm scared shitless. The same stomach-dropping feeling I had when not-actually Kim decided to show up next to me during that football game two weeks ago. What's going to happen when I'm actually near her?

I mean . . . I could do it tomorrow. Or even next week. After my mom gets home from running errands, I could even call Sam to . . . put it off. I'd just be putting it off.

"Don't be such a little bitch, Kyle," I mutter, and I head up the steps and out the door, hoping the super-long walk to the cemetery will be enough time to pull myself together.

Only, of course, today it feels like a block.

Too soon the wrought iron gates come into view, big trees casting shade over the sea of gravestones, a heavy sadness in the drooping branches. I slow down as I walk along the path, taking in each headstone while I put off my destination. Mothers, fathers, sons, grandparents. Even kids.

Fuck, I do *not* want to be here.

Some of the plots are carefully maintained, fresh flowers looping around the stone, trinkets from friends and loved ones placed underneath.

Others are overgrown, no one left to look after them.

Will Kim's grave be okay? I sure as hell hope so. While *I* don't mind looking uncared for, I don't think I could stomach seeing anything of hers that way.

I wouldn't want it looking like . . . well . . . like this one.

I stop to study a small headstone with dead ivy crawling over the corners, the inscription just a single word: GOODBYE. No name, no date, nothing.

Damn, that's sad. My head sears with pain and I have to steady myself, squinting at the individual letters, both of the *o*'s, the *e*, until the burning slowly starts to pass.

I wonder what kind of person a headstone like this belongs to. If anyone even remembers them.

When all of the pain dissipates, I pull a purple flower from the bouquet in my hands and place it carefully on the lonely headstone. I don't really know why I do it, but it just seems like someone should. Especially since the grave next to it is surrounded by a sea of pink flowers growing as far as the plot allows. The big triangular petals are vivid and eye-catching. I really don't know how I didn't see it first.

I lightly touch one of the flowers. I think I recognize them from my mom's garden. She tried growing them a few years ago, their smell strong enough to waft through our kitchen window on summer mornings.

But what were they called?

I'm about halfway through the alphabet of the dozen flowers I *do* know when I realize how hard I'm delaying.

I urge myself along. *Come* on, *Kyle.*

I continue on the path for a few more steps, my mind drifting from those pink flowers to the GOODBYE headstone. Something about it feels wrong. *Why* exactly? I'm so in my head that I almost miss it.

KIMBERLY NICOLE BROOKS. REST IN PEACE.

The wind is knocked right out of me.

Her plot isn't overgrown or neglected. In fact, there's a massive bouquet of blue tulips already there, the color rich enough to hold a twinge of lilac at the base of the even petals.

Blue tulips.

I look down at the irises in my hand. Shit. Blue tulips were definitely her favorite. I can hear her now, telling me that she loved them because they matched her eyes.

Irises were just the first flowers I ever got her. If Kim were here, she'd refuse to talk to me for the rest of the day. Or the week if she was feeling especially salty about it.

God, I loved her, but I hated when she did that.

Love her, I correct myself. I will always love her. What the fuck is wrong with me thinking about that right now?

I put my sad bouquet of irises next to the tulips, and my hand finds the coarse gray stone. My fingers trace her name, the past few months leading to this moment.

"Kim . . ."

I stop, placing my whole hand on the headstone, all of the feelings I've kept bottled up hitting me at once. I can't do it. I can't be here. Not yet.

But I take a deep breath and try to start again.

"I . . . I don't believe this." I shake my head, throat burning. "I *can't* believe it. But I face it every single day when I wake up and you're not here."

There's a stab of pain in my temple, radiating out from a single point, almost sizzling. I rub it with my fingertips and fight to continue.

"If I could do it over, I wouldn't have gotten so angry at the party," I say finally. "I wouldn't have forced that conversation in the car. I would have listened when you said you wanted . . ."

To turn around and not *see me there.* I swallow, her words echoing around my head. They still hurt, but it's a softer pain than what I'm used to.

And this isn't about *my* pain.

"I would have given you the time apart that you wanted. I would have . . . I would have let you drive," I say with a harsh chuckle. "You would have definitely laughed at that," I say, almost hearing the sound from somewhere just out of view. *Almost.*

I open my mouth again, wanting to say so much, but the thoughts devolve into a jumble of words and sadness, too messy to string together. I tighten my grip on the headstone, everything building and building until my broken brain finally erupts. A sharp, stabbing pain courses through my temple as tiny flashes of light radiate inward from the corner of my eye.

Holy fuck.

"Once upon a time there was a boy . . . ," a voice says from behind me, the words soft enough, gentle enough, to send a scattering of goose bumps up my arm.

At first, through the fog of pain, I think it's Kim. Another hallucination. But the voice isn't hers.

I turn quickly, expecting to see someone, but I'm met only with the rustling trees. My vision blurs, then clears. Pain bounces behind my eyes, so I slam them shut, rubbing my temples until it fades enough for me to reach into my pocket and pull out a Tylenol bottle.

I struggle with the child-lock lid before I finally free two pills into my palm and dry swallow them.

But the voice isn't gone. "He was sad and alone," it echoes behind me.

This time when I turn around, my head is clear enough that I see a girl in a sunshine-yellow pullover standing a few steps away, by the sea of pink flowers. She has long, wavy brown hair that seems to blow softly in time with the trees behind her.

She studies me with such uncertainty that I have to wonder if the voice came from someone else. But we're the only two people here.

I rub my eyes and try to get them to focus. Something about her is . . . familiar. Did she go to Ambrose? I don't think so. I knew just about everyone who went there, and I definitely think I would remember her.

"Hi," I say, raising my hand in the world's most awkward wave.

She turns to look over her shoulder, as if she's searching for the person I'm actually waving to.

"Do I know you?" I ask when she turns back to look at me. I'm still trying to place her face, my brain running through sports camps and football games and hallways. She shakes her head no, and though I could swear I've seen her before, I don't press the point. "Did you say something? Just now?"

The girl hesitates, her hazel eyes wide with curiosity. Or maybe surprise. Or maybe confusion that I just had to wrestle with a child-lock lid for a whole minute and a half. "I . . . didn't think you'd hear me," she says.

I take a step closer to her, noticing a smattering of freckles along the bridge of her nose. "I heard someone talking. That was you?"

She seems cautious, like she's unsure whether or not to answer. Her eyes search mine.

I should turn back to Kim's grave, the whole reason I'm here, but instead words come tumbling out of my mouth. "Once upon a time, right?"

Her eyes lock on mine, and the five words hang between us.

She pushes her hair behind her ear, face flushing. "I . . . tell stories," she says as she lightly touches one of the pink flowers.

"Stories? Like . . . fairy tales?"

"Yes," she replies, looking back up at me with a small, pleased smile. "*Just* like fairy tales."

"That's cool," I say as I stop across from her, the pink flowers between us. The toe of one of her yellow Converse traces a small circle in the dirt. When she doesn't say anything else, I start to talk again.

"What's your name?" I ask, but her voice overlaps mine, asking, "Does your head hurt?"

My head? I reach for my scar. I thought my long hair was covering it.

I trace my fingers along it. The pain still lingers, but it's more distant now. "How did you—"

"Marley," she says, our words overlapping yet again. "My name is Marley."

Marley. The name's not familiar, but her face is.

"I'm Kyle," I say, trying to keep us on one track of conversation instead of two. "Kyle Lafferty."

She nods and studies my face for a long moment before saying, "Food helps. With headaches." My gaze lingers unconsciously on her mouth, her lips delicate and pink, curved up at the corners like two rose petals. "Maybe you should eat? It's lunchtime," she continues.

A quick, sharp pain darts across my temple, gone before I can even reach up to touch it.

"Do you . . . want to get lunch?" she asks.

"*Oh*," I say, finally catching on. My stomach sinks. I'm not here to make friends. I'm here for Kim. I shake my head and start to turn away from her. "No. Uh, I should go—"

"But you're hungry," she counters.

I open my mouth to object, and as if on cue, my stomach lets out a long, low growl. Perfect. Marley smothers a smile. I have to fight the urge to smile back as a laugh tries to make its way out. It's such a foreign reaction to me right now, to laugh. But it feels . . . good.

And she's right. I *am* hungry. But . . . going with her to get lunch would mean leaving before I finish talking to Kim. Even though I have no idea what to say, it doesn't feel right to do anything else.

So if I can't do *that*, I should probably just go home.

"Thanks, but I really can't," I say, limping past her down the path as I head toward the gates, defeated.

"Oh. You're leaving," she says. Something in her voice makes me turn back around.

I'm more than ready to start my long walk home, but she pushes her hair behind her ear, her hazel eyes expectant.

Keep walking.

I want to, but I feel rooted here, my feet completely disobeying my mind.

Marley takes a step closer to me, but when I don't say anything, she stuffs her hands in her pockets and looks away.

Maybe she's lonely? A graveyard isn't exactly a cool place to hang at lunchtime.

I guess I can relate to that. My social life for the last three months has been hanging out with my mom. Sometimes Sam, more recently, but mostly my mom. Probably not the most normal thing an eighteen-year-old guy could be doing, but I don't even know how to be normal anymore.

I glance at her again. I mean, it's just lunch. I was going to go home and eat some cereal or something anyway.

She gives me a small smile, as if she knows what I'm thinking. "So . . . ," she prompts.

"Let's get lunch?" I ask.

The wattage of her grin could power nine suns. Her eyes seem brighter, the hazel color bolder. More vibrant. Greener.

It's contagious. Suddenly I'm smiling too. My first real smile in months. It feels good to make someone happy for a change.

"I would like that very much," she says, and the two of us head down the path together, toward the big iron gates. I hesitate, looking back at Kimberly's grave as we leave. I don't know what I expected would happen, but this is definitely not it. I promise her I'll come back, that I'll know what to say next time, but her voice stays silent.

9

A few minutes later, I stop short when I realize where we are.

Here? Really? Of all the places I could've taken us to, my feet automatically led me to this one, the winding paths of the park giving way to . . .

"Oh, I love this pond," Marley says.

I glance sideways at her. "You've been here before?"

She nods, and a puzzle piece clicks into place. Maybe that's why she's familiar. I must have seen her when I was here with Sam and Kim.

The pond was one of our favorite spots, mostly since it was usually pretty empty in the evening, and definitely empty at night. With no lights around the perimeter, the entire dark pool of water and the trees around it were usually ours and ours alone. We drank bad champagne out of red Solo cups when Kim earned her spot as cheerleading captain, and Sam stood on the rock in the middle, pumping his fist, when he was named to All-States after a killer junior season.

Sometimes Sam and I would come alone if we were killing time after practice, or Kim would meet me here to work through whatever we were fighting about.

Now I wonder if *they* ever came here, alone. If this was the spot where Kim told Sam about Berkeley.

"But I go to that side," Marley says, drawing my attention back as she points across the pond to a small army of ducks, their orange feet standing out against the green blanket of grass. "That's where my ducks are."

I don't know if my eyes are playing tricks on me, but I swear on my good leg that the grass looks greener over there. It's a stupid metaphor, but I need an excuse to get away from our bench and this clawing feeling in my chest.

"Let's go to your side, then." I start walking that way, my eyes meeting Marley's as I nod across the pond.

I stop to readjust my crutch, and when I glance up, I see that Marley is already halfway around, leaving me completely in the dust.

"Hey!" I call out to her. "Where's the race?" She spins around to look back at me, her long hair catching in the breeze, the sun outlining her face. It's like an engineered Instagram photo come to life. A perfect shot that would usually take a hundred tries to get.

I pull my eyes away and point a few feet off the path to a small snack shack, a red-and-yellow sign plastered to the side.

"Let's get lunch," I say, repeating the words from earlier.

She grins. We head over, slower now, to the small stand, where each of us buys a hot dog and fries. I get a Coke, but Marley goes for their iced tea with mint, grown fresh at the small community-run garden in the park.

"Mint iced tea is my favorite. Especially in the summer," she says as she glances past me to look at the yellowing trees along the path, the first signs of fall starting to appear all around. "I've only got a few weeks left to enjoy it."

I try to balance my plate and watch as she gets an extra tiny paper plate for her condiments. She carefully divides the ketchup, mustard, and mayo on it with a barrier French fry between, her brow furrowing with serious concentration.

"What's with the division? You think mustard and ketchup don't get along?" I ask as we sit on the sparkling green grass on her side of the pond.

"I like to think of it as . . . each deserves its own space," she says, tucking her foot under her leg as she holds up a fry.

So, because I'm an asshole, I dip one of mine into the mound of ketchup on my plate and drag it straight through the mayo. She grimaces as I pop the whole thing into my mouth.

"Okay, but did you taste the French fry at all?"

I chew, frowning as I swallow. Full mayochup taste, but not very much fry. I couldn't even tell you if it's made of potato.

I watch as Marley carefully touches the very tip of a French fry to her ketchup before she takes a slow bite. "Sometimes . . . less is more."

I shrug and force myself to look away, in the direction of the cemetery. I remind myself I'm just being polite. Doing a good thing. It's not like I'm ever going to see her again.

But the guilt starts to bubble up with every passing second, the food becoming tasteless.

This is *not* why I came here. I came to say goodbye to Kim, not to learn proper condiment protocol from a random girl I met *inches* away from my girlfriend's grave.

Ex-girlfriend, I correct for the millionth time, even more frustrated.

What am I doing?

I quickly finish off my hot dog, abruptly standing as I push my fries over to her. "Uh, you can have the rest of these," I say, avoiding her eyes, because I know if I meet them, I'll probably stay. "I have to go. My mom needs help with—"

"Maybe I'll see you again," she says, cutting off whatever lie I was in the middle of coming up with. Like she sees right through it but doesn't care. She gives me a small, shy smile.

"Maybe," I say, though I'm almost certain that she won't.

I turn on my heel and limp away down the path.

I'm still thinking about the divided condiments and her small dusting of freckles and the green grass by the pond when I walk in the front door almost a half hour later. As if on cue, my mom's head pops out of the kitchen to greet me, the door barely closed behind me. She eyes my pressed button-down and dress pants.

"Did you finally go to the cemetery today?" she asks, her grip tightening on the spatula in her hand. I let it slip after Sam left that I was thinking about going, and she's been asking me about it every day since.

"Yeah," I say curtly, but I don't elaborate. It wasn't exactly a rousing success.

"I'm just starting dinner. We can talk about it."

"I already ate," I say as I keep pushing toward my room. I'd rather rebreak my femur than talk about my day.

I hobble down the basement steps and pause in front of my closet to put my jacket away. When I open the door, my eyes land on the box tucked into the back corner.

The box filled with what they were able to salvage from my car after the accident.

I pull it out and place it on the floor of my room. I sit across from it for what feels like hours, trying to work up the courage to open it. If I couldn't get anywhere at the cemetery today, I could at least try to do this.

I find myself staring at a piece of filmy white fabric peeking out from underneath the folded corner. I don't know what it is, but something about it makes me afraid to unfold the flaps. To see what else is inside.

I work up the nerve to reach out and peel back the layers. As I slowly sift through the contents, the bit of fabric unfurls into a scarf. Underneath it, a purse. A single shoe.

Tiny parts of her, never to be worn again. Never to be wrapped gracefully around her neck, or slung around her shoulder, or kicked off into the corner of my room after a night out.

I dig some more and find the disco ball ornament, completely intact.

I hold it up so the light from my bedside table reflects off it and sends tiny shards of light around the room. A jolt of pain slashes across my scar, and I see the tiny disco ball ablaze as the headlights of the truck rush toward us, the freckles of light dotting Kimberly's horrified face. My heart rate picks up and my vision blurs.

I drop the ornament, closing my eyes, the pain receding as the memory fades away.

When I open them, my eyes land on a small velvet box at the very bottom. Carefully, slowly, I pick it up and open it to reveal the charm bracelet. I wrap my fingers around it, the cool metal sitting gently in my palm.

My finger traces the charms, finally making its way to the empty links, the spot I saved for our future memories. Memories that she would've made alone, at Berkeley.

Now I'm the one making my own memories without her.

I think of Sam's words the other night at my house. *What Kim would've wanted.* Of my mom and her "Always forward. Never back." Of Marley, standing by the pond. *Our* pond.

I place the charm bracelet carefully back inside the box and put it away. It's too soon. I went today because I thought it's what Kim would have wanted.

So why does every new minute still feel like such a betrayal of all the old ones?

10

A few days later I find myself back at the cemetery, at Kim's grave, just wanting to feel close to her. Not in the creepy-vision kind of way, but in more of an I-don't-know-what-else-to-do kind of way.

I lay a fresh bouquet of tulips next to my wilted irises, but a larger bouquet of them is already resting against the headstone. I wonder how many bouquets Kim's parents left before I even came once.

At least this time I brought the right flowers.

I take the silky scarf out of my pocket and drape it gently over the headstone, returning it to its owner.

"Well, Kim," I say as I pull away. "Like always, I'm finding it difficult to figure out what it is exactly you want. I keep thinking I know, but . . ."

I pause, half expecting her to answer me, but there's only the sound of the wind in the trees, the leaves rustling above me.

I sit down and rest my back against the headstone, silently waiting for a moment of clarity. Five minutes pass. Then fifteen. But nothing comes. And the same questions roll through my head like a news ticker that can't unloop.

I look around and spy the sea of pink flowers two plots away. Pushing myself up, I let my curiosity get the best of me.

I reach out and touch one of the flowers, the petal soft underneath my fingertips.

"Stargazer lilies," a voice says from beside me.

Jesus Christ. I jump, nearly having a heart attack as I look over to see Marley standing next to me, her long hair pulled back with a yellow hair tie. She plucks the Stargazer I was touching, her hazel eyes studying it.

My eyes study the headstone nestled within the pink blooms.

"My sister. Laura," Marley says softly, before I can ask.

"She was my hero. Loved me just the way I was," she says, as if we're picking up a conversation we'd already begun. She places the flower on top of the headstone. "It didn't matter to her if I was different. Or sensitive. Or quiet."

She looks up at me, and I can see finally where the intensity in her eyes is coming from. It's loss, buried in the deep hazel, a familiar pain wrapped around the irises. I know that pain. It's like looking in a mirror.

"I wanted to be just like her," she adds, breaking the gaze and turning her face back to the flowers.

"How old were you when she—"

"We'd just turned fourteen."

We? But before I can ask, she answers that, too.

"Twins," she says.

Shit. "What happened?"

"Oh, I don't tell sad stories," she says. Then she smiles sadly, and it's as if a curtain drops behind her eyes.

All right, then. That's *clearly* a sensitive topic. We stand in silence for a long moment.

"Oh!" She slips the yellow bag she's carrying off her shoulder and surprises me by pulling a single flower out of a side pocket. Her eyes clear, and she holds it out to me as if I asked her to bring it.

Cautiously, I reach out and take it, inspecting the circular yellow center, the petals around it perfectly even and white. I actually know this one.

"A daisy?" I ask.

"Flowers have different meanings," she says, sensing my confusion. She nods to the daisy in my hand. "This one made me think of you."

"Why? What's it mean?" I ask, honestly a bit surprised flowers have any meaning at all. I thought they were just nice to look at.

"Hope," she says simply.

Hope. Does she think *I'm* hopeful? I don't hope for much of anything anymore.

"I'm happy to see you again," she adds suddenly, not looking at me. "I wasn't sure I would."

I decide that I probably shouldn't say I wasn't planning on seeing her again. I just smile, and then almost as if we'd already planned it, the two of us find our way down the path and to the pond. We buy some popcorn from a vendor and then walk to her side of the pond, where the ducks are. They gather around her feet to reverently stare up at her, quacking so loudly I swear they must all be holding mini megaphones.

I watch as she reaches into the red-and-white striped container and throws some kernels to them, her hair falling in front of her face. I mimic her, taking a handful of my popcorn and scattering it in front of me. The ducks converge on it like they've never eaten in their entire lives.

"Do you come here a lot? To feed the ducks?"

She hesitates, a fistful of popcorn in her hand. "Not as much as I used to."

I nod, but I don't ask why. I know what it's like to stop doing things you loved.

A duck snaps at the popcorn in her fingers, and she squeals, breaking the tension with a laugh. She jumps back and releases the kernel before he can take off her pinky. Her shoulder brushes against my arm, lightly enough to leave a trail of goose bumps behind it.

I clear my throat and take a step back.

We follow the ducks down to the water, their quacks leading the way. A few feet from the edge, Marley pauses to look up, her hand frozen on top of the kernels.

"It's going to rain," she says thoughtfully, her head tilted back to see the heavy, dark clouds above us.

I follow her gaze, nodding. Something about it reminds me of the sky on the evening of the graduation party. The same ominous gray, the clouds dense with rain.

I'm struck again with the feeling that I shouldn't be here.

"Kim always liked it when it rained," I say, shaking my head at the sick irony of that.

As I pull my eyes away, I catch sight of a blue butterfly fluttering over the dark pond, its wings struggling to move.

Something's definitely wrong with it. It's airborne, but just barely. It painfully inches its way toward us, closer and closer to the water with every pump.

"Kim," Marley says. Hearing her name in Marley's voice makes my scar throb uncomfortably. "The grave you always go to," Marley continues. "She was more than just a friend, wasn't she?"

"Yeah," I say, an avalanche of memories rushing at me. I can feel my hand in hers as she pulled me down the empty school hallway during junior prom. See her running onto the football field after I'd thrown the game-winning pass. Feel her lips on mine that very first time, when she found my message in her diary. "She was more."

I remember the pain I saw in Marley's eyes earlier. Something tells me I can talk to her about this, that she could understand in a way that my mom and even Sam can't seem to. But I don't know how to even begin.

So I turn back to the butterfly and watch as it drifts closer and closer to shore. Almost . . . almost . . .

"Kimberly didn't make it," I say, forcing myself to try to talk about it, but I keep my eyes trained on the butterfly's blue wings.

They give out, and the butterfly drops onto the water's surface, so close to the bank but not close enough. It twitches, struggling against the current. I hurry to the edge of the water and carefully scoop the insect into my hand.

I glance down at the water. Something's not right. I look closer and realize . . . I don't see myself. I just see the tree branches above my head, the outline of the leaves. The stormy gray of the clouds in the sky just past them.

Frowning, I lean closer.

There's even the butterfly, but not . . . *me*.

Like I don't *have* a reflection.

I swallow hard and try to collect myself as the familiar pain blooms in my head. I fight to keep myself here and not let my broken brain take over as the words in Dr. Benefield's note pop into my head.

Chill out. It's not really happening.

I focus on my heart beating in my chest, my rib cage rising and falling all around it, the butterfly flitting around in my palm.

Another reflection appears in the water. Marley, her face concerned. I look quickly over at her, and the butterfly takes off, still struggling, but moving.

"Poor thing," Marley says as she watches it go.

I look back at the water, holding my breath, and this time my eyes stare back at me, dark and panicked. Instantly I feel like an idiot. I probably looked like I was freaking out over a butterfly.

These brain spasms keep getting weirder, not better. I reach up to touch my scar but disguise it by running my fingers casually through my hair. Dr. Benefield said this is happening because I'm protecting myself. Maybe it's because I was talking about the accident.

Marley leans over my shoulder to look at my reflection in the water. And of course, it's right there, looking back at us, just like it's supposed to be.

Her hair falls across my arm as she leans even closer, making my skin prickle. "With that scar, you look like Harry Potter. Without it, you'd practically be Prince Charming or something."

All thoughts of my head injury disappear, because . . . *Prince Charming?*

"Oh no," I laugh. "Is that the kind of fairy tale you write? Are you filling kids' heads full of *that* nonsense?"

If I learned one thing from what happened with Kim, it's that I'm definitely no prince. And love is not a fairy tale, no matter how perfect the story sounds. I don't believe that anymore.

Our images blur as it begins to rain, heavy drops rippling across the pond's surface.

"I hope it's not nonsense," she says, her voice quiet. "I hope there's something better ahead to believe in."

She raises her face to the sky. I take in the pink of her lips, the openness of her face to the rain. In that moment I want to tell her everything. Because even though it seems so impossible after all that's happened, I want to believe there's something better ahead too.

But the rain starts falling too hard, and before I can make up my mind, we have to leave.

✱ ✱ ✱

That night I sit at the kitchen table, twirling and untwirling spaghetti around on my fork, my hair still wet from walking home in the rain.

"Well," my mom says, scanning me with that X-ray vision all mothers have, "she sounds like a nice girl." She takes a loud, crunchy bite of garlic bread.

I stupidly told Mom about Marley when I walked through the front door, soaking wet and holding a daisy. She asked me where I got it from, and my broken brain couldn't think of any other possible reason I'd be holding a daisy.

I'm realizing now that any excuse would have been better than telling her the truth.

I tighten my hand around my fork as she presses for details.

"I barely know her," I say, stabbing another bite of spaghetti. "Don't make this a thing, okay? She's just . . . easy to be with. She . . . gets what I'm going through." I shake my head. It's not like I met her in the park or the mall. It was a cemetery. And not just *any* cemetery. It was in the middle of the cemetery where *Kim* was buried. "But, I mean . . . shit."

We stare at each other, and she reads my mind with yet another mystical mom power.

"Kim would want you to be happy."

"Mom, I told her I'd love her forever. Even just being friends with someone new feels wrong."

"That's not very fair to you, is it?" she asks.

I let my fork clatter against my plate. "How could you even say that?"

Not very *fair*? What isn't fair is that Kim's life was taken away from her because of a fight and a freak storm. The least I can do is keep this promise to her.

"Kyle," she says calmly, ignoring my outburst, just like she always does lately. "I just meant that you have a lot of life left to live. You never know—"

"No," I say as I push back from the table and stand up, the chair legs squeaking noisily against the ground. "I do know. Kim was the only one for me. And I'm the one not being fair to her."

With that, I storm downstairs to my room, and a new kind of clarity forms.

If I can't go to the cemetery just for Kim, I have to stop going. I have to stop seeing Marley.

11

I head to the cemetery a week later to tell Marley I can't see her, the warm fall day taking me through the winding paths of the park as I search for her around every bend, between every cluster of trees.

She'll probably think I'm some kind of weirdo, coming to find her just to tell her I'm going to be ignoring her from now on. I mean, what am I even going to say?

Hey, if you happen to run into me by my dead girlfriend's grave, don't expect a hello.

I roll my eyes, even though that's exactly what I'm going to do. Because it feels like that's what I have to do to do right by Kim.

My thoughts wander to my fight with my mom last week, frustration and guilt sitting heavy in my stomach.

She's been such a broken record lately. *You have to keep moving forward. Stop lingering in the past.*

I tried to talk to Sam about it during the morning run/walks we've started going on every Friday, but it's no use. He says it's not lingering in the past; it's just keeping her memory alive. They're always trying to tell me what I should do and how I should heal, without bothering to give me any useful specifics.

I take a long, deep breath, trying to shake the feeling that I'm trapped. Stuck somewhere between Kim and Sam and my mom, unable to cross the start line.

A yellow-and-white striped shirt catches my eye, the lines thin enough for the two colors to blur together.

Marley.

She's standing by a huge cherry blossom tree, her long hair catching the breeze and dancing around her shoulders, down to the small of her back.

I watch as she reaches up to carefully break a stem off the tree, something about the movement familiar even though I hardly know her. She smells the jumble of tiny pink flowers at the edge of the branch, face deep in concentration.

I find myself wondering what she's doing before I remind myself why I'm here. Maybe I should just leave it to chance. She hasn't seen me yet. I start to turn around and leave.

"You've decided not to see me anymore," a voice says, stealing the words right out of my head. I look back to see Marley studying me, her serene expression gone.

I pause. *How did she . . . ?* It doesn't matter.

I look down at the cherry tree twig in her hand as I avoid the question. "What's this one mean?"

"What do you want it to mean?" she asks, turning it right back around on me. It catches me off guard. She's the first person to ask me something like that in a long time.

A new start. I catch the words just before they come out, the answer suddenly right in front of me. A way forward that doesn't feel wrong.

"I don't . . . I don't know," I say instead. I should be shutting the conversation down, saying goodbye.

Only I can't. Her eyes don't buy it. They hold me in place, the green strands vibrant in the morning sun, the same color as the grass at the pond. Marley's side of the pond.

"I want . . . ," I start to say, watching as the cherry blossoms begin to tremble slightly. A few of the petals fall to the ground in a small shower.

Say it.

I can't, though. Because there's something there in her face. The exact thing I've been looking for. The unnamed thing we both understand.

"I want . . . a friend," I say, my own words taking me by surprise. "Someone who didn't know me before all of this happened. Someone who I can be myself with, the me that I'm becoming. Not who I was. The me I *want* to be."

"We all want that, don't we?" she says, nodding the way you do when someone says exactly what you're thinking.

But I have to draw a line. For myself. For Kim.

"But that's all I can be. Just friends."

She bites her lip and nods. Something like relief settles in her shoulders. Like it's a safe compromise for her, too. "Definitely. Just friends. Nothing more."

She brightens then and holds out the cherry blossom twig to me. I take it, letting out a small laugh. "So . . . what does it mean, really?" I ask her.

"Cherry blossoms? They mean renewal, a new start," she says.

Her words send goose bumps up my arms. Another wind gust pulls the cherry blossoms off the tree behind us, then tugs at the branch in my hand. Her eyes are bright as she smiles at me through the whirl of pink and white petals, the sunlight glittering through the trees all around her.

Later, when I get back home, I take off my jacket and find a cherry blossom petal clinging to the sleeve. I pluck it off and hold it in my palm. The color always makes me think of Kim at our senior prom, in a dress the same soft pink. I told Marley that earlier as we sat under the cherry blossom tree, and she nodded, her face thoughtful.

Her sister had liked the color pink too. That's why she'd stopped by the cherry trees in the first place.

Until that moment I'd kept all the reminders of Kim to myself, but talking about it with Marley somehow made the memories less painful. I haven't felt that comfortable with anyone in months.

This isn't at all how I thought things with Marley would go.

I kick off my shoes and crawl into bed with a groan, pulling the covers up over my head. Part of me feels weak, like I betrayed Kim so I could feel better, but the guilt doesn't rush over me like it once did.

Frustrated, I roll over. I don't know what the right thing is.

I don't know anything anymore.

I stare into the darkness beneath the blanket, letting it envelop me. I don't know how much time goes by, but I eventually jolt awake to the sound of a phone ringing, the dusky twilight outside my bedroom window now replaced with midnight black.

Groggily, I fumble around on my nightstand until my fingers finally find my cell. It must be Sam.

I look at it, surprised to see the screen is black. There's no incoming call, but the ringing doesn't stop. If it's not my phone, then where is it coming from?

I sit up, trying to figure it out.

I don't have a landline in my room. The upstairs phone is *upstairs*, and my mom's cell would be with her. Still, there's a phone ringing somewhere nearby.

A wave of dread rolls through me as my gaze falls on Kimberly's purse, sitting on my desk. *No way.* I walk over, my heart hammering loudly in my chest. The ringing is definitely coming from inside. I yank the purse open. Kimberly's cell phone, with its blue glitter cover, sits at the bottom, the screen blinking the words UNKNOWN CALLER as it rings. This is impossible. Kim's phone was almost never charged. How has it stayed on for months?

It keeps ringing.

Tentatively, I press the green button and hold it up to my ear. "Hello?"

The phone crackles noisily, the sound of buzzing and distant voices pulling through the static.

"Can . . . ear me? Don't . . . have to . . ."

"Who is this?" I ask, pressing the phone to my ear, straining to hear. But the line abruptly goes dead. I pull the phone away to see the screen is dark. I hold down the power button as hard as I can, but it refuses to turn back on. The battery is completely drained.

I limp quickly back to my bed, rip the cord out of my phone, and plug it into Kimberly's.

I pull my desk chair over and plop down, staring at the phone as it charges, the battery symbol appearing, red line blinking. I lean against my nightstand, watching. Who the *hell* would be on the other end of that call?

I wait and wait, but the phone refuses to boot back up. My eyes start to droop. I remember pestering Kim to get a new phone, one that might actually charge, but she never got the chance. So I sit and I wait.

I wake with a start, realizing I'm back in bed, the covers wrapped firmly around me.

I don't even remember lying down.

Frustrated with myself, I roll over and reach out for Kimberly's cell, feeling my way up and down the nightstand. I can't find it anywhere.

Did I knock it off in my zombie state?

I lean over the edge to peer around on the floor, but the blood rushes to my head and sends a throbbing pain across the length of my scar. Note to self: brain is still not ready for a head rush.

There's nothing on the floor.

I mean, a few lingering Pop-Tart wrappers, but no phone.

I clamber out of bed, looking at my desk for her purse. But . . . it isn't there. The spot where it was resting just last night is vacant.

That doesn't make any sense.

Slowly, I turn toward my closet. Now that I think of it, what actually makes no sense is that the purse was even on the desk in the first place. It was *never* on my desk. It's still . . .

I open the closet door and zero in on the box immediately, tucked away in the corner, just like it's always been.

I pull back the lid to see the shoe, the disco ball, and . . .

The purse, cell phone inside, screen dark and quiet.

12

"It didn't happen. It's just your head," Sam calls to me on our run the next morning, struggling to keep up with my scared-shitless pace, which is coming pretty close to an Olympic marathon runner's even with my less than fully functioning leg.

On our first mile on the track, I told him about the phone, the unknown caller, the garbled voice, struggling to put into words whatever the hell happened last night.

He's always been the logical one. Maybe he can help me make sense of this.

"Sam, I *saw* it ringing. I *heard* someone on the other end. I could tell you every detail. It didn't feel like a dream."

My leg buckles and I stop abruptly. My hands grab my knees as I struggle to catch my breath, spots forming in front of my eyes.

"I didn't say you were dreaming, dude," Sam says as he stops next to me. "But you *did* have a brain injury."

"Why is this still happening? I'm doing everything the doctor said. Taking the pills, doing the memory exercises, staying active. But *every* time I turn around, I see her," I say, frustrated. I straighten up, meeting his gaze. "She didn't even want to be with me, but now she won't leave me alone?"

I don't know who's more shocked by these words. Where did *that* come from?

Sam just looks at me, his expression unreadable.

The guilt bubbles back up, but part of me can't help but feel there's truth in what I said. Kimberly said she didn't want to be with me anymore, and yet the moment I breathe a little easier, there she is, haunting every headache and twinge of pain. Every memory of the accident. Every thought about the future.

I'm trying my best to stand on my own and do what she wanted me to do. Why won't she just let me?

"What if this never heals?" I ask as I jab angrily at my scar. "Am I going to keep seeing things and hearing things until I go crazy? It hurts too much seeing her. Thinking she's here."

"It hurts *you?*" Sam snorts, looking back at me. "Did it ever occur to you that you're not the only one grieving, Kyle?" I notice now the rigid set of his shoulders. "I would kill to see her again."

"Sam, I—"

"Did you ever even bother to see how I was doing? To see if I'm okay?" he asks. "You only call me when *you* have a problem. You never want to talk unless it's about you."

Hearing that makes me feel like shit, but at the same time, it was different for him. I was the one *there* that night. The one driving the car my *girlfriend* died in.

We stare at each other for a long moment, years of friendship struggling against these last few fucked-up months.

"She was my friend too," he says, his voice low. "She was special to me, too."

"I'm sorry, Sam. I know she was," I say. I take a deep breath and gaze past him at the track. "I've been a shitty friend. I—I don't know what I'm doing."

He shrugs and lets out a long sigh. "Me neither, man. That's why we can't lose each other," he says, patting my good shoulder. "The only thing making you crazy is *you*. You had a nightmare. Let it go."

I want to tell him that it's not that simple.

"All right," I say instead, agreeing with him. I can't lose him, too. "Come on." I fix a smile on my face and nod to the track. "These laps aren't going to run themselves."

Later, in the shower, it happens again. In the streaming water, I'm brought back to the drenching downpour the night of the accident. I see Kimberly's face right in front of me, like in the parking lot at the hotel, her hair soaked completely through.

I close my eyes, take a deep breath, and when I open them, she's gone. But the memory of that night lingers.

When I step out of the shower and wipe the steam from the bathroom mirror, I flash back again to the car, to my hand rubbing the fog from the windshield.

Chill out. It's not really happening.

I say it over and over until the pain in my head subsides, just like Dr. Benefield told me to. I push back my long hair to see my scar in the mirror, the skin healing nicely, the color still a fragile pink. I trace it, trying to convince myself that the brain and the heart aren't like skin. They take a little longer to heal.

But it won't ever heal if I keep thinking what I'm seeing is real. I think about my conversation with Marley. How for the first time in months I was able to talk about Kim. The *real* Kim, not what my broken brain keeps conjuring. So how can I get my brain to stay on the real Kim instead of imagining her ghost around every corner? My reflection doesn't have an answer for me.

I know one thing I can fix, though.

I tug at my hair. Time for a haircut. I look like I'm about to be cast in some kind of Revolutionary War reenactment as George Washington's cousin.

Now, *that* would be a nightmare.

13

Marley leans in closer to me, studying the scar, a full three days after my last vision and my first haircut in three months. It's super visible now, and as she leans forward, I try to distract myself by staring at the grass, or the trees, or the people out for a stroll around the park. Then . . . she reaches up to touch it, her fingertips barely skimming my skin. She does it so gently that it leaves behind an electric feeling.

It feels strange, like my body is waking up.

"What happened?" She pulls her hand away, and I realize I've been holding my breath this whole time.

"I don't tell sad stories," I say, teasing her.

She raises her eyebrows, challenging me. "Oh, is that how this works? I give, then you give?"

I pause, realizing that that's 100 percent *not* how I want this to work. I want to tell her. About the accident. About *Kim*. She's the first person I've wanted to talk to about any of it.

"I guess . . . ," I say, shifting my position to rest my back against the cherry tree, my voice trailing off. "I just don't really tell stories."

"Yes, you do. We all do," Marley says as she crosses her legs underneath her. "We're telling a story right now. Deciding how to be, what to say, what to do." She pushes her hair behind her ear. "That's . . . telling a story."

"That's living."

"Okay, so someone's *life story* isn't really a story?"

She has me there and she knows it.

"Can you stop being right?" I ask her, because it sure as hell seems she's been right about nearly everything. "Please?"

She rolls her eyes and nudges me, a faint red appearing on her cheeks. "You know the best thing about telling stories?" she asks.

I shake my head, my eyes still on the flush of her cheeks.

"The audience," she says. "Without an audience, a storyteller is just talking to the air, but when someone's listening . . ."

"Ah," I say. "So you're saying you're a good listener."

She tilts her head and shrugs like it's a no-brainer. "I am. And I'd love to hear your story. If you want to tell me."

For the first time, I think maybe I can.

"God." I exhale, trying to find a good jumping-off point. "Where do I even start?"

"Start at the beginning," she says as she leans back against the tree, her shoulder brushing mine.

I give her a look. The *beginning*? Does she want to be here until

Christmas? Though I guess I don't really have any plans between now and then.

"Okay," she says, arching an eyebrow. "How about the middle? Two-thirds?"

I laugh, trying to think of a good place. The *right* place. "How about . . . ?" I say, picturing the way Kimberly's lower lip would jut out when she wanted something from me. "How about I start with Kim?"

So I tell her. About the two of us fighting over the same swing at recess and Sam giving up his so we'd stop fighting. About getting up the nerve to write "I ♥ U" in her diary in middle school. I tell her about how Kim and I would ditch school on our anniversary every year and take a small road trip to a surprise location she chose in advance. The beach, the aquarium, a national park. She'd always pack the best snacks and put together the perfect playlist for the drive.

All the firsts. All the plans. All the little fights and makeups.

"I mean, we were perfect. I know we were a cliché—head cheerleader and the quarterback. But we were the couple everyone wanted to be." I look out at the fallen cherry blossoms scattered around us in the grass. "And even when we weren't, after my shoulder got wrecked, everything was okay because I still had Kim."

I turn my head toward Marley, but she doesn't say anything, just waits for me to go on, a soft, unhurried look on her face.

So I tell her about my football career ending. How broken I felt when I saw the X-ray, years of training and dreaming destroyed in a fraction of a second, Kimberly holding my hand in the ambulance and at the hospital, too. She never left my side.

"Don't get me wrong. We fought, too," I admit. We'd argue over going out with the team after my injury, when I just wanted to hang out at my house. Or when she wanted to do an epic college road trip to see a bunch of schools, but I didn't want to because I was sure I already had a full ride to UCLA. Or when . . . Well, we argued about a lot of things. "Probably more than most couples. But I always thought it was just because we cared so much."

I scrape my heels across the grass. "I don't know. It seems so stupid now. It was all so . . ."

"Trivial," Marley says, looking up at me, and I can tell she gets it. She doesn't press for more after that. Doesn't ask me the big questions, what happened to Kim, to me. And maybe that's why I keep talking. I tell her everything. From the graduation party to the visions.

Marley listens, without interruption, until my words trail off. Her eyes are thoughtful as she bites her lower lip, like she's replaying my words in her head.

"Did it ever feel like that to you?" she asks, looking over at me. "That you were controlling everything?"

"No," I say firmly, but it sounds false to my ears. Especially when I look at it now. Something about telling the whole story makes all the tiny cracks more visible. There were more of them than I remembered, enough that could lead to a big break. "I don't know," I say finally. "I think maybe, after I lost football, I felt kind of helpless. Like my whole future was gone. I guess I thought if she was there, I wouldn't be alone in that. Maybe I just wanted to be in control of *something*."

"Most days, I *still* feel that way," she says, nodding, her eyes distant. I want to ask, but I don't pry any further. I know for a fact that her *not* asking helped me. I have to trust she'll tell me when she's ready.

"Still want to hang out with me even though my ex-girlfriend is haunting me?" I ask to lighten the mood.

Marley laughs at that as she sits up and gathers a handful of cherry blossom petals. "Maybe she isn't," she says, making a fist before letting them drop from her hand one by one. "Maybe you're still trying to be in control. Trying to keep a part of her here."

I watch the petals drift slowly to the ground. "Pretty pathetic," I say as I shake my head. "I mean, she *dumped* me."

"I'm so sorry, but . . . ," Marley says, and I look up to see a smile forming on her lips. "I mean . . . Kim. Come on. What an idiot."

What? Did Marley just say that? I cringe, but completely unconsciously, a laugh bursts out of me. "You can't say that. She's dead."

I'm pretty certain that's an unspoken cardinal rule. You can't talk shit about dead people. Unless they're, like, a dictator or a serial killer.

"Well, she broke up with you," she says, standing and brushing away the small flecks of dirt and grass clinging to her yellow skirt. "Not smart."

Her words catch me off guard, but her expression isn't flirty. I think she's just being a good friend.

It's nice to be able to talk to someone about the breakup. Someone who will actually acknowledge I was dumped without making me feel guilty about it.

I stand, and she looks up at me, reaching out to lightly touch my arm, the point where her fingers touch feeling like a ripple of water vibrating out across my body. Her expression grows serious again.

"I'm sorry you're hurting," she says. And it doesn't feel like an empty phrase, a generic sentence that everyone repeats out of politeness.

It sounds genuine.

And it's exactly what I needed to hear. She's not pushing me to just be better already. Not judging how I feel or what I'm doing. She's just letting me feel it.

"Doesn't hurt as much as it used to," I say back, surprised to find I mean it.

After a while we walk around the park, a few of the leaves on the trees already turning orange and red and yellow. Some drift off their branches and fall in front of us, and our feet crunch noisily over them.

Marley pulls a half-finished red-and-white box of popcorn out of her bag, leftovers from an earlier pond expedition with the ducks. She holds it out to me. I take a handful, popping a few kernels into my mouth.

"Do you have any dreams outside of all of that? Outside of football? UCLA?" she asks. Our shoulders are almost touching as we walk, like some invisible barrier between us has disappeared.

I swallow, looking away at the pond peeking through the trees. It's what my mom's been trying to ask me. The question I haven't had an answer to.

"I don't know. Football was always my first choice. But since that's out, and since my plans with Kim are out . . . ," I say, shrugging. "I don't really know where to start."

"What do you want?" she asks. "Not Kim. Not Sam. Not your mom. *You.*"

I take a deep breath, saying the first thing that comes into my head, completely unfiltered. "I think right now I just want to *be.* I don't want to go to UCLA and pretend I have it figured out. But I don't really want to go anywhere else, either."

"I get that, but you don't have to leave to start thinking about what you want. Just because you can't play anymore doesn't mean you can't do something football related," she says, a few popcorn kernels disappearing into her mouth.

"Like what?"

She chews thoughtfully. "Coaching?"

I consider it for a minute, but the idea of being on the bench still feels kind of raw. "I don't know about coaching. But . . . I mean, they did ask me to write a couple of football articles for my school paper since I was stuck going to the games anyway. I liked doing that, and I think they were pretty good. But I don't think anyone actually read them."

"You should try," Marley says eagerly. "Be a writer. Or a journalist. Then we'll *both* be storytellers."

I smile, her enthusiasm infectious. I try to picture it. My name in print, in something more than just the Ambrose school paper. Giving teams the coverage they actually deserve instead of some shitty clickbait.

"They're never really gone, you know," she says unexpectedly, stopping dead in her tracks. I look back to see her face has grown serious again. "We keep them with us, just like you and football. They're still part of our lives."

Still part of our lives. That's all I've wanted since the accident. To find a way to live without leaving Kim behind.

My fingers unexpectedly brush against Marley's hand, and I pull back instantly, the feeling strange and familiar all at once.

I stuff my hands in my pockets, and we walk silently for a while, but not in the painfully awkward way where you're desperately trying to think of something to fill the silence. This is actually nice. Comfortable.

"Thanks, Marley," I say as we round a corner of the park, tall oak trees reaching for the sky.

"For what?"

I shrug, not knowing how to put my gratitude into words. For being easy to talk to? For understanding? "It hasn't been easy for me to really talk to anyone . . . since . . ."

She nods, already knowing. Of course she does.

"You think you'll be back here tomorrow?" Marley asks.

"Actually, um . . ." My voice trails off, my brain trying to pull itself together and form a coherent sentence. "I was thinking maybe we could get out of the park for a night? Dinner at my house on

Friday? As a thank-you." I give her a big smile as I try to butter up the experience. "I'll cook."

Marley shoots me a side-eye. "I didn't know you cook."

"Of course I cook," I say, looking offended. "I'm a pizza rolls aficionado."

14

"All right," MY MOM says, grabbing a grocery cart, a look of determination on her face. "Divide and conquer. You get the rib eye and some turkey from the deli, I'll get the veggies, and we'll meet at the checkout counter in ten. Good?"

I nod, eyeing the cart. "You're using a whole cart just for a small bag of potatoes?"

She glares at me. "I may grab a few other things. See where the wind takes me."

"See where the *wind* takes me," I repeat, laughing and shaking my head. Classic. "Maybe the wind will take *me* to the dessert aisle!" I call over my shoulder to her, her sarcastic laugh trailing behind me.

I move off in the direction of the meat counter and get two fresh-cut rib eyes. Marley and I decided on six o'clock for dinner tomorrow. I'm going to make my mom's secret family rib eye recipe, which . . . could definitely go either way. It'll be good to hang somewhere other than the park. At least, that's what I tell myself. I don't want to think this impromptu invitation from me was anything more than just a change of scenery.

I make my way to the deli counter, where I grab a number and wait behind an old lady getting four pounds of American cheese. She's in for a *night.*

I take a Tylenol while I wait, warding off the return of the nagging headache I've had for most of the day. I'm getting better at figuring out how to manage the pain, but some days I still can't get ahead of it.

"Sir?"

I look up, realizing the deli clerk has been talking to me. He wipes his hands on a towel and repeats his question. "What can I get for you?"

"Sorry," I say, stepping closer to the display case. "Half a pound of turkey, please, thin cut."

"You got it," he says, snapping on a pair of fresh gloves. I watch him grab the hunk of turkey and drop it onto the slicer with a loud *thump.*

"Kyle?" a voice says from behind me.

I turn, but I see only an empty aisle of the grocery store. Light glints off plastic soda bottles and metal cans. Uh-oh. Not now. I will the Tylenol to kick in as I nervously turn back to the deli clerk. He reaches up to put his hands on the machine, his shadow moving on the wall behind him.

But . . .

They aren't in sync. My eyes shift from the man to the shadow, his movements a second faster in silhouette.

He leans over the machine just after the shadow does, but now there's long hair flowing over the silhouette's shoulder.

I take a step closer, confused. The height and shape of the shadow is suddenly shockingly familiar to me. Too familiar.

Kimberly.

I see the electric blade spin, but the sound isn't right. Instead of the whirring of metal, I hear an odd whooshing sound.

Chill out. This isn't real. This *isn't* real.

I think of what Marley said, about how I'm trying to control things. Trying to keep a part of her here.

The shadow's arm reaches for the slicer again, and I close my eyes, focusing on that. It's in my head. It's—I jump when a hand touches my neck.

"What the . . ." I whirl around, coming face-to-face with my mom, her hand in midair.

"I'm sorry," she says, studying my face. "I thought you heard me."

I glance back at the deli clerk to see him making a normal slice, with a normal shadow.

It's been almost a week since my last weird vision. I'm pissed at myself.

"You okay?" my mom asks, feeling my forehead. She's been better at giving me some space to figure things out now that I'm not staying in bed for twenty-three of the twenty-four hours in a day, but that still doesn't stop her from poking and prodding me after the slightest trace of a headache.

"Yeah," I say as the deli clerk puts the wrapped meat onto the counter. I grab it, put it into the overflowing cart with a *thunk*. "My head's just bothering me today. What else is new?"

I can still feel her looking at me, so I try to reassure her again. "Nothing a little Tylenol and some food can't fix." I look down at the pile of groceries in the shopping cart, the bag of potatoes hopefully buried somewhere at the bottom. "Where'd the wind blow you?"

She shrugs coyly and holds up a tub of ice cream, making the both of us laugh as we head to the checkout.

Exactly twenty-four hours later, I'm in *way* over my head. The steak? Looking great. Veggies? Steaming. My mom's béarnaise sauce recipe?

A catastrophe.

I'm surrounded by two empty egg cartons, shells and yolk guts littering the entire counter, and for what feels like the millionth time, the sauce comes out lumpy.

Why is it so lumpy?

My mom always makes this look so easy.

I glance at the clock, panicking a bit when I see it's 5:45. I only have fifteen minutes to get this sauce right, reheat everything, and probably change my shirt, since I've sweat clean through this one trying to figure out how to make this fancy-ass sauce.

After speed-watching a YouTube how-to video, I finally realize that I've had the temperature too high this entire time. I scan through my mom's handwritten recipe card for the thirtieth time, and there is no mention of temperature. So I toss it back onto the counter, doing a double take when I catch sight of a tiny note scrawled on the back: *lower temp before eggs.*

Great. Just great.

I lower the temperature this time, and when I whisk the yolks and then beat in the butter, my wrist screaming, it actually turns into a smooth sauce instead of a lumpy mess.

"Holy shit. I did it," I say, breathing a sigh of relief as I give it a taste. Creamy. Perfect. I add a pinch of salt just to be safe.

Moving quickly, I put down the plates and fold napkins underneath the utensils and even make sure to have a flower centerpiece.

A branch of cherry blossoms.

I ran to the park earlier just to make sure they'd be here, so a few of the blossoms look a little worse for wear.

While the rib eyes reheat, I pour the sauce into tiny ramekins instead of over the meat, since Marley is particular with her sauces. The second one takes a long time to fill, the sauce pouring out at a glacial pace. Impatiently, I tap the bottom of the saucepan, and of course, it all comes rushing out at once, overflowing past the top of the ramekin and onto the countertop like a damn mudslide.

I'm crushing this cooking thing.

Sighing, I grab a towel and clean it off, then plate the meat and get everything on the table with just enough time to sprint downstairs to change my shirt before the doorbell rings.

Marley.

I smooth down my hair as I take the steps by twos, then slide into the entryway to pull open the door.

She's wearing a lemon-yellow rain jacket, the color standing out against the cloudy gray sky, the rain falling all around her.

"Hey," I say, leaning casually against the doorframe.

"Hey," she says, squinting to look at me through the rain. She nods up at the steady downpour. "Can I maybe . . . come in?"

"Oh, right. Yeah," I say, pushing the door fully open. She steps inside and pulls her hood down, her hair wavier than usual because of the rain. I find my eyes zeroing on a stray strand trying to break out of her ponytail.

I want to tuck it behind her ear like she always does, but instead I take her jacket from her. I hang it on the basement doorknob to dry while she looks around the entryway at all the pictures. She stops in front of me, peering down the steps.

"What's down there?" she asks.

"A couple of dead bodies," I joke, to which she rolls her eyes, nudging my shoulder, the tiniest bit amused. "My room's down there."

She looks intrigued. "In the basement?"

"Yeah. I moved down there my sophomore year of high school, after my mom got it finished," I say as I nod down the steps. "Sam and Kim used to sneak in through a door down there. Leads straight to the backyard."

She smiles at that, definitely amused now. "Ah, a bad boy," she teases.

I roll my eyes. "You ready for dinner?"

"Am I?" she asks warily, understandably doubting my cooking abilities.

We head into the kitchen and Marley smiles at the cherry blossoms on the table, so at least my manic, limping run to the park this morning was worth it.

I'm about to sit down when I realize I forgot to put water on the table. Pulling open the cabinet, I hear a car door slam shut outside.

"Hey, my mom's home early," I say as I crane my neck to look out the window, catching a glimpse of her getting her stuff out of the backseat, the rain barely a mist now. I knew she had a mischievous glint in her eye when I asked her to get out her recipe card last night. Of *course* she couldn't stay away. Classic Lydia. "She's going to be so excited to meet you."

I head out of the kitchen and into the entryway, then pull open the door to greet her. "Hey, Mom, this is . . ." I turn around, but the hallway behind me is empty—no Marley. My mom's excited expression fades to confusion, which I return with the same kind of energy.

"One sec," I say as I backtrack to the kitchen, but even the seat where Marley was sitting is now empty. What the . . . ?

I pause, noticing the door to the basement is ajar, her yellow rain jacket gone.

"Marley?" I call as I push it fully open, jogging down the steps. I'm met by silence, the French doors in the corner of the room flung wide open. I peer out into the backyard for a trace of her yellow jacket.

"Marley!"

Still nothing.

I grab a hoodie from the back of my desk chair. "Hey, Mom!" I call upstairs as I pull it on. "I'll be right back." I jog outside and around the house, squinting as I search for her.

Where did she—*the pond.*

I run-limp out of my neighborhood and along the path, my chest heaving by the time the glittering surface of the water comes into view, the air warm after the rain, the sky a blend of pinks and oranges and purples.

I skid to a stop when I see her yellow jacket, doing a double take when I notice there's a duck sitting in her lap.

Like . . . an actual live fucking duck. Sitting. In her lap.

I pull off my hoodie and walk over. I place it on the slightly damp ground before sliding down next to her.

"Well," I say with an exhale. "This is probably the first time I've ever seen anyone cuddle a duck."

"I'm sorry," she says, not looking at me. She remains focused on the duck, gently petting its white feathers, her eyebrows knitted together.

"What happened? You didn't even get to taste the food. I mean, I'm no chef, but it couldn't have been *that* bad." The bird turns its head to look at me, its beady black eyes sizing me up. I scoot a little farther away, not looking for a fight.

Marley shrugs and looks out at the water, the familiar glimmer of pain in her eyes.

"Is it part of the sad story?"

She lets out a heavy sigh, her shoulders rising and falling with the breath. "I just . . . I got nervous," she says as she pushes her wavy hair out of her face. "Your mom came home. New people make me nervous. I can't seem to find my voice. I don't ever know what to say."

I smirk and scoot closer to nudge her shoulder, the bird eyeing me. "You talk plenty."

"Only to you," she says as she looks over at me. "With you it's . . ."

Her voice trails off as she searches for the word.

"I don't know. It's . . . us. You get it."

Us. My heart thumps loudly in my chest at that word. I swallow and watch as she tucks her fingers under the duck's wings and scratches, its feathers ruffling for a few seconds before settling back down. It rubs its beak against her arm, more affectionate than I knew a duck could even be.

I cross my legs, one over the other, and lean back, trying to ignore the feeling her words have just given me.

"Well, the way you ditched me at dinner was super not cool," I say, attempting to be serious. "I spent a full hour on that sauce and you didn't even try it."

I glance over to see her eyes are wide, her face flustered.

"So," I say, the word "us" still ringing in my ears. "I deserve a do-over."

"A do-over?" she asks, both she and the duck staring at me.

"No parents allowed," I say, meeting the duck's gaze. "Or ducks. Just you and me."

The duck quacks in response, its feathers ruffling as Marley and I laugh.

"Just you and me," she says thoughtfully, hesitantly, until that shy smile pulls at her lips. "Okay."

We stay another half hour, watching the sun set, our legs almost touching. I jog home after, still trying to figure out how I feel about all of this.

This is not at all how I expected this night to go.

I thought she'd tease me about the messy sauce or my subpar napkin-folding skills. That maybe she'd open up and tell me a little more of her sad story.

But now I just have more questions.

The thing is . . . I do know exactly what she means by "us." We just *get* each other. And even though it feels like something I shouldn't admit, I can't help but be excited about our do-over. Excited about *us*.

I shake off my jumbled feelings and slow down as I head through the front door and into the kitchen, the uneaten rib eyes still on the table, my mom leaning casually against the counter like she didn't just come home three hours early to catch a glimpse of Marley.

"Everything all right?" my mom asks.

"Yep," I say as I fill a glass with water and take a quick sip. "It's all good." I can feel her eyes on me, prodding for more. "Maybe," I start to say, and she perks up, eager for more information. "Maybe you can promise me you'll *actually* work late next time? Instead of, you know, ruining my plans."

She gives me a guilty smile before agreeing.

"You hungry?" I motion to the uneaten plates.

She laughs, scooping them up to reheat. "Starving. I've been eyeing them since you left."

We've barely started eating when there's a knock on the back door. We look over, the hinges creaking as Sam steps inside, grinning wide and holding a six-pack of beer.

Crap.

Sam knows my mom usually stays late at work on Fridays, but he hasn't just shown up like this since before the accident.

"Hey," he says as he holds up the six-pack. "Thought we could hang."

I frantically gesture to him to hide it, but it's too late. His eyes widen instantly when he sees my mom, and he quickly tries to hide the beer behind his back, but nothing gets past Lydia Lafferty.

She gets up and grabs them right from his grip, clutching the six-pack to her chest. "How thoughtful, Sam! How did you know I love a good IPA?"

"Oh, come on, Mrs. L.," Sam says, smirking and throwing an arm over her shoulder. Sam could charm anyone. "I feel like I've aged three years in the last three months. How about you, Kyle? You feeling twenty-one?"

"Maybe even twenty-two," I say, grinning at him as my mom rolls her eyes at the both of us.

"Nice try, boys," she says, pretending to not find our antics even a little bit funny, but I can see the corner of her mouth pulling up into a smile.

Sam sighs and plunks down on one of the kitchen chairs, nodding to the remnants of dinner.

"That's a fancy meal," Sam says, leaning over to give the rib eye a sniff. "What's the occasion, Mrs. L.?"

"No occasion," my mom says. She glances over at me, hesitating.

"What? What's that look?" Sam asks me, his gaze confused, and my stomach sinks.

I know, even before saying it, that he isn't going to understand.

15

I pull my backpack farther up on my shoulder the next morning, finally taking up Sam's invite to join the Saturday touch football game at the park. I told him a few days ago I'd come, but after last night . . .

I see his jaw lock as he looks over at me from the middle of a group of guys. As I get closer, he spins on his heel, intentionally walking away from them. Away from me.

. . . I kind of wish I'd bailed.

I catch sight of Dave and Paul, two guys from our team who have stayed in town and started working. I hesitate, my stomach twisting a little more. I never replied to any of their texts. I really don't need more people on this field to be pissed at me.

The worry is instantly washed away, though, when Paul looks straight at me, his face breaking out into a huge smile. "No shit."

Dave spins around to see what he's looking at, his mop of blond hair pulled up into a man bun. "Lafferty! Good to see you, man."

"You too," I say as Paul throws an arm around my shoulder.

At least someone isn't pissed to see me. I can practically *feel* Sam's passive-aggressive rage radiating at me from his fake-ass hamstring stretches a few feet away.

He knows now that I've been hanging out with Marley, but I can't figure out why he's being so weird about it. Maybe because he just left instead of letting me explain.

The silent treatment was always Kim's move, not Sam's.

"You look good," Paul says as Dave nods in agreement.

"It's been rough, but I'm getting back out there," I say, which is somehow both an understatement and an overstatement at the same time. This is the most people I've been around in months.

"That's awesome, bro. Glad you came," Dave says, smiling as he hands me the football he's been holding.

I look down at it, rolling it between my hands, the feeling like coming home. We divide into teams, the rest of the players people from last year's JV team, now promoted to varsity after our departure.

When we circle up for the first play, Sam stands off to the side, making a show of disagreeing with everything I say.

Great. Here we go.

As we get into formation, he brushes past me a little too hard to be accidental. "It's just like changing channels for you, isn't it?"

"What?" I ask as he sets up on the line, his back to me.

"You know what."

I ignore him and call the play, my eyes following him down the length of the field, a defender hot on his tail. I opt to throw a short pass to Paul for the sake of gaining a couple of yards. He catches it, but he's tapped by a lineman almost immediately, ending the play.

Sam jogs back over, his chest heaving. "Nothing?" he asks, raising his eyebrows expectantly. "You've got *nothing* to say? Maybe we should ask Marley what she thinks."

There it is. Out in the open. Fucking *finally*.

"Let it go, Sam," I mutter as Paul hands the ball back to me.

"Expert advice, huh? You sure know how to let go, don't you?"

Did he really just say that?

Scowling, I call the next play. The ball is hiked to me, and Sam's supposed to run a hook route for the touchdown. Instead he just strolls right through the play, his back turned away from the pass.

What the *fuck*?

Fury explodes across my chest. I fire the ball at him with enough force to make my shoulder twinge, watching as it bounces off the back of his head and his neck jerks forward. He whips around and is already running at me before I have any time to take off. He slams into me. I hit the ground hard. Not any harder than I have millions of times in a football game.

But it stuns me for just a second. I've *never* seen Sam like this.

"How many times did Kim break up with you? Do you even remember?" he says, standing over me.

I push myself up, refusing to be intimidated. "I'm guessing you do. How many?"

He grabs my collar, twisting his fists into it with a raw anger that's clearly been boiling for a while now. "Seven. Seven times since the ninth grade—"

Suddenly all the frustration I've been shoving down the last few months erupts all at once. At him. At what happened. Who the *hell* does he think he is? How dare he tell me how to feel?

"And she was about to do it again, Sam! But she died," I say as I shove him away, his fingers releasing the fabric around my collar. "What am I supposed to do? Pine forever? Stop breathing?"

"*I would*," Sam says, all of the anger rushing out of him, his shoulders dropping as a heavy weight settles down on them. A weight that I recognize. Then . . . he confirms it. "I loved her too. *Really* loved her. And I would *never* let her go."

We stare at each other, his words knocking me speechless. But he isn't done.

"You don't deserve her, Kyle," he says, his voice low. "You never did."

He turns and stalks off the field, his broad shoulders fading farther and farther away into the distance. I watch Sam disappear completely from view, my head spinning.

Sam loved Kimberly?

I see it now, the pieces clicking into place. The way he would stand behind her protectively. The way he always deferred to her. How broken he was after she died.

How the hell did I miss it? How, in all these years, did I not notice that my best friend was in love with my girlfriend?

The other guys act like they weren't watching the fight go

down. No one comes over, and I don't expect them to. I haven't been close to any of these guys for a long time. I didn't see it until now, but when I left the team, I left them behind too.

Everyone but Kim and Sam.

So how did I not notice he loved her?

Because I was selfish.

The words ring around my head, crystal clear. Painfully true.

All I did was see the world, my friends, my girlfriend, through *my* lens. I didn't once bother seeing it through any of theirs.

Later that night, Mom finds me in my room, my eyes fixed on a small dot on the ceiling.

"You wore it, you help fold it," she says, dropping the laundry basket on the floor by my door. I groan and roll out of bed to follow her upstairs, one hand clutching a bag of frozen peas to my bruised side, the other juggling the basket.

Mom keeps glancing at me as the two of us start folding together in her bedroom.

"I thought this was supposed to be a touch game."

"It was for me. Sam, though . . ."

I didn't plan on saying anything, but my mind hasn't stopped going over it all. So I tell her everything. About the fight. And Marley.

"Sam's right," I say after a moment of silence, a worn Ambrose High football sweatshirt in my hand. "Maybe I never deserved Kim at all. Maybe she was too good for me."

"What does Sam know?" she says, rolling up a pair of socks and tossing them at me. "You're allowed to have other friends. Even other . . . more than friends."

My stomach lurches, but I can't go there right now. I can't stop thinking about what Sam said. "He was in love with Kim," I say finally, expecting her to look up. To be surprised. But instead she nods. *She knew.* This whole time, was I the only one oblivious to it?

Did Kim know?

It's just another question I'll never be able to ask her.

I watch as Mom folds a towel, her face becoming thoughtful. "So . . . what are you going to do?" she asks.

"About what?"

Mom rolls her eyes at my lack of response.

"You're a hopeless romantic, honey. I've watched you with Kimberly since you were eight years old. Once you set your heart on her, no one else would do, even when you drove each other crazy," she says finally. "But because of that, you never let yourself imagine your life without her. You always centered everything around her, and . . . that's a lot of pressure in a relationship. A lot of pressure on a person who's still figuring out who they are."

"Mom—" I start to say.

"Just listen. Why did you get Kim that bracelet?"

"Because I loved her," I say adamantly. "I wanted to show her how much I loved her." She just stares and raises one of her eyebrows like she's waiting for me to continue. I let out a long exhale, looking away as I slowly fold a pair of sweatpants. "And . . . because I could tell something was up. I thought the bracelet would remind her of everything we'd already made it through. Show her we could fix whatever was wrong."

She nods. "You were *always* trying to fix things instead of thinking about why they were broken. It's hard to build anything if the foundation has cracks." She pauses to grab another shirt. "And that doesn't mean that you two didn't love each other. It just means that maybe you two were operating on two different wavelengths."

Operating on different wavelengths. Sometimes when we'd fight, it really did feel like we weren't having the same conversation. I think about that night. Our conversation in the car. Were we on the same page then?

How many times were we on different pages without even realizing it?

"Kim's always going to be part of you, Kyle, but you have to live your own life. She doesn't get a say anymore. You've got a lot of days ahead of you. They could all be like this one, folding laundry with your sweet, devoted mother. . . ." She folds a shirt while my hands remain frozen, clutching mismatched socks. "Or you could try to live your life *without* her, allow yourself to *really* live," she says, looking up at me. "See where the wind takes you."

I smile, but I'm silent for a moment, reaching out to take a pair of jeans. That's what Kim said. *Exactly* what she said. Kim wanted to see who we were without each other too.

She'd realized it. *Mom* had realized it.

It was me who hadn't.

This time, though, it makes sense. This time . . . I might actually understand.

And with that understanding comes the realization that Sam's both right and wrong at the same time.

We do need to remember Kim. And . . . well, it would be impossible to forget her even if I tried. She's tangled up in every part of who I've been. I wouldn't be here without her.

But we can't be stuck, immobilized without her. Immobilized by what she wanted.

We have to figure it out for ourselves now.

"I've been talking to Marley about what I might want to do. Since football is out now," I say slowly, and Mom's eyes light up instantly. "Do you think I'd be a good sportswriter? I thought I could take a class or maybe apply for an internship or something."

"I think you'd be a great sportswriter." She smiles, looking happier than I've seen her since . . . before. "And I think anyone who can help you find your way forward is a good person to have in your life."

She scoops up an armful of towels, calling over her shoulder as she heads toward her bathroom, "Guess I'll have to find a new laundry partner."

The next morning, I pack up the box of Kimberly's stuff and carry it upstairs. Mom follows just behind me, her hand wrapping gently around my arm when I make it to the entryway.

"Are you sure about this, honey?" she asks, turning me to face her.

I nod, looking up from the box to meet her questioning gaze. "I'm sure."

She pulls me into a hug, her arms wrapping tightly around me. I lean into it. I need to do this to start moving forward. Whether that's getting an internship or mending things with Sam or . . . anything else.

The memories of that night aren't the ones I want to hold on to. I have to let go of the guilt. I have to stop trying to keep her boxed up here with me.

Gently, I lay a hand on top of the box, one last goodbye, before handing it to Mom to give back to Kim's parents. As she turns, I feel the heaviness of the charm bracelet in my pocket. The final reminder of that fateful night.

The one I didn't think I could let go of.

"Wait," I say as I pull it out, the metal charms clinking together. It hurts to let it go, but as I gently place it inside the box, a weight lifts off my chest and lets me take my first deep breath in almost four months.

16

I lie on my back on the grass a few days later, watching the sunlight trickle through the tree branches, the sparkling light dancing in front of my vision. Marley and I meet up at noon to feed the ducks like we usually do, the warm late-September weather leading us to the cherry blossom tree, the petals fading now to an off-white.

"What are you thinking about?" Marley asks from next to me.

"Just . . ." I take a deep breath. "Sam."

Talking to my mom helped me figure out a lot of shit, but it didn't fix anything with Sam. And I still can't figure out how to talk to him about it.

I turn to look at her, the sunlight casting a warm glow on her face, making her hazel eyes bright, the color giving way to a glowing green around her pupil. She reaches out toward my face, and I find myself wondering what it would be like if she touched me.

Instead, she plucks a dandelion from between us and gives it a sniff. The guilt rises up, but without much strength, like it's too exhausted to keep fighting. Maybe I am too. But Sam's hurt face doesn't recede from my mind.

"We got into a fight this weekend. I—I haven't been a very good friend to him since Kim died. I wasn't being honest with him. . . ." I pause and let out a long sigh. "Or with myself."

"It's hard to be the one who messes up, isn't it?" she says, her face growing sad.

I push myself up onto my arm. It takes a lot for Marley to open up. She notices my reaction and offers a weak smile. "Sorry. I didn't mean to say that. It's funny. I was always quiet. *Super* shy. To the point that sometimes Laura even spoke for me." She looks away, in the direction of the cemetery. "She always knew what I wanted to say. Maybe because we were twins."

She's always avoided talking about her sister. No sad stories. This is big for her.

"We were identical. In almost every way," Marley says, and the dark cloud behind her eyes comes over her. From the furrow in her brow to the battered hunch of her shoulders, it consumes her. It's like an entirely different person is sitting in front of me. "When I lost her, I lost my voice. But now, with you . . ." She stops, looking back at me, her eyes clearing just the tiniest bit. "I feel like talking again."

"Talk all you want," I say. "I'm here for it." There's a magic in this moment where she's letting me in, and I don't want to break that spell, so even though I want to take her hand and comfort her, I don't.

She twists the dandelion around in between her fingers. "A life without Laura," she says, her voice soft. "It feels more impossible the longer she's gone. It feels *wrong*."

I wait a little while, but she doesn't say anything more.

"I get that," I say, sitting up. And I do. Everything about life after the accident has felt wrong. Except this. "But maybe we can both try to find something that makes it feel a little less wrong. Together."

"How?" she asks.

The words hover on the tip of my tongue, but I don't know where to begin. Then I think of how we met that day in the cemetery, an idea coming to mind. "Stories. You said we could both be storytellers, right?"

She nods, her face thoughtful.

"Well, I want to hear one of yours," I say. She straightens up and crosses her arms. "All I got that first day was 'Once upon a time.'"

"No way," she says, her shoulders tense. "I have no idea if they're good or not. I mean, what if you hate them?"

"I'll love them. I know I will," I promise her.

"You can't promise something like that," Marley says with a laugh.

"Please?" I ask, and I can see the hesitation in her face. The silence stretches between us until she finally breaks it, letting out a long, dramatic sigh.

"Okay . . . but only if I get to read some of your stuff too."

I'm so happy she said yes that I'm already nodding before I realize what I've agreed to.

Damn, she's good.

She holds up her pinky. I wrap mine around it, promising. Our hands linger, fingers sliding toward wrists until her hand is completely in mine.

It feels like waking up again. Every fiber in me feels alive, wanting me to close the gap between us, the smallest shift an earthquake.

"Marley . . . ," I start to say, but she quickly pulls away, her eyes lingering on my lips.

"Do you feel that?" she whispers.

I do. The air around us buzzes, the space between us crackling.

I reach out to take her hand again, but just as my fingers meet hers, she moves away from me, pulling herself out of the moment. She stands quickly and brushes off her clothes, abruptly stuffing her hands into her jean jacket. "I should go."

"Marley," I say, collecting myself. "You don't have to go."

She starts walking away, her yellow shoes standing out against the green of the grass.

"This is a sad story waiting to happen," she mumbles, her voice barely audible. When she gets to the path, she turns to look at me. "Just friends, Kyle," she calls to me. "That was the deal."

I nod, watching as she leaves, disappearing between the trees. I look down to see one yellow dandelion sitting next to me.

I pick it up, wondering what it would have been like to kiss her just now, her eyes on my lips a moment ago. Maybe Sam was right about something else.

Do I really want to be just friends with Marley?

* * *

On Thursday morning I walk to the cemetery. I still have a lot to figure out, but I think I finally have the right words to say to her. To Kimberly.

I stop short when I see a figure kneeling at her graveside, a long arm reaching out to place a big bouquet of tulips against the headstone.

Sam.

Of course.

"The tulips," I say as I come closer. "They were from you."

"They were her favorite," he says, his eyes focused on the headstone. KIMBERLY NICOLE BROOKS.

I kneel on my stiff leg and run my hand across the uneven stone.

"It's not fair," Sam says, watching me. "You're moving on. She can't. That might be a dick thing to say, but . . ."

"I get it, Sam. Trust me, I've felt like a dick constantly. Going to get ice cream. Watching movies on my couch. Even *laughing*. It all felt wrong, doing it without her. But if that's true, the two of us will spend the rest of our lives stuck right here," I say, gesturing to the cemetery around us, to Kimberly's headstone.

He doesn't say anything, but he doesn't stop me either.

"I finally realized what Kimberly was saying. I didn't get it before. I didn't listen to her before. But I finally, after all this time, understand what she wanted from me. *For* me. The best thing I can do to honor her is to stand on my own, Sam. Like she wanted. I need to let go." I pause, looking at him for a long moment, realizing he needs this just as much as I do. "So do you."

He pushes himself up onto his feet while I struggle to get to mine. When our eyes are level, he gives me a long look, before glancing guiltily away. "I'm sorry you had to find out like this."

"Yeah," I say, nodding as I think of his words at the park. "A lot of things make sense now. How you always defended her. Took her side."

"I took *your* side too," Sam says. "I never went after her. I never told her how I felt."

"You never told me, either," I say. "You could have."

"Would it have changed anything?" he asks.

I shake my head, knowing the truth. "Probably not."

He smiles at that, and I know both of us are hearing her voice in our heads. Not in a brain-injury way, though. Not this time.

"But," I continue, "I think it changes something now. I see the truth in what you said before. We have to be honest with ourselves."

We stare at each other, unsure of where to go from here. We opt for a quick bro hug, and then Sam nudges my arm, giving me a wry smile. "Wonder what your mom did with that beer?" he asks.

I nod toward the path, grinning back at him. "You want to find out?"

We walk together out of the graveyard, just the two of us. Even though I was talking to Sam, I'm sure Kim was there. I feel like she heard me. That I got it right at last. And even as we're leaving her behind, she feels closer than she has in a long, long time.

17

I shuffle around the kitchen, fixing the silverware on the napkins, the mint iced tea in the corner of the place mat. I'm just about ready.

This attempt at making dinner is going about a million times better than before. Probably because I ditched the rib eye recipe and tried something a bit more . . . Marley.

Hot dogs and fries. But fancy ones, with a Marley twist.

I carefully set up her side plate, putting eight empty baby ramekins down, encircling a slightly larger bowl filled with popcorn. Then I fill the ramekins around it: one with yellow mustard, one with bacon bits, and the others with ketchup, barbecue sauce, two different kinds of pickles, shredded cheese, and diced onions.

I push them together and add a big stick of celery extending from the bottom. Just as I hoped, the plate is transformed into a condiment flower. I carry it to the table and gently set it down. I want her to feel comfortable tonight. I want her to see that I see her. The way she always sees me.

That this isn't going to be a sad story.

I plate the hot dogs and the fries, making sure they aren't touching, just in time for the doorbell to ring.

I head out of the kitchen, trying to calm my nerves. *Why* am I so nervous? We're always so comfortable around each other.

I open the door to see Marley standing on our welcome mat, wearing a pair of jeans and her yellow cardigan, her hair pulled back into a bun.

"Hi," she says softly. She holds out a bundle of flowers. I do a quick scan, trying to guess what she's telling me with these.

I peer at the clusters of tiny white petals, but I'm out of luck when it comes to a name. All I know is that they're the poofy ones planted outside of granny houses.

"What's this one mean?" I ask her.

"They're hydrangeas," she says, clutching the strap of her bag with one hand, the other reaching out to touch one of the enormous floral puffballs. "It means . . . gratitude."

"Well, I am filled with *gratitude* for the flowers," I say, cringing hard at myself. Could I *be* any lamer?

Luckily, she laughs and comes inside, sliding her shoes off.

"You hungry?" I ask.

She nods and turns her face toward the kitchen, sniffing. "Smells good."

There's something suspiciously like relief on her face.

"Hopefully it actually *tastes* good," I say as we follow the warm smell of the food out of the entryway and down the hall.

As we step into the kitchen, she takes in the carefully laid out table, the folded napkins, the candles I pulled from the top shelf of the hallway closet. Her hand reaches out to touch the flower-condiment plate, a smile finally appearing on her lips.

"Because each deserves its own space," I say, and she blushes as we sit down.

There's an awkward pause, a new tension between us. A warm electricity. Does she feel it too? I try to shake it off, keeping my voice light as I suggest we dig in.

I grab my hot dog and take a huge bite. That eases the tension a bit more, and soon Marley's laughing and trying out all the different condiments in little bites.

Somehow her favorite, though, isn't even a condiment at all.

"Just *popcorn?*" I ask, incredulous, as she carefully puts another piece on top of her hot dog and takes a bite. "Of all of these toppings, popcorn is your favorite?"

She shrugs playfully. "I must be part duck."

I can't help but smile at that. I spend the rest of dinner grossing her out with different condiment combinations, though my bacon, barbecue sauce, and shredded cheese is literal genius.

As our meal disappears, the conversation stalls. I pop my last fry into my mouth. Marley puts the last few bites of her hot dog aside. Both of us fall silent as the nervous energy we've been fighting off fills the room. I know Marley hasn't shared her stories before, and I've sure as hell never shared my articles with anyone before.

Well, not in person.

But . . . I don't think this is about the writing.

I clear my throat and stand to take the plates to the sink. From the corner of my eye, I see her fidget with her napkin, folding it and unfolding it.

I turn to watch her fingers twist the material.

"Are you nervous?" I ask.

She looks up in a way that says, *Abso-freaking-lutely.*

"Good. Because *I'm* nervous," I admit.

She seems surprised. "You are?"

"I am crazy nervous," I say, studying her face, from the freckles on her nose to the fullness of her lips. Every feature somehow looks different in this new setting, sending my heart beating faster. "I mean, you're *here.*"

"I make you nervous?" she asks as she looks down at her napkin. "I . . . really?"

I hesitate, knowing that I'm balancing on a ledge, one side the past, one side the future. I have to choose. "You make me . . . ," I start to say, and as I take a step closer to her, I decide to just say it. "You make me want more, and *that* makes me nervous."

She looks up, her eyes glowing in the flickering candlelight, but she doesn't say anything. Maybe I should have just kept my mouth shut and let her enjoy her dinner.

"So, um," I say, changing the subject. "How 'bout dessert?"

I get the ice cream out of the freezer, relieved to see Marley light up even more when she catches sight of the strawberry. Guessing people's favorite ice cream flavors is a talent of mine, and Marley is definitely a strawberry lover.

We each fill a bowl, Marley laughing when I pile most of the gallon of chocolate into mine and steal a scoop of her strawberry to top it off. Then I lead us into the basement, the both of us sitting on opposite sides of the worn couch.

"You ready?" I ask her as I grab my wrinkled pile of articles off the dinged-up coffee table.

I'm not sure *I'm* ready, but she nods and puts the half-eaten bowl of ice cream down, nervously pulling her worn yellow notebook out of her bag. She hesitates before holding it out to me, crossing over some invisible line as she lets go of it.

I open to the first page. Her neat, even cursive pulls me in, making me forget she's reading my articles as I'm instantly drawn closer to the hidden parts of her, the secret pieces of Marley that make their way into every single fairy tale.

One story is about identical twins feeding a gaggle of ducks at the pond. More and more ducks come, until they are both swept away, flying high above the pond and the park and the cemetery.

Another is about a young girl who plants pink flowers that won't stop growing, until one day they turn into a whole person: a flower reflection of the girl.

Marley's stories are so good they make me want to lean over and snatch my lame articles back from her.

"Marley," I say. She peers at me over the top of one of the articles, her eyes wide, questioning. I hold up her notebook. "You have to share these with more people than just me. Kids would go crazy for these stories."

She shimmies up on the couch, eager, her nervous energy bubbling over. "You really think so?"

I nod, looking down at the page in front of me, where there's a doodle of the flower girl from her story. "Absolutely."

"Yours are great too," she says, holding up the article she's reading. "I don't even like sports, and you actually manage to make it interesting. These player profiles you did are my favorite. I feel like I really know Sam after reading this," she adds, Sam's black-and-white picture staring at me from the top of the pile. "You make them more than just stats. That's what you should use for your internship application."

I laugh, relieved that she doesn't hate them. She's silent for a long moment, staring at the yellow notebook in my hands.

"People will like them?" she asks softly.

Our eyes lock.

"They're gonna love them," I say, meaning it.

She looks past me to the French doors, the moonlight reflecting off the glass. "Do you want to go outside?" she asks as she tugs at her collar.

I know how she feels. The room seems to have contracted around us, filled to the brim with that still-unnamed feeling swirling between us.

"Sure," I say, and I grab a thick, quilted blanket from my room.

We head to the backyard and lie down on the blanket, gazing up at the ceiling of stars. Her hand brushes lightly against mine, and the night comes alive. Everything brighter. Everything buzzing.

She pulls away to point at the moon, a perfect circle hanging in the sky. "They say people don't sleep as well when there's a full moon."

I study the shining surface, knowing I sure as hell won't be able to sleep tonight, full moon or not.

"Werewolves?" I ask, and she laughs, nudging my arm.

"I wrote a story about the moon," she says as the electricity from her touch still hums softly through me. I look over to see her face shining in the faint glow, the pale moonlight outlining her features. "A new story."

"Tell me."

"It's a . . . love story," she says hesitantly. "My first one."

"Then definitely tell me."

She looks over at me, her eyes dark pools, deep and vulnerable. I push up on my elbow, waiting.

"Okay," she says finally. "Once upon a time—"

"Why do all stories start like that?" I ask. I don't want to break the spell, but the question is out before I can stop it.

She smiles. "Not *all* of them. Only the best ones."

"That's the first thing you said to me, remember? Once upon a time."

We stare at each other for a long moment, an invisible force pulling me closer. I swear I stop breathing. Marley clears her throat and looks away, the pull fading but not disappearing.

"Story," I say, turning my eyes back up to the moon. "Right. Go on."

"Once upon a time, there was a girl," she says.

"I like it already," I say, encouraging her, and she punches me lightly on the arm, her expression half-amused, half-exasperated. And like I hoped, it spurs her on.

"Every night she walked a path through a dark, dark forest to the base of a beautiful waterfall, and there, she looked to the moon and made her wish," she says. "It was the same wish every night."

Marley's words weave a spell and I imagine I see the girl. *Really* see her, gazing up at the moon from the base of the waterfall, her lips parting as she wishes for . . .

"She wished for love," Marley says, as if reading my mind. "She was a dreamer with no one to share her dreams with."

I feel it, the loneliness of the girl, sitting deep in my bones.

"But it happened that on that night, the moon was full. Brighter than it had ever been," she says softly. "Looking down, she saw something on the path. A pearl. She picked it up and heard a man say, 'Excuse me, but I believe that is mine.'"

"Was it?" I ask. "His pearl?"

She nods. "So she held out the pearl, and he saw in the bright moonlight tears in her eyes," Marley says as I hang on every word. "The man asked her, 'Why do you cry?' And the girl answered him quietly, 'I thought for a moment it might be for me.' But the man took the pearl and kept walking the path."

"Dick," I say.

"Just wait," she says to me with a knowing smile.

"He better not be a dick."

"The next night, while making her wish, the girl heard a

sound behind her," Marley says, ignoring me. "It was the man, and in his palm was the pearl. 'I traveled many roads to find this lost treasure, this piece of me, but it was you who found it and returned it to me. Now I wish to give it to you,' he said, placing the pearl in her hand. And every night for the next month, she met the man at the waterfall."

"Not a dick," I say, relieved.

Marley smiles and shushes me. "They talked of everything, shared their secrets and their dreams. The girl had gotten her wish. She had found love," she says, the word making me turn my head and look at her, something inside me shifting. "But on the thirtieth night, the night of the next full moon, the man was not there. In his place . . . was a pearl."

My heart sinks. The sadness weaving through her words is familiar.

"For the next twenty-nine nights, nothing. She didn't wish. She just kept going, kept searching, but he was never there. But on the thirtieth night . . ."

"The next full moon," I whisper.

"Another pearl," Marley whispers back. Her eyes meet mine, the energy between us crackling. After a long moment, she continues. "The girl cried and cried. Then she wiped her tears, looked to the moon, and made another wish. A different one."

I hold my breath, my eyes on Marley's lips.

"'*Bring him back to me.*'"

Chills move up my spine as Marley says, "The moon brightened, its rays reflecting off the waterfall, making it look like a million falling pearls. The girl looked back at the moon, and suddenly . . . she remembered what the man said."

Marley stares reverently at the full moon like she's making her own wish right now.

"What did he say?" I ask quietly, when I can't wait any longer. I know I'm being a terrible audience, but I need to know what she's wishing for.

"He said, 'I traveled many roads to find this lost treasure, this piece of me. . . .'"

This piece of me—holy shit. I start losing my mind a little.

"Each full moon for the rest of her life, the girl received another pearl . . . ," Marley continues.

"The man in the moon," I say, and sit up, totally shook. "He was the man in the moon!"

Marley smiles. ". . . and she knew that he was watching over her, shining down on her, lighting her path through the dark, dark forest. And every once in a while, off the water's reflection, she could see his face. There in the moon, smiling at her."

Her voice is barely more than a whisper as she finishes the story. "And she knew that she was loved."

Our eyes lock, and I know this isn't friendship. All my excuses fall away. I don't think about if it's wrong or right or anything. I love her. I love her like the man in the moon loved that girl.

She flushes, sitting up, suddenly bashful, totally and completely misinterpreting my silence. "It's stupid, isn't it?"

I shake my head and take her hand. "It's not stupid," I say, meaning it more than I've ever meant anything. "It's beautiful."

I expect her to pull away, but she doesn't. Our fingers lace together, and we stay like that until it's time for her to go, gazing at each other underneath the glowing stars. Then I walk her to the door, leaning against the frame while she looks up at me from the welcome mat.

"They're good," I say, meaning it. "Your stories are really good, Marley. It was almost like . . ." My voice trails off, and I smile at her. "Like magic. You take me somewhere else entirely."

I can feel that crackling between us again. Her eyes are warm in the soft glow of the porch light. More open. She takes a step back, but the magnetic pull stretches, and instead of breaking, it fills the space between us. "I hope you always think that," she says. The tiniest shadow passes over her face. I just wish I knew why.

"I will," I say as she walks down the steps and across the front lawn, turning back to give me a small wave before disappearing completely around the corner.

I stand on the porch for a while after she leaves, still feeling that energy even though she's out of sight. I shiver, the cool fall night sending goose bumps up and down my arms, but I don't want to move. I don't want this feeling to disappear.

Soon, headlights appear in the driveway. My mom's car slows to a stop, and then the car door creaks noisily open. She steps out, giving me a once-over before ducking back inside to grab her bag.

"You look happy," she says when she reaches the steps.

And she's right. I am.

18

I wake up the next morning feeling pretty damn great.

So great that I grab my iPad from my bedside table and open up Google to start my internship search during breakfast. At first it's less than promising, mostly unpaid gigs that aren't that thrilling. I find one that's pretty perfect, working for the sports section of a magazine, but it would be a two-hour drive one way.

I hear my mom shuffling down the stairs, so I throw another slice of toast in the toaster and pour a cup of coffee with cream for her just as she rounds the corner into the kitchen.

"Morning," I say as I hold it out to her.

"Morning," she says, taking the cup. She widens her eyes at me as she takes a sip. I turn my attention back to my iPad, frowning as I scroll through another page of openings. "What's with the frown? Your head hurting again?"

"Nah, that's been getting better," I say. And it has. The flashes have faded a bit since I started actually talking about stuff with Marley, proving Dr. Benefield's point about them being emotional more than physical. I sigh, tapping the button so the screen goes dark. "I'm just looking for an internship."

"Oh!" she says, smacking her forehead. She books it out of the room and returns a second later with her overflowing purse. I watch as she sifts through it, pulling out receipts and a first aid kit and a couple of granola bars. I swear, the shit she has in there could get a small village through the apocalypse. "I ran into Scott Miller yesterday morning at Starbucks. You know, the guy from the sports section of the *Times* who used to cover your games?"

"Yeah, I remember him," I say, sitting up in my chair. Scott actually did a profile on me the week before my injury. He was really encouraging when I saw him a month after everything went down.

I don't know why I haven't thought of him before now.

"Well," she says as she brandishes a business card from the very bottom of her purse. "I told him you were interested in writing, and he said you should definitely give him a call."

She holds it out to me, and I grab the card, jumping up to give her a hug. "You're the best," I say as I plant a kiss on her cheek.

I pull out my phone and head into the hallway to call him, but a text notification pings in from Sam as I'm dialing.

Football today at 10. You coming? Need a ride?

I hesitate over the keyboard before typing out a quick response. Today's probably the best I'm going to feel, so if I'm ever going to try, it might as well be now.

"Hey, Mom?" I call into the kitchen. "Can I borrow the car?"

* * *

By the time I meet up with Marley at the park on Wednesday, I've already scheduled an interview with Scott for this Friday *and* driven my mom's car a grand total of three times. I'm practically invincible.

The park is crowded today, the warm fall day bringing with it a slew of kids playing all along the grass.

"I used to love flying a kite," Marley says, watching as a boy sprints past us, trying to get one to take flight.

I turn to look at her, the rest of the park fading.

She looks beautiful today. Her hair is down around her shoulders, a deep-yellow sweater matching the thin headband in her hair. Every time she talks or turns to smile at me, I have an overwhelming urge to reach out and take her hand. I didn't know what was going to happen after the other night, but this thing between us has only gotten stronger during our few days apart.

We cross the small street that leads to the pond, and the closer and closer we get to the water, the braver I get. I think of the story she told me. The girl wishing for love. The man in the moon answering that wish.

Do it, I tell myself, watching her hand as it moves back and forth next to mine, centimeters away.

I take a deep breath and reach out, taking it, a sharp pain jolting through my head at the same time. Damn, my head has been pretty good all week.

"Okay?" I ask as I fight past it, focusing instead on her rose-petal lips and the fact my heart is about to hammer straight out of my chest.

149

She hesitates for a second, so I take a step closer to her.

"Our story won't be a sad one, Marley," I whisper to her. "I won't let it be."

She doesn't say anything, but she twines her fingers tighter in mine. I tuck her hair behind her ear, my hand lingering on her face, her lips inches away from mine. I lean slightly forward, barely even breathing, unsure if she's going to lean forward or bolt.

She doesn't bolt.

She closes the gap and we kiss, and it's a rush of everything all at once: her face framed by the flurry of cherry blossom petals, her eyes the day we first met, a waterfall of pearls.

I pull away, smiling at her, her face aglow in the afternoon sun. "My friend rule was a terrible idea—"

She muffles the rest of my sentence, laughing as she leans in for another kiss. I move to wrap my arms around her, but her eyes widen as she looks past me and suddenly jerks away, my hands grasping at empty air.

She rushes across the grass, frantic, pushing past a group of kids playing soccer. She races into the street to grab a little girl from the middle of the road, pulling her onto the sidewalk.

What the hell? Did I miss something?

I hurry to catch up as Marley marches the child toward a group of older kids. She deposits the kid next to a tween girl who shares the same shade of hair as the little girl.

"Is this your sister?" Marley asks angrily.

The girl nods, clearly frightened. She can't be more than twelve.

"Do you know what could have happened to her running into the street like that?" Marley is yelling now, her hands on the girl's shoulders. Her eyes are wild, but I can't tell if it's with anger or fear. This is a side of her I've never seen. "What is she . . . ? What if . . . ?"

I step in, reaching out to touch her shoulder. "Marley," I say firmly, but she ignores me.

"You're supposed to watch out for your sister. She could have been *killed*."

I stand there, confused, my eyes taking in the other kids, their scared expressions as they simultaneously try to hide behind one another *and* get a closer look.

"Take your hands off my daughter!" a voice calls suddenly, and a woman who could only be the girls' mother is storming across the grass, out for blood. We have to get out of here.

"Marley," I say, pulling her away. "Stop. She's fine. Let's go."

She looks around at the group of kids, at the terrified girl, the angry mother, her eyes finally landing on me, her wrists now grasped firmly in my hands. Tearfully, she rips out of my grip, running off across the grass, in the direction of the cemetery.

"What is wrong with you?" the mom calls after her.

I watch her go, taking a second to process whatever the hell just happened.

I make a quick apology to the lady and the frightened girl and run after Marley, cutting quickly through the park, knowing exactly where she'll be. I head straight into the cemetery, where I find her slumped next to Laura's grave, her head down, long hair hiding her face.

"She's right, you know," Marley says as I come closer, my chest heaving. "Something *is* wrong with me."

I bend to gently push her hair behind her ear so I can see her face. "What's going on?"

"No sad stories," she says, shaking her head.

"Okay," I say as I sit down next to her. All I want is to understand what just happened. But I know better than anyone what it takes to be ready to tell that story. "You don't have to tell me. But if you want to, I'm here."

Her body has totally huddled in on itself. Then she looks up, touching what I now see is a pink sapphire pendant around her neck. Usually, only the chain is visible; I've never seen the stone before.

"I always wore yellow," she says, and I think about all the touches of it I've seen her wear. The headband, her shoes, the cardigan, the raincoat. "At first it was just something my mom did when we were really little to give us our own special look, since everything else about our appearance was exactly the same, but . . . later it became more than that. Yellow made me feel happy, light. Even when I was anxious."

Her fingertips touch the pink Stargazers growing around the grave. "But Laura . . . she loved pink. The brighter the better. Always."

I try not to move, afraid that even the slightest breath will stop her from talking. It's rare to get more than a sentence out of her when it comes to Laura.

"I was never like her. She was fun, you know? Outgoing. She could talk to anybody, for hours." She plucks one of the flowers off, smiling sadly. "I didn't mind that everyone loved her more, because I loved her more too."

I reach out and take her hand, silently encouraging her to continue.

"We looked out for each other, always. Well, Laura looked out for me, mostly. On that day . . . she was . . ." Her voice breaks, and I tighten my grip around her fingers, giving her strength.

"She was going to teach Jenny Pope a lesson," she says, returning the squeeze as she continues. "She wasn't going to hurt her, just embarrass her, the way Jenny embarrassed me." She pauses and shakes her head. "God, I was terrified. I just knew that *someone* would know that it wasn't me, but that it was Laura, pretending. Then I'd be even more embarrassed." She looks over at the grave, the name on it. "But Laura . . . she was so sure. So calm. So ready to take charge. I couldn't say no to her."

I notice a pile of petals at her feet, the Stargazer shredded into tiny pieces with her free hand. I swallow, afraid of where this story's headed.

"So we were in each other's clothes. She had my yellow; I had her pink. Her hair was down; mine was up. We . . . *were* each other."

She stops, her breath going ragged. She tries a few times to continue, but she can't. There's something stopping her, some barrier she can't break through.

"If . . . ," she manages to get out. "If I'd been looking. If I'd just been paying attention. I . . . I . . ."

"What? Marley, what happened?" I urge her to keep going, to fight through it.

She shakes her head, but her voice continues on. "We . . . we had these stupid necklaces. Pink and yellow sapphires. Laura knew that if we were going to pull this off, we had to be perfect. We were waiting by the road, at the bus stop, when she remembered." She reaches up to her neck. "I was still wearing my yellow sapphire—she was wearing her pink one."

I watch as she starts to tremble, her memories consuming her.

"She took it off and asked me for mine. But . . . while she was putting it on, it . . . it got tangled in her hair. She was so used to having her hair up—and mine, mine was always down. But hers was . . . Shit." She starts to shake harder. "I . . . Shit. . . ."

"It's okay. Marley. . . ." I try to hold her, but she's angry now. Frustrated.

"It's not okay!" she says fiercely. "That fucking yellow pendant—*my* yellow pendant—got tangled in her hair. Her hair that was down because of *me*. She was pulling it and yanking it and laughing, and it snapped. The pendant rolled into the street."

She stops, the memory alive in her eyes.

"I saw the car before she did. She . . . never even saw it. But *I* did. I saw it and I froze. I didn't even try to warn her. My voice was frozen too."

I lean back in shock. Holy shit. She tenses, as if she's hearing the screeching tires, the sickening thud.

"Marley. It wasn't your—"

"Then I heard screaming," she says, cutting me off. "I thought it must be me, but it was our mom. I don't even remember how she got there. She was just *there*, on the ground, holding Laura.

Screaming . . ." Her voice goes high and shrill, the pain of the words, of the memory, embodying itself in her. "'You're supposed to watch out for each other! How did this happen? Marley, how did this happen?'"

She's silent for a long moment as she struggles to catch her breath. "That was what she screamed, over and over."

She wraps her arms around her knees, burying her face as she fights the tears that threaten to fall. Her voice drops to a whisper. "I've been screaming that same question to myself every day since. Every minute. But I scream it *inside*, where no one can hear me."

I see it now. Hidden behind her every movement. Her every breath. She still blames herself for what happened, even though it isn't true. It's not her fault.

It's the truth to Marley.

"I've never cried. I never even talked to anyone about it. I don't tell the sad story. I just try to disappear," she says finally. "Because if Laura can't be here, neither should I."

"Marley," I say, reaching out to touch her hand. "It wasn't your fault." I have never wanted to make someone realize something so much.

"It was," she says, looking down at where my fingers meet hers. "My mom was right."

"Sometimes . . . ," I say. "Sometimes when we're hurt, we say things we don't mean. We say things without thinking about the consequences. I'm sure she didn't mean it."

But she's not convinced.

"Laura *always* looked out for me. She was trying to save me, and I didn't even try to save her," she says, angry with herself. "I just stood there."

I squeeze her hand, thinking. "Marley. Do you think the accident that killed Kim was my fault?"

She looks up, confused. "No. That was an accident. You *know* that was an accident. I mean . . . you were hurt too."

"Then how is this any different?"

"It just . . ." Her voice trails off, and she looks away. "It just is. You got hurt. I didn't. Laura was just trying to help me, and I couldn't . . ." Her eyes grow distant. "She was just better. In every way," she adds. "It's not fair that I'm here and she's not. I want to be like her, but I'm not. I never will be."

I lightly touch her cheek, her face turning toward me. "You don't need to be like her, Marley. You're already everything."

She shakes her head and looks down at the tiny bits of torn Stargazer on the ground.

"You *are*," I repeat, thinking of all the things we've shared since we met. "Marley, you've made me feel understood in a way that no one ever has. You're kind, and you're such a good listener, and you're so fucking strong. I think your stories are as incredible as they are because you know loss. You know *love*. You know what it means to feel," I say.

She keeps her head down, silent.

"For me, you're the best part of everything. I was such a mess when we met, and you made me feel *alive* again. Can't you see how special you are?" I try to lean forward to catch a glimpse of her face, but she doesn't budge, so I lighten it up. "I mean, who gives people flowers based entirely on their meaning? Who else has a small army of popcorn-loving ducks ready at their beck and call?"

I know that one moment won't convince her, but we have more than just today. More than just this moment. We've got time.

"I meant what I said, Marley," I say, pulling her close, relieved when she leans into me, smelling like jasmine and orange blossoms, warm and familiar. I wrap my arms around her, holding her tight for the first time.

"No more sad stories. I promise," I whisper.

And just like that we start a new one.

19

"Try this one on," Mom says, holding up an oversize pin-striped blazer. I squint at it, unsure of how to break it to her that she's successfully found the ugliest item in this place.

Sometimes my mom is right on the money when it comes to picking out clothes. And other times she holds up a blue pin-striped blazer for me to try on.

Luckily, she registers my expression and holds up a casual dark-gray sports coat instead. "You want to look casual but professional."

I take it from her, shrugging on the jacket, the fabric clinging comfortably to my shoulders and arms. I check myself out in the department store mirror.

I wonder what Marley would think. Would she think I look good?

I try to smooth down my hair, and my eyes find the thin scar on my forehead, the ever-present reminder of all that's happened in the last few months.

The longer I look at the sports coat, at my reflection, the more nervous I get for this interview tomorrow.

Mom adjusts the collar and gives me a once-over.

"I know that face," she says, patting my cheek lightly. "That's your worried-on-a-big-game-day face."

I look down at her. "Is it that obvious?"

"What? The expression of existential dread?" She shakes her head, smiling back at me. "Not at all."

I look to the mirror, turning right and left to get a better view of the jacket. I let out a long huff of air. "What if I don't get the internship?" I ask her. "What if he thinks my writing sucks?"

Her face gets serious, and she reaches up, turning my face away from the mirror and back to her. "Kyle, you had to hit the reset button not once, but *twice* in this last year. Your shoulder injury was rough," she says, taking a deep breath. "But what you went through with that doesn't even hold a candle to when you lost Kimberly."

I swallow, my shoulder and scar suddenly aching at the thought of it all.

"If you can get through that, you sure as hell can get through this," she says, meaning it. "You'll always find a way to reset if you have to."

I clear my throat, looking away, while she sniffs loudly, wiping quickly at her brown eyes, an exact copy of my own. "All right," she says, smiling and nudging me. "Let's get you a shirt."

I sling an arm over her shoulder as we cut through to the shirt section.

"Always forward," she says, patting my chest.

"Never back," I say, smiling down at her.

The next morning I'm sitting in the lobby of the *Times*, wearing my new gray sports coat, waiting for Scott Miller to come out of his office to interview me.

In the meantime, I'm trying not to make awkward eye contact with the receptionist while I scan the walls, taking in the framed editions and clippings occupying every square inch.

I catch sight of a couple of headlines: AMBROSE HIGH WINS THE STATE CHAMPIONSHIP, GORDON RAMSAY DID NOT HATE LOCAL RESTAURANT, TOWN SAFETY MEETING ENDS IN ACCIDENT.

A door opens down the hall and I quickly wipe my hands on my pants, because although I normally don't have sweaty palms, my body apparently has decided it's going to give it a go right here and now.

Scott pops his head into the lobby, flashing a quick, toothy smile at me. "Kyle! How've you been?"

I stand up to shake his hand, tucking the folder with my articles and résumé under my arm. He's a little bit taller than I am. About Sam's height, with close-cut silver hair and a pair of stylish black glasses.

"I've been good, sir. Thanks so much for meeting me today," I say as we head down a long, thin hallway and through a door into a busy newsroom filled with cubicles and people talking and the sound of typing. Scott nods hello to a few people, leading me to his spot in the corner, the space littered with sports memorabilia, an Ambrose High pennant tacked loyally to the wall.

He slides into a swivel chair, pulling over another one from an empty desk.

I hold the manila folder out to him as I sit down. "Uh, here's my résumé. I brought a couple articles I wrote—"

He gestures to his computer and pushes his glasses farther up on his nose. "I've read them. I subscribe online. Your senior player profiles are really something."

If my palms weren't sweaty before, they definitely are now. What did he think of them?

"You been back to Ambrose for any of the games this year?" he asks.

I hesitate, remembering the game I went to, when I turned to see Kimberly sitting beside me, dead but not dead. "I caught part of one."

"Well," he says, leaning back in his chair, the hinges squeaking loudly. "I would love for you to do the same kind of profiles for the seniors this year."

"Like . . . for the *Times*?"

Scott laughs, nodding. "Yeah. Like for the *Times*."

"Yeah!" I basically shout. *Be cool, Kyle. Be cool.* I clear my throat, taking it down about eighteen notches. "Yes, sir. I'd love to do that."

"Great," Scott says, swinging around to his computer. He moves the mouse and the screen comes to life. He minimizes the Word document he has up, a calendar coming into view. "I was thinking fifteen to twenty hours a week, twelve dollars an hour. Obviously, when you do the profiles or we go off-site for a game, that counts as paid time. That good for you?"

"Wait," I say as he looks over at me. "So . . . I'm hired? For the internship?"

He grins. "You were hired the second I read your player profiles. You managed to bring each player to life on the page. I was very impressed," he says, and it feels like making varsity all over again, except this time I'm getting paid.

We work together to fill out the schedule, adding my name to certain empty blocks, while I make sure I can still meet Marley over lunches or in the afternoon when I get off. When we're finished, he prints it and holds it out to me. Still warm. It feels good to have a schedule in my hands again, to have people counting on me.

It feels like a step forward. A step toward the person I am becoming.

I call Marley the second I get out of the building, and we make plans to meet at the park in half an hour. It's hard to play it cool when I feel like I'm going to literally burst from excitement.

I have some time to kill, so I stroll down Main Street, window-shopping. I stop when I see a big yellow kite on display. A few minutes later I'm carrying it with me to my mom's car.

The drive to the park is quick, and I get out to wait for Marley, texting my mom and Sam the good news about the interview.

I tuck my phone back into my pocket and breathe out a big sigh of relief, my warm breath turning to fog in the chilly air. When it clears, I see Marley walking toward me on the path, a reddish-pink flower clutched in her hand. The trees around her are nearly naked in the autumn air, their brown and orange leaves crunching noisily under her feet. I hold up the kite in hello and her face breaks out into a smile. She runs the rest of the way to me, pushing her mustard-yellow beanie higher on her head, ignoring the kite completely.

"How was it? How did it go?"

I lean against my car, trying not to appear too excited. "Well, he seemed to like my articles," I say casually.

"So?" she urges impatiently.

"So . . . you're looking at the new sports intern at the *Times*," I say, my cool demeanor cracking. "I was hired on the spot."

Marley squeals and throws her arms around me. "I told you. I knew you would be."

I laugh. "You were right about the player profiles. That's what he liked the most."

"Of course I was," she says, handing me the flower she's holding, a pretty round puff with dozens of pale-pink petals, getting smaller and smaller as they near the center. "It's a peony. It means good luck and fortune, but I guess you kind of don't need that now."

"Can never have too much good luck."

She smiles and leans back to get a better look at me. "You look cute, by the way."

I smooth out my sports coat, smiling back at her. She's never said anything like that to me before. "Why, thank you. Maybe not exactly the best thing to wear for flying a kite, though."

"I haven't flown a kite in years," Marley says as she smooths a hand down my lapel.

"I thought it might be fun," I say, holding it up. "You mentioned you used to love to do it when you were little. And . . . it's super windy today."

As if on cue, the wind tugs at her hair, whipping it this way and that. She lightly touches the thin wood of the kite frame, nodding in agreement.

It takes a lot of work for us to get the kite going. We unwind some of the string and take turns running across the grass, the breeze catching it and then letting it go just as quickly, the kite nose-diving into the ground.

Finally, on my fifth run, it lifts smoothly into the air.

I whoop as the string slides through my fingers. The kite tugs right and left, the wind making it dance across the cloudy autumn sky.

Once it's steady, I pass the tiny wooden bar to Marley, watching as she stares up at the kite, her face beautifully open.

"You got any plans for Halloween next Saturday?" I ask.

"Not really," she says as the kite dips. She pulls back on the string, steadying it. "Other people . . . aren't really my thing."

"Well," I say, unsurprised. "My mom is going out of town, so I could use a little help handing out the candy."

She looks over at me skeptically.

"It'll be fun," I say. "We can wear Halloween costumes and everything," I add, really trying to hype it up. "I mean, what's not to love about that? You can be anyone or anything you want."

I see her mind working, thinking it all over.

"Okay," she says finally. She presses into me and I kiss her forehead. "But only because you seem really into the dressing-up thing. I'd hate to crush your fantasies."

Her small, teasing smile is too much. I pick her up in a huge hug, the both of us laughing as the rest of the string unfurls from around the tiny wooden bar, the kite drifting, untethered, into the clouds as I kiss her. Her lips are cold, but the rest of her body is warm, and she wraps her arms around my neck.

"We lost the kite," she sighs after we come up for air.

I laugh. "I'd rather hold on to you anyway."

A drop of rain lands smack on my forehead, and we pull apart, laughing as we run along the path back to my car, the rain pouring down all around us. We're almost there when Marley yanks her hand from mine.

"Wait!"

She bends to pick up something from the ground. I get closer to see a trail of tiny dots on the path. They're baby snails, and Marley's picking them up one by one and moving them off the path.

"What are you doing?" I ask, squinting at her through the downpour.

"I don't want anyone to step on them," she says as we slowly make our way up to the car, me redirecting runners and walkers around us as Marley moves every single one of the snails out of the way.

Every life, even the life of a snail, matters to her. My heart is full as I watch her, the both of us getting drenched. When we make it safely into my car, she looks at me, and without saying anything, I lean over and kiss her. I've never met anyone quite like her before, and I don't need peonies to tell me how lucky I am that I did.

20

I sit on the front porch holding a basket full of candy. The fog machine next to me lets out another puff of smoke, clouding my vision. I wave my hand to dissipate it as another horde of kids come screaming up to me, their parents lingering on the streetlight-lined sidewalk.

"Trick or treat!" a tiny ghost shouts.

"Uh, treat?" I say as two Elsas greedily dig into the candy before scurrying off and out of sight.

I put the basket down on my lap and pull off my football helmet, quickly checking in my phone camera that the zombie makeup my mom helped me apply is still in place. My scar is now an oozing gash across my forehead.

I almost asked Mom to take it off when I saw it, and honestly, I still can't look at it without cringing. All I can see is my reflection in Dr. Benefield's glasses the night of the accident, when my head was *actually* broken open.

But I'm trying not to run from it anymore.

I tense as my vision blurs, and for a moment I can hear a voice, whispering to me, telling me not to let—

"Boo!" a voice says, pulling me safely out of the flash before it can completely overtake me.

I put my phone down to see . . .

What on earth?

Marley's voice is coming toward me up the stairs; she's almost swallowed whole by a lumpy brown snail costume. It's got it all. Long antennae, a big, swirly shell, everything about it identical to the snails we picked up on the path a few days ago.

Laughing, I stand up and reach out for her. She wiggles away and swings her shell around to whack me in the side.

"Hey, I'm not laughing *at* you. . . ."

She glares at me, crossing her arms over her chest, her antennae even staring me down. "All right. Fine. I won't say anything." I smirk and turn an invisible lock on my mouth while she rolls her eyes, looking adorable.

Never thought I'd be attracted to a giant snail, but here we are.

I unlock my mouth and clear my throat. "Wait, I just have to say . . . you're the cutest damn snail I've ever seen."

"Yeah, sure," she says, but she softens and does a tiny twirl. I move to hug her, but her giant shell is in the way, blocking my arms from wrapping completely around her.

"So, uh. Why a snail?"

"Well, you know," Marley the Snail says, reaching out absently to touch my tattered zombified football jersey. "We're quiet, we're shy, and we hide."

I lean closer to her, one of her long antennae almost poking my eye out.

"You never have to hide with me, Marley," I whisper to her.

I watch as a million expressions move across her face, too quick for me to even keep up with. Finally her features settle.

She reaches up, hesitantly touching the two buckles on her shoulders. "I guess I dressed up as the old me," she says, looking up to take in my tattered football jersey, the football helmet tucked under my arm, the fake bloody gash on my forehead. She takes a step forward and reaches out, touching it lightly, while I stare at her lips, wanting to kiss her.

"And you dressed up like the old you," she says softly, and I close my eyes at her touch, wanting more.

The magic of the moment is broken by a giggle.

I look over to see an audience of tiny costumed kids watching us like we're a plate of broccoli.

"Ew!" a little Dracula says, and there's a chorus of giggles.

I look between them and Marley, giving her a wry smile. I toss the entire candy-filled basket in front of the kids, and a mob scene breaks out on my lawn, the parents' eyes wide with horror.

Grabbing Marley's hand, I pull her inside and flick off the porch light behind us.

It's dark inside except for the glow of the streetlights outside, the yellow light pouring in through the windows. I take a step closer to her, the air electric as she looks at me, her lips slightly parted. "Looks like we're out of candy."

"How did that happen?" she asks, breathless.

She slowly reaches up, my heart pounding as she unsnaps the buckles at each shoulder, letting the shell slide to the floor.

"I'm not this anymore," she says, moving closer to me.

I pull the jersey over my head, wiping away the bloody gash on my forehead, the injury that doesn't define me anymore. "And I'm not this."

She pulls off the antennae. I kick off my shoes.

She stares at me for a long moment; then my heart leaps into my throat as she slowly pulls her leotard down, revealing her smooth skin underneath. Her eyes never leave mine, the electricity between us growing and growing until I can hardly stand the space separating us.

Soon we're standing in just our underwear, all of the old parts of us stripped away. Her soft buttery-yellow underwear clings to her hips, her breasts. I'm dying to touch her, but I don't dare. We've never been alone like *this*, never even talked about it. Anything that happens next is up to her.

So I wait. But I can't stop my eyes from drinking her in. She's beautiful.

"I've . . . I've never done this before," she says softly.

I pull my eyes up to meet hers. "We don't have to. Marley—"

"I want to," she says. Her cheeks flush bright red the second the words are out. Her gaze, though, is steady. Certain.

"With you," she continues, stepping closer, her eyes moving

shyly over my body as she explores my arms, my neck, my chest. I'm sure she can feel my heart pounding under her fingers, practically exploding beneath her touch.

"I'm dying here," I say as her hands travel down, over by abdomen.

"I—I don't know what I'm doing," she whispers, looking up at me, unsure for the first time.

"You're killing me, that's what you're doing," I say as I inhale sharply.

We start laughing, some of the nervous tension melting away. I pull her close, her arms wrapping around my neck, her fingers lacing into my hair.

"You sure this is okay?" I ask. I want to be sure. I want *her* to be sure.

"Yes, I . . ." Her grip tightens in my hair, her pupils large in the pale-yellow glow of the light. "I love . . . ," she starts to say, but her voice trails off. She kisses me softly, barely a whisper on my lips. "I love . . . it," she says, finally resting her head against mine.

I stare at her lips, our breath mingling between us. The entire world fades away except for her. I hold her face in my hands, my thumbs gently moving along her cheeks, understanding.

"I love *it*, too," I whisper back, knowing what *it* means. Knowing I feel the same.

She pulls my face down for a kiss, and I pick her up, her legs twining around my waist. I carry her down the hall and open the basement door, and soon the last things that keep us apart fall away.

* * *

Hours later, the darkness gives way to the sound of shrieking metal, rain hammering noisily on the roof of a car. My eyes fly open and I see a huge hole in my windshield, rain pouring through it onto me, soaking my clothes, soaking the seat under me.

I see the disco ball wrapped around the mirror, red lights bouncing off it, making the falling rain look red.

Like blood.

I try to move, try to get out, but I'm stuck, pinned in.

"Help!" I try to scream, but nothing comes out.

I claw at my seat belt, the sound of a ringing phone pulling my attention to the center console, where a cell vibrates, inching its way toward me. My heart stops when I see the name on the screen.

KIM CALLING

My eyes fly open. I frantically look around. I'm in my room, in my bed.

But knowing it was only a nightmare doesn't stop my breath from coming out in ragged gasps. As I calm down, I hear the wind whipping on the other side of the window. It whistles across the glass, low and creepy, the perfect soundtrack for a nightmare. It was just my fucked-up head again. This time, though, I know it's just a dream.

Marley's pressed against my back, warm and comforting. I let the final touch of fear and panic fade in a long sigh of relief.

Behind me, Marley burrows closer, her warmth soothing me even more. I roll over to pull her closer and feel an icy grip tighten on my lungs.

It's Kimberly. We're nose to nose. Her breath tickles my face.

Warm. I reel back, but her hands clench around my arms, keeping me close to her.

"Don't do this. Don't let go," she says to me urgently.

"No!" I scream, and sit bolt upright. I struggle to catch my breath, my chest heaving. I feel her move behind me. I shove her away.

"Kyle. Hey, what's going on?" I hear her. I smell her.

It's not Kimberly.

"It's okay," she whispers. It's not Kim.

Orange blossoms and jasmine. *Marley.* I open my eyes and take in her face, the familiar freckles, the soft curve of her jaw, and her delicate lips.

"It was just a dream," she says, resting her hand over my beating heart. "I'm here. I'm right here."

I pull her close as the nightmare fades, the images of the car accident and the bloodred rain finally dissipating, drifting away, replaced with what's real.

21

The days fly by. Between working at the newspaper and spending time with Marley, December sneaks up on me. Soon, Main Street is completely transformed into a winter wonderland.

And every day Marley comes a little more out of her shell.

I look up to see the snow lightly falling, drifting down onto the street lined with people, the annual Winter Festival in full swing. Wreaths wrapped in red ribbon hang from every streetlight, a choir sings carols on a street corner, and the smell of pine and cinnamon is so strong it permeates the entire place with enough force to rival Sam's discovery of Axe body spray in ninth grade.

A group of kids crowd around the window outside the toy store, their breath fogging the glass as they gaze at the train set in the window, chugging along its miniature track.

"Do kids even play with trains anymore?" I ask Marley. Her

cheeks and nose are a soft red, and a thick yellow scarf is bunched around her neck. "Is that a thing?"

"I guess so." She tucks her arm into mine, taking in a deep breath of that cinnamon and pine, a smile tugging at her lips. "I didn't expect to love this. Every year, Mom tries to get me to come with her, but since Laura . . ."

I kiss the top of her head. "Thank you for coming with me."

This one took a bit of convincing, but she finally relented yesterday, our trips to the movie theater and to the coffee shop by the *Times* making this step just a little bit easier.

She gazes at a group of preteens buying roasted chestnuts from a vendor, her hand reaching up to touch the pink sapphire necklace hidden under her scarf, her eyes distant.

Laura.

Every now and then a dark, inescapable cloud rolls over Marley, the heaviness of her guilt still keeping its grip on her.

I squeeze her tightly, my eyes landing on a teal-and-white booth, my high school football team's annual fundraiser at the Winter Festival. I watch as a guy with brown hair wearing a letterman jacket picks up one of the footballs and throws a perfect spiral through a dangling hoop, giving his blond-haired girlfriend the stuffed-animal prize.

Kim, my brain thinks instantly. She loved this festival, even though she made fun of it.

Marley and I are both still healing, I guess. But I think we've come a long way over the last month, the weight of the grief lifting with every passing day.

I mean, Marley is actually *here*, at the crowded Winter Festival. That's . . . pretty freaking huge.

"Hey," I say as I grab Marley's hand and pull her to the booth, breaking free of the dark cloud threatening us. "You see anything you like?"

We scan the prizes. A bear holding a candy cane. A red-nosed reindeer. Marley grabs my arm and points to a yellow duck wearing a red coat and a Santa hat. I mean, how could we not go for it? I pull a dollar out of my wallet in trade for a football.

I take a deep breath, staring at the hoop. Sam and I ran this booth our freshman year during a total snowstorm. We were so bored and cold during the first hour, we spent most of our shift playing the game ourselves, lobbing the ball through the hoop hundreds of times.

I've got this.

I launch the ball at the hoop, the spiral wobbling as the throw swings wide.

I pull out another dollar and try again, this throw worse than the first one, the ball soaring over the hoop and out of sight.

Maybe . . . I don't have this.

I shrug and turn to grin sheepishly at Marley. "I'm sorry. Maybe I can buy you one. . . ."

She's focused, though. Her eyes are locked on that Santa duck as she digs into the pocket of her jacket and pulls out a dollar. She drops it down on the counter, then grabs the football, and . . . holy shit.

A perfect spiral sails right through the hoop.

I whoop as the freshman behind the booth hands her the duck.

Then I scoop her up and spin her around, her yellow scarf coming undone.

"Marley," I say when I put her down. I'm more than a little impressed. "That was awesome. Can you do it again?"

I pull another dollar from my pocket, and she grabs the football, the same laser-focused look on her face. Without a second thought, she launches it perfectly through the hoop again, this time with even more zip on it. Who *is* this girl?

She gives me a mischievous look I haven't seen before, the green in her eyes bright against the white snow falling all around us.

Five minutes later, a Santa duck and a red-nosed reindeer in hand, we stroll proudly away from the booth, my arm slung over her shoulder. To think, last year I'd sulked over not being able to hit that hoop with my left arm.

Now I'm celebrating my girlfriend absolutely destroying me. *Twice.*

I kiss Marley quickly on the head, and she nuzzles closer to me, everything feeling absolutely perfect. We just need one thing.

"Hot chocolate?" I ask Marley, redirecting us toward a booth of treats and sweets, filled with enough candy to keep our local dentist in business until next Christmas.

She nods, eager, her teeth chattering in the cold.

"Two hot chocolates, please," I say to the bundled-up barista behind the counter. "Extra whipped cream. Extra marshmallows."

Marley watches as the barista makes the hot chocolates, shaking her head in disbelief. "That's a lot of sugar," she says.

"Are you talking about the chocolate melted in milk? Or just the whipped cream and marshmallows on top?"

She turns to look at me, the both of us laughing. "When you put it that way . . ."

"There's no such thing as too much sugar," I say, tugging lightly at her scarf as the barista hands us our hot chocolates, a thin trail of steam drifting off the frothy top. "Not at the Winter Festival."

The hot chocolate is incredible, rich and creamy and sweet, exactly like I remember it.

Marley takes a small sip, a blissful smile appearing on her face. I reach out and grab her free hand, her fingers cold in my palm, as the two of us wind through the crowd to the holiday light show.

It's awesome, lights of all different colors forming trees and reindeer and snowmen, a blanket of white underneath them. The twinkling colors guide us to the heart of the display, a long, glittering tunnel of blinking lights hanging down around us like falling stars.

We come to a stop in the center, and Marley takes a long sip of her hot chocolate, letting out a sigh. "You're right. There's no such thing as too much sugar."

She pulls the cup away, whipped cream clinging to her upper lip. I reach out to wipe it off, but her voice stops me. "Oh boy."

"What?" I ask, and she points up, tilting her head back, her rosy cheeks glowing in the waterfall of lights.

I look up to see mistletoe hanging just above us in the exact center of the tunnel.

"You know what that means," Marley says, her gaze warmer than the hot chocolate in my hand.

I raise my eyebrows, surprised as I look around at all the people. Marley, who almost didn't want to come out today, wants to kiss *in public*?

"Yeah?"

She nods, the whipped cream still lingering on her lip. "Yeah."

I bend to kiss it off, and her hand twists into the front of my jacket, pulling me closer, the kiss intensifying. I lose myself in it, her lips cold but sweet. When we pull away, I'm short of breath, dizzy in the best kind of way.

I tuck her scarf closer to her neck, glancing to the side to see a familiar pair of brown eyes at the end of the tunnel.

Sam.

"Shit," I say as he shakes his head at me, like he's disappointed.

"What?" Marley asks, surprised.

"Sam."

Her head whips around, but Sam's already walking away, his broad shoulders fading into the distance between the twinkling holiday lights.

The moment is kind of deflated after that, so we head out from under the lights, walking slowly along the path to my house, Marley's hand lacing into mine.

"I'm sorry," she says, tugging gently on my fingers. "About Sam."

"No, it's fine. I've been trying to tell him," I say, looking up at the snow, a few flakes landing on my forehead. "It's just . . ."

"He's never seen you with anyone else," Marley fills in.

I nod, lowering my head.

"Will it be okay?" she asks.

I stop and pull her into my arms, reaching up to brush the hair out of her eyes. "It will be okay. Sam just has to get used to it."

I say the words with total conviction, but I'm not entirely sure it's the truth.

22

"Happy New Year," Sam says, ducking inside the back door of my house. The holidays were so hectic I haven't gotten a chance to see him since the Winter Festival a week ago.

He peers around, clutching a huge lump under his jacket. "Where's Lydia?" he asks, walking past me to peek into the hall-way, his head turning right and left.

"She's out. I told you," I say, watching as he hams it up, making a show of checking under the kitchen table. I'm relieved he isn't being weird.

"All right," he says, unzipping his jacket to reveal a six-pack of beer. "It's game time. UCLA going for bowl glory. Kickoff was ten minutes ago."

A car drives past outside, and he quickly zips his jacket up, craning his neck to peer out the kitchen window.

"She won't be back until tonight," I say as he unzips his jacket again. I smirk as he clutches the beer to his chest the entire way to the living room, his eyes darting suspiciously around.

"You scared of my mom, dude?" I ask, elbowing him.

"Who? Mrs. L.?" he says, plopping down on the couch. "Absolutely."

We laugh, and I flick through the guide, clicking on the game. UCLA is already up by six, going for the extra point.

"How's Marley?" Sam asks casually, his eyes fixed to the TV screen. I study his face, waiting for the snark. The punch-in-the-gut comment.

But it doesn't come.

"She's fine," I say. This is the first time he's asking about her freely, but I don't give him too many details.

Sam nods, popping open his beer and drinking the entire thing down.

Like . . . the *entire* thing.

"Dude," I say as he grabs another beer and pops it open. I lean forward and grab it away from him.

"Look, Sam, if you're pissed about seeing me and Marley last week, then—"

"I'm not," he says, cutting me off. "I mean, I wanted to be. I *tried* to be, but . . ." His voice trails off as he avoids my gaze, his eyes darting around the room, to the TV, the window, the bookshelf in the corner. Everywhere but me.

"Is that a new lamp?" he finally asks, pointing to a lamp that has been in this room since we thought girls had cooties.

"Come on, Sam," I say. I thought we weren't going to be like this anymore. I turn to him, and the light from the TV reflects off the glass bottle in my hand, hitting me square in the eyes and sending my head throbbing.

It's been weeks now since it's hurt, but when the pain does come back, it's as bad as ever. Isn't this supposed to get better the more time passes? I grit my teeth and fight through the ache for my words. "Whatever it is, just say it."

He finally looks at me, eyes serious. "I'm leaving."

"What do you mean?" I ask as he starts to fidget, his leg erratically bouncing up and down. I kick it like I have since we were kids, telling him to knock it off.

He chuckles uncomfortably and forces his leg to be still.

"Is this because . . . because of what you saw?"

He pins me with a look. "You know, not everything is about you."

I blink, replaying what I just said. Shit. But if not that, then why . . . ?

"Kim did it," he says with a small smile. "Her essays helped get me into UCLA. I leave next week."

Next week?

"That's . . . that's great." But it doesn't feel great at all.

I stop, realizing I've done it again. I've made this about me, when it's actually about Sam. And if Sam is ready to move on, then I have to let him move the hell on.

Just like he's let *me* move on. It's what I wanted for him. But I somehow didn't imagine it quite like this.

"I need to do this, man," he says, sensing my confused thoughts, a skill from more than a decade of friendship. "The last year and a half has been . . ." He stops, swallowing hard.

Year and a half? What is he talking about?

"Damn it." He reaches up to run his fingers through his thick, dark hair. "You know I didn't mean to do it, right?"

"Do what?" I ask, confused. "Didn't mean to do—"

"The block," he says, frustrated. "I lost focus for one freaking second and he got past me. When I heard that crack . . ." His voice trails off, his eyes wide. Haunted. "I thought I'd never get that sound out of my head." He rubs his face with his hands, shaking his head. "Now everything you lost, everything *we've* lost, goes back to that one moment. The moment I fucked up."

"Sam, this isn't on you," I say, wanting to make him see. "I know you didn't mean to miss that block. . . ." I stop. *Why* does he feel this way? I think of Kim that night in the car. What she said. "But I still made you pay for it, didn't I? You and Kimberly both. I leaned on you guys for everything."

Sam gives a harsh, rueful laugh. "And again, it becomes about you."

But isn't that what he's talking about?

"Yes," he says, nodding. "I regret that block. I hate what it did to your career. I'd take it back if I could, but . . ." He pauses, his voice trailing off. "Maybe not *only* for the reason you think."

I lean back on the couch, confused.

"If I hadn't missed that block, then I would have had no reason to make it up to you. And since then, that's all I've been trying to do—make it up to you. . . ."

The pieces start to align.

"And because of that, I chose you over Kimberly. I chose you over *myself*." He puts his hand over his chest. "Your feelings had to come first because I fucked up," he says, swallowing. "Every time she cried, I wanted to tell her I loved her. Every time you fought, I wanted to step in and shield her."

I see it now. The bouquet of blue tulips resting against the grave. The way he looked at her the night of our graduation. All these things that were invisible to me for so long, simply because I hadn't been looking.

"I *still* love her like that. I can't shake it. And if I'm honest, I don't want to," he says, his fists clenched in his lap. "I'd rather love her forever and hurt the entire time than let her go for even one second. Maybe someday . . . maybe someday I'll be able to. But for now I can't. . . ."

He's quiet for a moment before he looks over at me.

"The minute you said Marley's name, I knew she wasn't just your friend. I knew because that's how I feel about Kim."

I drop my head, rubbing my face with my hands. Shit. This is a lot to process.

"God. I'm sorry, Sam. I'm—"

Sam puts his hand on my bad shoulder, cutting me off. "*This* was my fault, and so were the choices I made after. But . . . I'm letting that go. I have to."

I shake my head as I look up at him. "You both should have tossed me to the curb a long time ago."

Sam snorts and rolls his eyes. "Shut up. As if either of us could have gotten rid of you. You don't give up on people, so we don't give up on you," he says, giving me a rueful grin. "Besides, Kim tried. Seven. Times."

We both break down in laughter. It feels good, though. Healing and sad all at the same time.

"So . . . you're doing it," I say as our laughter dies down. "You're leaving."

He nods. Solemn but hopeful. "Yep. I'm outta here."

"You know I'll be coming to visit, then?"

"You better." Sam smiles, and we look at each other for a long moment. Sam, the glue that held the trio together, held *me* together, is taking his place in the world.

"I guess this is what growing up feels like," I say, hating it.

"It kinda sucks, if I'm honest," Sam says, echoing my thoughts. Instinctually, we do our handshake, pausing during the last fist bump to smile at each other.

"Always forward," I say as I reach up to clap him on the shoulder, knowing that our friendship will stretch and change for years to come, but if it didn't break after all this, it never will.

23

Things are strange without Sam around.

All winter long we make it a point to talk every Saturday morning, FaceTiming while I take blue tulips to Kim's grave, the weather slowly getting warmer as bundled walks through snow-storms give way to April showers.

Between spending time with Marley, and my internship, and starting journalism classes at the local community college, it feels like I blinked and the seasons changed.

Pretty soon, it's 75 degrees out, and the park is filled with people running around in tank tops and sunglasses, acting like it's summer.

I set up the last of the folding chairs and stand up to stretch, my shoulder a little sore from all the lifting. I do a final once-over of the outdoor classroom I've spent this entire May morning setting up, nodding when I see the rows are perfectly straight. A few minutes later the middle schoolers start to trickle in, but the teacher . . .

Missing in action.

I scan the perimeter, searching for that familiar trace of yellow. My eyes catch sight of a yellow skirt, its owner pacing nervously back and forth by the pond, a tiny gang of ducks trailing behind her.

I grab a single yellow Doris Day rose from my bag and head over, stopping to straighten the hand-painted sign reading HOW TO TELL A STORY in cursive far neater than I could ever dream of writing. The ducks turn to look at me as I get closer. I mumble my "excuse me's" to them as they part, a clear path forming straight through to Marley.

"Hey," I say as I reach out to take her hand. She gives me a panic-stricken look, her features frozen with worry. "You've got this."

She lets out a long sigh, clearly not convinced. "How did you talk me into this?"

"You're the best storyteller I know," I say, meaning it. "You can do this."

She looks doubtful, but I know it's going to be great. I know more than anyone how special she is. Every day she opens up a little bit more, becoming more and more herself.

And now, today, she's going to share a small part of herself with more people than just me. Something that we've talked about since she let me read her stories last fall.

I pull the rose from behind my back and finally get a glimmer of a smile. "My favorite," she says as she takes it from me. "I love . . . it," she adds, taking me back to Halloween night, our little catchphrase.

"You talking about me or the rose?"

The smile grows, and she squeezes my hand. "Both."

Hand in hand we head up to the tent, almost all of the seats taken by eager students wielding notebooks and pens. Old-school. No laptops or tablets. Writing the way Marley does it.

I made sure to put that in the free advertisement Scott was nice enough to include in the *Times* two weeks ago since he's trying really hard to get me to stay on another semester.

I kiss her cheek and slide into an empty seat while she walks to the front of the makeshift classroom, a sea of eyes staring up at her. She freezes and I hold my breath, silently willing her to talk while internally screaming, *You can do this, Marley!*

"What," she starts finally, her eyes locking on mine, "is the first thing you need to tell a story?"

"A character?" a girl in the front row calls out, and Marley's attention turns to her, a smile appearing on her face.

"Characters are important, for sure," she says, nodding. "But even before that. What do you need?"

Someone calls out, "Something for them to do?"

Then a voice from the back shouts, "An idea! An idea! You need an idea."

"*Yes*," Marley says, excited. "You need an idea." She pauses for a second, holding my gaze. "You need a dream." I do a quick scan of the crowd to see all the middle schoolers at the edge of their seats. She's crushing this. Just like I knew she would.

I watch in awe for the rest of the class.

With every minute that passes, she gets more and more confident, the Marley I know and love finally breaking out of her shell for everyone else to see, her enthusiasm inspiring everyone here to tell the story they are longing to tell.

After the class ends, a small crowd of middle schoolers overtakes her, asking her questions, hoping for another class in the future. I take a Tylenol and start to clean up the chairs, smiling to myself.

Shoulder pain and all, this has been more than worth it.

Two arms wrap around me after I finish, the last of the students heading out of the park, notebooks tucked under their arms.

"That was amazing," Marley mumbles into my shoulder.

"*You* were amazing," I say, turning around to kiss her, my hand finding the familiar dip of her waist. "We should celebrate. Do something fun."

"Like what?" Marley asks, reaching up to touch my face, her fingers gentle against my cheek.

"Anything!" I say.

She thinks, her eyes lighting up, a smile appearing on her lips. *"Anything?"*

We pull up to the animal shelter, and Marley peers out the window, excited.

This is definitely not what I had in mind when it comes to

celebrating, but . . . this is big for her. She's been talking about getting a dog since winter, but something always stops her.

I smile at the determined look in her eyes. *Nothing* can stop her today.

Plus, I'm pretty excited myself. While I'd never say it out loud to her, a dog is way cuter than a fully grown duck hell-bent on getting popcorn snacks.

She turns to look at me, hand on the door handle.

"What's up?" I ask, reaching up to push a strand of hair behind her ear.

"You'll help me, right? Take care of the dog?"

I nod, reassuring her. "Absolutely."

"Because what if I can't and something happens to it . . . ?"

"You just saw what you can do, Marley, even when you think you can't. You're amazing." She still looks doubtful, so I add, "But I've got you. Always."

She grins, her enthusiasm returning.

We head inside, and Marley stops along the way to examine the budding flowers as we go, the warm spring afternoon making everything feel new and happy and right in the best way. I nudge her lightly as she leans forward to smell a blossom, catching her before she topples over, the both of us laughing.

We head to the front desk, and I poke around while Marley asks to see the dogs. A chunky orange tabby with a tag that says OLIVER lumbers up to me and rubs against my pants, purring until I give him a quick scratch behind his ears.

One of the employees takes us back, and Oliver trots around

behind us, clearly in charge of the entire operation.

As we peer through the cages, Marley looks more and more somber.

"I wish we could take them all," she says, using her pointer finger to pet the nose of a Lab mix, big brown eyes staring sadly up at her.

Then there's a squeaky yip from the cage behind us, and we spin around to see a tiny silver Yorkie puppy, its little body the size of one of my hands. The dog barks again, straining to get through the links to her.

Marley gasps, and I witness what I can only define as an out-of-body experience, sheer cuteness overload.

She runs over, and the employee comes to unlock the door and get the small puppy out of its cage. "This one just got here last night. We found her abandoned by that pond over on Hickory Street."

The dog launches herself into Marley's hands, and she cuddles her sweetly, almost reverently. She grabs a tiny ball from the front of the cage, and the two of them begin to play with it, the puppy's little paws attacking Marley's fingers as she rolls the ball back and forth.

"This is exactly like the puppy I've always wanted," she says, looking up at me, her eyes glistening.

"I think we found a winner," I say, watching as Marley holds the pup up, staring at it lovingly.

After she fills out the application and pays the adoption fee, we run around on the grass by the parking lot, the puppy's tiny silver head popping up in between the flower bushes while she crashes through them, petals clinging to her ears and nose.

Soon she collapses in front of Marley, huffing and puffing from all the exercise. "Someone's sleepy," Marley murmurs as she scoops her up, giving me a kiss on the cheek.

"Her name is Georgia," she says, holding the puppy up to me. Georgia mimics Marley's kiss, licking my cheek with her tiny tongue, her fluffy fur tickling my skin.

"Nice to meet you, Georgia," I say, patting the pup's little head as she yips a response.

Yep. Way better than a duck.

"We should take a picture," Marley says, excited. She pulls her phone out of her pocket and holds it out to take a photo of us.

I smile as there's a quick flash, and then another, and a surprising jolt of pain slices through my head. For a moment I see my mom standing in front of my eyes in the same white floral dress that she had on the night of the accident, her phone in her hand.

Fuck.

My first vision in well over a month. Every time I think they're gone for good . . . something happens.

I collect myself, pulling Marley closer as she takes one more, the two of us peering at her phone to see the result.

It's a cute picture. Marley looks beautiful. Happy. Her nose and cheeks are flushed from all the running, the green in her eyes standing out against the grass all around us. We both look so different than we did when we met all those months ago at the cemetery, the weight of our grief lifting slowly off our shoulders, pain no longer shadowing our faces. In her arms, there's tiny Georgia, miraculously looking in the direction of the camera.

"Send that to me," I say to her as we walk back to the car, the feeling of her hand in mine outweighing the pain in my head and the uneasy feeling in my chest.

24

I hold Marley's hand as we walk down Main Street a month later,
the sky above us dark and ominous. The humid summer air clings
to my arms and legs as Georgia stops to sniff at a patch of grass
next to the sidewalk, giving me time to turn and look up at the
clouds, the wind tugging at my hair.

"I think it might—"

There's a clap of thunder, and the sound drowns out the rest of
my sentence as rain begins to fall all around us.

Marley squeals and grabs ahold of Georgia, pressing close to
me as we duck under an overhang to keep dry.

I rest my chin against her head, tensing when I see a car whiz
past us. A silver Toyota. Identical to the one I was driving the
night of the accident.

The car that Kim died in.

Sometimes it feels like forever ago. Sometimes just a minute.

Marley takes my hand as she studies my face. "What's wrong?"

"That car," I say, a shiver running through my body. "It's just like the one I was driving when . . ."

I pull away, staring at the curve the car disappeared around, my vision blurring as I see windshield wipers trying desperately to push away the rain, Kim in the passenger seat. "I . . . I drove past here. On a rainy night like this."

There's another boom of thunder, and I flinch at the noise, lightning splitting the sky in two. "*Just* like this."

Wait.

I pull out my phone, and the screen lights up, the date appearing in white letters. June 7. "A year ago today," I whisper.

A year. It's been a whole year since that night.

"Let's go home," I say, my eyes focusing on Marley, Georgia clutched to her chest, raindrops clinging to her cheeks.

The second our eyes meet, I feel calmer. Safe.

Our fingers twine together and we make a run for it, ducking between awnings and overhangs until we get to the path leading to my house. When we arrive, we head straight for the basement, and I move to start a fire in the fireplace, the flame catching almost instantly, white and yellow and orange eating away at the wood, warming us.

I lean forward to stoke the fire as it grows across the log, swallowing it whole. There's a clap of thunder outside, and at the same time a quick, sharp pain streaks across my forehead. The fire poker clatters noisily from my hand.

Ow. Holy shit.

I pick up the fire poker and put it back on its stand as I keep my eyes focused on the fire. That was—

An ember pops, a flash of red. For a split second I see the flare of red emergency lights on wet asphalt, a dizzying pain.

No. I'm not going through this again. I stand up, shaking it off as the room comes back into view.

I run my fingers through my hair and let out a long sigh. All these months later and I still don't like storms. I don't know why this one is triggering my head pain like this. It must just be the anniversary.

"You feel it too, don't you?"

I turn to look at Marley on the couch, her long hair still damp from our run through the rain. Her face is aglow in the light of the fire, but her eyes are focused outside, staring at the storm through the French doors. Georgia is wrapped in a towel in her arms.

I sit down beside her, studying her face. There's a distant, haunted look in her eyes. One that hasn't been there for months.

One I thought we'd gotten rid of.

"Feel what?" I ask.

"Like we were never meant to be this happy. Like one day all this will be gone? Like . . ." Her voice trails off as she looks down at Georgia and then at the fireplace, her eyes taking in every corner of the room before landing on me. "Something this good can't last."

I cup her face in my hands and she tries to smile, but the

sadness lingers around her eyes, the corners of her lips. So I kiss her everywhere I see it. One eyelid and then the other, her lips, then, softly, her forehead. She looks up at me, and I know this is the moment. More than ever before, I feel the words I've wanted to say for months threaten to bubble out, my heart pounding at the idea of telling her.

No more I love *it*. I love *her*. Marley. More than anything.

I repeat it over and over again in my head, my breath catching in my chest as I prepare to say the words I never thought I'd say to anyone ever again. The words I never knew could mean so much. The ones I've felt since that night under the full moon.

But the nerves are gone the second I open my mouth, and the words flow out more naturally than anything I've ever said. "I love you, Marley."

She starts, pulling back to look at me.

"I never knew love could feel like this. That it could get so deep inside me that I have two hearts beating in my chest. . . ." I pull her hand up to rest above my heart. "Yours and mine. As long as we love each other, Marley, *this will last*. Nothing is going to stop or change that. I will love you forever. I promise."

Before I continue, I kiss her softly, so gently it feels like a whisper.

"So I guess it really depends . . . on whether or not you love me, too."

Her eyes brim with tears, and she reaches up to push the unruly strand of hair out of my face, a small smile forming on her lips. "I do," she says, kissing me between the words. "I do, I do, I do."

She pours herself into my arms, her yellow dress soft beneath my fingertips as I pull her closer, tugging her on top of me. I kiss her, the electricity between us crackling louder and more powerfully than the bolts of lightning on the other side of the glass.

Everything we've been through passes in front of my eyes as I hold her. So much has changed since that very first day at the cemetery, since the accident a year ago, this person entirely changing what I thought was even possible for my life.

We sit by the fire, curled up with Georgia under a blanket, ignoring the thunder and rain outside, focusing only on each other until the warm, crackling flames pull us closer and closer to sleep. As my eyelids grow heavy, I look at Marley, tucked safely in my arms, her cheeks rosy from the fire. "I love you," she says softly. Hearing those words for the first time from her lips puts the biggest smile on my face.

"I love you too," I whisper again before sleep pulls me under. I love her too. I always will.

I don't know how long we're asleep, but a loud crash of thunder wakes me with a start, my arms empty, the basement dark, the fire gone cold. I sit up, rubbing my eyes, squinting as Georgia sits at the French doors, whining. She paws at the little panes of glass.

I push myself up and go over, looking out into the storm. It's still raging furiously.

"Marley?" I call out toward the empty basement.

Only silence answers me. Georgia paws again and my stomach tightens. Is Marley out *there*? In this mess?

I throw open the door. A cold wind rips through the bare trees and almost yanks me along with it. The rain pours off the roof as I run around the house, the downpour instantly soaking my clothes. Dread creeps up the back of my neck. A dread that's familiar in a way I don't want to think about.

"Marley!" I call as I run, the sound of electricity sizzling in the air, lightning flashing angrily across the sky. A searing pain stretches the length of my scar, and I try to will it away, ignoring the memories that start to intrude as I stagger forward, calling her name again and again. "Marley, where are you?"

I stumble into the street, looking up and down the block, the streetlights burning bright through the rain, fighting back against the stormy darkness that threatens to overtake them. There's another explosion of light, a flash in front of my eyes, the bolt hitting a transformer at the far end of the street and showering the neighborhood in fireworks of sparks. I struggle to see through the rain and the wind, but it batters my eyes and my face, my head searing with pain as the streetlights pop off one by one, the darkness racing closer and closer to me until the street is completely black.

Yip-yip! Georgia.

I spin in the direction of the house, and all of the lights go on at once, illuminating the front lawn, the porch, the path to the basement. Is Marley back inside?

There's another crack of lightning across the sky, and I see a silhouette in front of me for just a moment before the pain hits me, ricocheting around my skull and all across my body. A pain so blinding all I can do is shout as I tumble forward, face-first. There's no stopping my fall. My head slams hard against the ground. Then it all goes black.

25

A bright light, a nurse reaching out to take my hand as I fight to raise it.

Shattered glass.

Kim's face.

Screaming.

The seat belt locking around her chest.

"Page Dr. Benefield immediately!"

Long brown hair surrounded by a halo of light. Hazel eyes.

Marley?

Marley. Where's Marley?

26

I open my eyes again to see Dr. Benefield studying my face intently. She smiles, pushing her glasses onto her head.

"Welcome back, mister," she says loudly, the sound crisp and clear. I wince, taken aback. "You gave us quite a scare. Can you hear me?"

I open my mouth, but my throat feels like sandpaper, raw and dry and scratchy. "M—" I croak out, but it's like there are tiny shards of glass rubbing against my vocal cords.

"Don't talk," Dr. Benefield instructs.

But I need to. I need to ask where Marley is. All I can remember is blinding lightning, the storm raging, and her, nowhere to be found.

"Mar—," I rasp, wincing in pain. Dr. Benefield reaches out, touching my arm and shaking her head, her face serious.

"Shh," she insists. "I'll get your family. They're going to be so excited."

I watch her leave, fighting to keep my eyes open, the lights still uncomfortably bright, my vision cloudy. Hazy.

I focus on the voices outside the room, but my body feels so weak, completely depleted. Next to me a machine beeps loudly, tracking my pounding heart rate.

"Someone's very happy you're awake," Dr. Benefield says from the door.

Marley.

My eyes swing back to Dr. Benefield, her outline still foggy, but I can make out a girl next to her, arm in a sling.

She pushes open the door farther and . . .

The entire room spins. I grab on to the rail on my bed, my breath seizing. I shut my eyes and wait for it to subside, to come back into reality like always. I must have really hit my head, because this flash is bad. More real than any of the others.

But when I open my eyes, the air rushes right out of me again.

Because it isn't Marley who walks through the door.

It's Kimberly.

And this time she doesn't fade.

But I do.

27

When I wake up, I keep my eyes squeezed shut, the nightmare with Kim slowly ebbing. I hear the machines beeping next to me, the sterile smell of hospital sheets filling my nose, a hand stroking my arm lightly, gently.

I must've hit my head *bad* in the storm. Bad enough to need to go to the hospital again. Bad enough to have a flash like *that*.

"These summer storms are drowning my roses. Why won't it—"

"Mom," I croak as I open my eyes, relieved, the image of Kim replaced by my mom's profile, the colors sharp and bright. I look around the room, too weak to sit up, too disoriented to take everything in, my mind moving in slow motion.

Her eyes swing over to look at me, and she gasps, then plants kisses all over my face, tears swimming into her eyes. "I thought I'd never hear that again."

"What's wrong?" I ask as the tears fall all over me. I groan, reaching up to touch my head. "I fell. Hit my head, I think."

She hesitates, frowning slightly, her hand pausing on my arm. "Do you remember anything?"

I stare at her. What does she mean do I remember anything? I just told her.

"Yeah, I fell and hit my head looking for Marley during the thunderstorm. Right?"

Her face falls. What else is there to remember? My heart stops. Please don't let anything have happened to Marley.

"Marley? I—you were in a car accident, Kyle," she continues, her eyes boring into mine. "With Kimberly."

I blink, shaking my head. As if I could ever forget. Why is she bringing that up now?

"Yeah, Mom," I say, reaching weakly up to hold her hand, the IV tugging at my skin. "That was a year ago. Last night I busted my face in the backyard."

She stares at me. "You're confused, honey. You've been . . . asleep," she says, her eyebrows knitting together. "In a coma."

"In a—what?" I pause, taking in her expression. How hard did I hit my head last night? "A coma? How long?"

"Eight weeks," she says.

What? If it was that bad for me, Marley might have had it even worse. Did something happen to *her* in the storm? "Where's Marley?" I ask her, feeling more worried every second that she isn't there.

Mom looks at me, her eyes filled with worry. Finally she asks, "Who?"

I freeze, a sinking feeling growing in the pit of my stomach.

The shriek of the metal. Kimberly's horrified face. Fluorescent lights flashing overhead as I'm wheeled down the hallway.

But . . . this doesn't make any sense.

Where is Marley?

"I've gotta get out of here," I say as panic claws at my chest. I try to swing myself up, but my right leg refuses to move. I look frantically down to see a full cast enveloping the entire length of my leg, and when I move it, pain radiates through the bones. A sense of déjà vu overwhelms me. Déjà vu and horror.

"It's over now," my mom says, grabbing ahold of my arm. "Things will be back to normal in no time. You'll see."

I yank my arm from her grip and rip the IVs from my hand. As I try to stand, my left leg crumples under the weight. I tumble forward into my mom. She breaks my fall, trying to keep us both upright.

"Nurse!" she screams out. "I need a nurse. Someone, please!"

I struggle to keep moving, but strong hands grab me and something sharp stabs my upper arm. A nurse . . . with a needle. I fall back onto the bed, my arms and legs like lead weights. Everything is suddenly slow and heavy as my mouth fights to form words.

"I . . . don't . . . ," I manage to get out, my eyes focusing on my mom. "Kimberly's . . . alive?"

"Of course she is, darling," my mom says, confused. "She's been here every day."

I wait for the flash to end. For the world to reset. I close my eyes, and Marley's face burns against my eyelids. Her hazel eyes, the freckles scattered across her nose, her long brown hair. The smile she gets on her face when she's telling a story. The way she chews her lip when she's thinking really hard about something. But when I open my eyes, I still see the hospital. Marley's not here.

The world goes black as the sedative pulls me under.

I hear voices all around me. My mom. Nurses filtering in and out.

I keep my eyes closed and I wait. For silence. For the chance to get out of here and find Marley.

Soon it's the middle of the night, and I hear the door close, the air still and quiet except for the beeping of my heart rate monitor.

In an instant, I sit up and rip the IV out of my hand again, ignoring the thin trail of blood that drips down to my wrist.

I take a bracing breath, then ease my legs out of bed, my vision doubling as I put weight on my right leg. The pain is so blinding, a wave of nausea roils through me. But I push through it. I have to.

I stagger out of the room and down the long hallway, my fingers clutching at the wall for support, cold sweat molding the hospital gown to my back. Every step is agony, the world around me tilting as I reach the elevator, the thought of Marley's face pushing me forward. The pond. It's the only thing I can think of. I *have* to get to the pond.

The big metal doors slide open and I lurch inside. I shove down more nausea, relieved to have made it this far. But I can't stop now.

The buttons blink at me, demanding I choose a number, a floor. I try to think, but the searing ache in my right leg is making that impossible, and my left leg is starting to tremble under the strain of supporting all of my weight.

The buttons blink, blink, blink. Lobby? Is that the one with . . . the . . . star . . . ?

Suddenly my good knee buckles. I collapse against the wall, tiny pinpoints of black filling my vision as my leg gives out completely.

Only one thought is left in my mind as I slide to the floor.

I . . . have . . .

. . . to find . . .

Marley. . . .

"Kyle," a voice says. A hand firmly clutches my shoulder, shaking me awake. *"Kyle."*

I open my eyes, and Dr. Benefield's face slowly swims into view. She lets out a long exhale and shakes her head at me.

"Really?" she says as I look around from the floor of the elevator.

"How long have I been here?" I groan as I sit up.

"You tell me," she says, crossing her arms over her chest. "What the hell were you thinking?"

Marley.

I try to push myself up, but the pain radiating from my leg is so overwhelming, I crumple to the floor again. Dr. Benefield stands over me for so long I start to think she's not going to help me. Then she sighs.

"Wait here," she says.

I slump down and try to fight the bile that's just at the back of my throat, pushed up by the pain vibrating through my entire body.

A shadow falls over me. Dr. Benefield. With a wheelchair.

When she gets me back into bed, she has a nurse reattach my IV, increasing my dose of pain medicine in an attempt to give me some relief.

She grumbles under her breath as she checks my eyes with her penlight. I stare straight ahead as she clicks the light off and scowls at me, her eyes somehow both angry and sympathetic at the same time.

"I had no idea you were going to be so much trouble," she says as the nurse leaves. When I don't say anything, she reaches up to probe the healing wound on my forehead. "Blurry vision? Headache? Dizziness?"

"No," I say. And it's true. After all these months of wishing they'd go away, of waking up from nightmares with blinding headaches, it's all just gone.

She sighs and sits down at the edge of my bed. "So, you want to explain the freak-out?"

No. I don't. But I try anyway.

"This isn't where I'm supposed to be," I tell her. I try not to sound so frantic, but I can't help it. I have never felt so completely wrong in my life.

"No one ever belongs in a hospital," she says with a wry smile. "Except people like me, of course."

"That's not what I mean."

"Where else would you be?"

I should be back at home, eating pancakes with Marley or walking to the diner in town for breakfast, the ground still wet from last night's thunderstorm. I should be looking at all the different yellow notebooks in bookstores, deciding which is just right to get for her birthday. I should be taking Georgia for her walk and getting ready to cover preseason practice at Ambrose High and playing touch football in the park next Saturday with my friends.

I should be with Marley.

Not right back where I started.

A fresh wave of pain ravages its way through my body, and I squeeze my eyes shut, willing the meds to kick in.

A coma. I was in a coma.

"Dr. Benefield," I say as I open my eyes to look at her. "Do people in comas . . . dream?"

"Tell me why you're asking," she says, "and I'll tell you what I know."

"Okay. I have . . ." I pause, trying to find the right words. "I don't get how I'm . . . *here*. For me, it's been a whole year since the accident. I have another life. Kim died. I have a girlfriend. Marley. But now I'm here and everyone is telling me that I was in a coma. That reality is"—I gesture at the hospital room, but also at this entire world—"this."

She gives me a calculating look I can't read.

"I know it sounds crazy," I say.

She nods. "Certifiable. Go on."

"I have to get back there, to my real life," I say, thinking of Marley and Georgia and our spot by the pond, missing them with all the agony of a missing limb. I don't care if my leg never heals, if my brain stays broken. I don't need them. It's Marley I need.

She frowns. "I don't understand. When was this?"

"Yesterday."

She studies my face. "Yesterday you were *here*. And the day before that, and the day before that."

I shake my head, thinking of the handful of doctor's visits I went to, the times I came *here* to get my head checked, to make sure I wasn't losing it. "You were there too," I say to her. "You were my doctor."

"You opened your eyes a lot," Dr. Benefield says. "Looked right at me. Those dreams . . . You probably incorporated me, or other people, into them." She motions to the beeping heart monitor. "Things you heard or saw could have found their way into your subconscious. It's not uncommon in comas. Your synapses were healing, reconnecting, coming alive. I can only imagine what that looked like to you in there."

"What about Marley?" I counter.

She thinks for a long moment, her voice quieter when she speaks again. "Your life with Marley, did it seem like the perfect version of your life?"

I feel a wave of dread wash over me.

Yes.

I had a job I was good at. A life. I was *with* the person I was supposed to be with. I was becoming the best version of myself, and every day got better.

She takes my silence as the answer she was expecting.

"Kyle, your life is here," Dr. Benefield says, giving my shoulder a squeeze. "Your friends, your mom, have been in this room every day, waiting and praying for you to heal. Perfect or not, they love you."

I let her words sink in, but it's all too confusing, the pain too much, the feelings too overwhelming.

Where is she?

The medicine starts to take over, and the world slows down around me as my eyelids get heavier and heavier.

"Get some sleep now, okay?" she says. She flicks off the lights as she leaves, my vision growing hazy as I drift off.

28

It's night by the time I wake up again. The whole day drifted by in an agonizing blur, the medicine barely taking the edge off.

I hear a knock on the door and turn to see Dr. Benefield, strands of her red hair slipping from her loose ponytail after a long day.

"How are you feeling? You slept a long time," she says as she pulls a chair over to my bed and slides into it, resting her arms on her legs.

"You really doped me up," I say.

She shrugs and nods. "You were hurting."

I'm still hurting. Just not the kind of hurt she's talking about.

I glance at the clock on the wall. It's pretty late.

"Do you live here or something?"

She snorts. "First few months on a new job, you spend a lot of time at the office."

My mouth drops open. And *she's* the person who operated on my brain? Is that why I'm so fucked up?

"First few months at *this* hospital." She smirks, and I breathe a sigh of relief. "I've been digging around in people's brains for a long time now. You're in good hands."

She nods to my broken leg, the white sheet outlining the huge cast.

"You have any idea how lucky you are you didn't reinjure this?"

I turn my eyes to look out the window, not wanting to think about last night.

Besides, I've already healed this injury. With Marley. This is insane. How can no one know where she is? *Who* she is?

"Charts say they're still going to remove the cast tomorrow, even after that little stunt you pulled. Good news, huh?"

Good news?

I open my mouth to say something, but my words get cut off as thundering footsteps sound from the hallway, quickly approaching my room. Both of us turn our heads as the door almost flies off its hinges and Sam bursts inside.

"Bro, you're awake! That's what I'm talking about." He starts doing his football touchdown dance, grooving around the room, his arms and legs moving to an imaginary beat.

For a moment I remember him crying, placing those tulips on Kimberly's grave. It's such a stark contrast. Besides . . . he's not even supposed to be here. He should be at UCLA.

He stops mid-hip-thrust when he sees Dr. Benefield and quickly straightens up, clearing his throat. "Oh, uh . . . I'll come back."

"You stay right here, *bro*," she says, standing and looking over at me. "We'll talk more later. Any symptoms and you have one of the nurses call me, got it? *Don't* move."

When I nod, she heads out, closing the door quietly behind her.

He spins around to look at me, absolutely ecstatic. "Dude, this is so—"

"How long have you been in love with Kim?" I ask abruptly, figuring the only way to get the truth is to shock it out of him. His mouth falls open in surprise, which tells me I was right. I couldn't have just made it all up. I *knew* it.

He recovers quickly and gives me a skeptical look, pointing to the IV drip next to me. "What kind of drugs are they giving you?"

I stare at him for a long moment, but he still refuses to fess up.

I let it slide and try to smile, pointing to my forehead. "Coma brain. Sorry."

His shoulders ease, and he plops down in the chair Dr. Benefield was just sitting in. "Dude, you've been out for *weeks*. Where the hell did *that* come from?" he asks, eyeing me.

I pause. He's probably going to think I'm crazy, but . . . everything is already so crazy, what does it matter? I have to be dreaming anyway. I'll wake up soon and be back with Marley.

"You told me at football one Saturday. After Kim died," I say, his eyes widening. "In the accident." His mouth drops open and he starts to speak, but I keep going. "I woke up, Sam. I woke up an entire year ago in this room, and *you* were here and you didn't say anything but you were crying and—"

"That's insane. Kim's fine—"

"Just listen," I say, cutting him off.

Then I take the leap and tell him everything. About Kim being gone. About the months lying around wishing I was gone too. Our fight in the park. The tulips. How we realized what we had to do, who we had to be. What we had to let go of.

Mostly, though, I tell him about the girl at the cemetery in that yellow pullover. The girl who saved me. The girl I fell in love with. I tell him about Marley.

He listens as I finish, his face stunned.

After a long, silent moment, he says, "A hallucination? A dream, maybe?"

I start to argue, but he stops me.

"*Nothing* you just said really happened," he says. "You were in a coma. I was here. I *saw* you, dude, and I promise, you didn't leave this bed."

I shake my head, my heart pounding loudly in my chest. He's wrong. "Still feels real," I say, thinking of Marley. "*She* feels real."

He snorts and pulls his phone out. "Easy way to find out," he says.

Yes. Of course. I sit up, watching as he opens a browser, typing out the letters in Marley's name and looking up at me expectantly.

"Marley . . ."

I freeze. Marley . . . ? What's her last name? I *know* I know it. I rack my brain, trying to remember a moment when she said it.

I can't, though. I can't think of one moment. How is that possible?

I swallow, faltering. "I, uh. I don't know," I admit quietly.

Sam puts his phone down, raising his eyebrows at me. "You were in love with some chick who has no last name? You didn't think that was weird?"

"She has a last name," I clarify, getting pissed off. "I just don't remember it because it didn't matter. . . ."

"The only place that shit doesn't matter is in *dreams*, man," Sam says, sliding his phone back into his pocket. He gives me a serious look. "I'll tell you what *is* real. *Kimberly* is real. Kim is alive. Not this dream girl of yours. Aren't you happy about that?"

I can still feel how coarse Kim's headstone was underneath my fingertips, the unending weight of grief, heavy on my arms and legs.

"Of course I'm happy, but—"

"Hey, fam!" a voice says, pulling me back to the present. "This where the party's at?"

Kimberly's standing in the doorway, a duffel bag slung over her good arm. Sam stands quickly, the chair screeching against the white tile floor.

"Yep! You know it."

I squeeze my eyes shut, like I've done dozens of times, but when I open them, she's still there, her blond hair shining. I didn't realize it until now, because they felt so real, but the flashes always had a fog to them. A blurriness lingering around the corners.

Now . . . she's crystal clear. I can see every strand of hair on her head. The faint dark circles under her eyes.

And that tells me it's true. She's *alive*.

All of the things I wanted to say to her when I thought she was dead come rushing back to me. My throat closes around a million words.

But I don't . . . understand.

Her eyes meet mine and her smile gives way to tears, spilling out from her eyes and down her cheeks. "God, Kyle, I was so scared," she says.

"Kimberly . . . ," I start to say.

"I know, I know," she says. She drops the duffel bag on the floor and runs to the bed, her arms wrapping around me. But she doesn't know at all.

Sam motions for me to hold her, but I can't because I am fully freaking out. I don't know how to explain that it's like she's come back from the dead, when for them *I'm* the one who did that. That hers aren't the arms I feel around me when I close my eyes. Marley's are.

She lifts her head, wiping her tears away. "Look at me—I'm a hot mess." She laughs, looking from me to Sam. "Were you guys arguing?"

"What?" Sam says, shaking his head quickly. "No way."

"We were just—" I start to say, but Sam cuts me off.

"Kyle had a nightmare. Or something."

Kimberly rubs my chest, smiling at me. "It's okay. I'm right here," she says.

I flinch, my whole body stiff, because all of this feels wrong. All I can see is Marley, her head on my chest as we lie by the fire.

I look up at Sam over Kim's shoulder.

"That's all it was," he says, his eyes boring holes into me. "Just a dream."

And of all the things Sam has ever said to me, that one hurts the most.

29

After Sam leaves, an uneasy silence settles over Kimberly and me. I want to grab my phone to look at anything else, but I can't look away from Kim.

It's like seeing a ghost. Again.

My eyes follow her as she sets up a cot by the window, pulling a fuzzy white blanket covered in blue butterflies out of her duffel bag.

I have a sudden memory of her sitting on the sofa, wrapped in that exact blanket, when I thought she *was* a ghost.

Dr. Benefield's words come back to me. *You opened your eyes a lot. Looked right at me.*

"Let me see that," I say. Kim straightens and turns, giving me a confused look. Then she holds out the blanket to me.

I take it, frowning as I feel the fabric, real and tangible in my hand.

"Did you sleep here while I was . . . ?"

"Sometimes," she says, brushing her blond hair out of her face as she studies mine.

"Did you say anything to me?"

She exhales, looking down at the blanket as she nods. "I'd ask you to wake up. I'd tell you, 'Don't—'"

"'Let go,'" I say, finishing her sentence. "You said, 'Don't let go.'"

"That's right," she says, surprised.

I did hear her. I even *saw* her.

Which means all the visions I had, the things I thought were nightmares, all the strange moments I told myself were in my head . . . were they all real?

But then, what does that mean about the rest of my life? About Marley?

"I'm so sorry. For everything that happened," she blurts out, her hand reaching to touch mine. "What I said, in the car—"

"No," I say. "You were right."

She looks taken aback. She shakes her head and opens her mouth to argue.

"Don't. Please," I say, looking down at the butterflies on the blanket. Memories keep rushing in. The butterfly struggling on the pond. I should be so happy, but this overwhelming sadness tugs at my chest, making it hard to breathe. I hold out the blanket to her, unable to meet her eyes. "I just . . . I'm sorry. Can I be alone?"

She watches me for a second. This girl I loved, one of my closest friends, brought back to life as if by magic. It's a complete miracle, and I'm such an asshole because it also feels like I've lost someone all over again.

"Okay," she says finally, taking the blanket. I can tell she's upset, her jaw locked, her eyes narrowed. It's a face I've seen hundreds of times over the course of our relationship, a silent storm brewing. She stuffs the blanket into her duffel bag, zipping it closed. Standing, she gives me a long, calculating look. "I guess I'll just see you tomorrow?"

As I watch her go, the pain of it all crashes down on me. I press the call button, and the nurse comes to give me another dose of pain medicine.

I don't want to think about what's real or not real. I don't want to think about why Kim is here and Marley isn't. I want to be knocked out.

Finally the drugs start to do their job, and for a moment there's relief.

"And her happily ever after was over. . . ."

Before I even open my eyes, I know I'm back where I belong.

I feel her fingers in my hair, lightly tracing the outline of my cheek. I press my hand over hers, holding it firmly against my face. I know this skin, this touch. *This* is real.

Marley.

Her fingers feel small beneath mine. Delicate. I squeeze them and gather my courage, praying with everything in me that when I open my eyes, she'll still be there. I let my lids open slightly, peeking, hoping.

Marley's face is inches from mine, so close I can count her eyelashes. I smile and pull her even closer, overjoyed at the feel of her, the *realness* of her.

"God, I missed you," I whisper into her hair. "Where were you? Everyone was telling me that—"

Suddenly she sobs and pulls away.

"You promised me," she whispers, her voice strained as she looks at me, her eyes full of pain and betrayal. "You said no more sad stories. You promised."

It guts me.

I did make that promise.

My eyes close as I think of how to tell her what's happening, how I woke up in a hospital room and my world was turned upside down. I grip her fingers and pull her hand back to my cheek, wanting to tell her that I won't ever fail her again. That I'm back and everything is fine now.

"Marley, I . . ."

But when I open my eyes again, she's gone. *Oh no. NO.*

Then I see her shadow leaving the room.

"Marley, wait!" I bolt from the bed to chase after her.

But the second I move, I jolt awake. Back in the hospital. Alone. My good leg hanging off the side of the bed.

I struggle to catch my breath as I look around at the beeping machines. I feel the tug of the IV in my hand. The stupid cast wrapped tightly around my leg.

"Marley," I whisper.

I *heard* her, *felt* her touch on my cheek. I can feel the exact spot her fingers had been, the skin still buzzing.

She was real. I'm awake now. My brain couldn't have just made her up. Right?

I see her face, the tears, the clouds consuming her expression.

You said no more sad stories. You promised.

I hear the hollowness in her words, matching the emptiness I feel every second without her. And it's all my fault because I can't get back to her.

I turn the light on, fumbling in the bag of stuff my mom brought me earlier for my iPad. I pull it out and open Facebook. Tapping the search bar, I type in her name, thousands of results cascading down the screen.

I scroll through, faces blurring in front of my eyes, blond hair, brown hair, blue hair, none of them the right Marley.

But I keep looking. Because she's real.

I know she is.

30

The next afternoon I stare at a commercial with toilet paper
dancing across the TV screen, trying to ignore the tension that's
been building between me and Kim since she got here fifteen
minutes ago.

My mom left to give us some "alone time," and I . . . really wish
she hadn't.

Out of the corner of my eye, I see she's sitting with her arms
crossed, her leg shaking, her jaw locked in a way that screams she's
biting something back. Finally she grabs the remote off the bed
and the TV goes dark.

"Kyle. *What* is going on?" she says as she tosses the remote
onto my bedside table.

"I don't want to talk about it," I say as I avoid her gaze.

She pushes her chair back and stands up, the legs squeaking

loudly against the floor as she grabs her duffel bag and spins around to face me.

"If you'd just tell me what's going on with you, maybe I can help," she argues, clutching the bag to her chest.

"You can't," I insist. It would be impossible for her to understand. How am I supposed to tell her I'm in love with someone else when she thinks we just broke up?

"You don't know that," she fires back, her blue eyes flashing in a way that I almost forgot about, her cheeks blushing in anger.

I think of Marley, and all the days, all the hours, we spent together, how we never fought like this. A wave of longing comes over me as I watch Kim fume.

I remember our relationship before. Before the accident. Before Marley. The charm bracelet. Always trying to patch the holes instead of looking at what was making them.

Not this time. This time we have to deal with it.

"Look at us. Fighting again. Just like we always did," I say, trying to keep my voice level. "We don't have to anymore, Kim. I mean, we almost broke up *seven* times. Eight, if you count the night of the accident. We were terrible at communicating. About dealing with our problems. And that's probably why you didn't say anything about Berkeley. Because it would have started a fight, just like it always did, right? It's ridiculous."

"So I'm ridiculous now?" she challenges.

"Yes!" I say, throwing up my hands. "We both are. But let's pretend for a second that we're not. Let's pretend that we can say anything, as long as it's honest, and the other person will listen and understand. Without judgment."

She looks stony, but she stays silent.

"Why didn't you tell me about Berkeley? For some reason, you were able to tell Sam but not me. Why?"

"I don't know what you mean."

"I think you do," I say. "I can take it. Tell me why. 'I want to know what it's like to turn around and *not* see you there.' You were right. Why are you acting like you never said it?"

"If you're trying to get back at me," Kimberly says, looking hurt, "it's working."

She storms out, slamming the door behind her. I stare at the spot she was in, letting out a long, frustrated sigh.

"Brilliant."

In the hours after she leaves, I feel restless, the four corners of the hospital room closing in around me the longer I sit here.

Should I have said something different? I spent so much time thinking about what I would say to Kim if I saw her again, and I screwed it up because I'm so hung up on the fact that Marley isn't anywhere to be found.

I feel like I don't have space in my brain for anything else. Every corner of my mind is dedicated to possibilities. Places she could be. Explanations. Memories.

I reach into the bag my mom brought from home to take out the dented blue jewelry box, salvaged from the accident. Flicking it open, I stare at the charm bracelet inside. It looks so different to me now. I remember staring at it for hours, thinking I could make her see what we had.

I don't even know how to explain to her what I see now. Especially when I've had a whole year to figure it out and she's only had a minute.

A whole year. I've had a whole year to let it go, to heal. I've lived what feels like an entirely new life, and I don't know how to get back to it. To find Marley. To find our life together.

They keep telling me *this* is real, but how can it be without her?

I'm relieved when a nurse rolls a wheelchair into my room to take me to my first physical therapy session seconds after my mom texts she'll be back tomorrow morning for another five-star breakfast at the cafeteria. I stare down at my phone as the nurse helps me into the chair, her long brown hair moving in my peripheral vision, reminding me so much of Marley I have to squeeze my eyes shut.

Frustrated, I leave my mom on read and pocket my phone. I can't talk to anyone right now.

Although, maybe being *relieved* about going to physical therapy is the wrong way to feel, especially when it turns out to be a grueling half hour of me discovering how weak a fractured femur and eight weeks in a coma can make a guy. Even the exercises we do sitting in a chair are rough. Basic leg extensions. Stretching.

Stuff senior citizens in an aerobics class at a nursing home could apparently now lap me in.

If I thought recovery was hard the first time around, this is a whole other animal.

"You're doing great," Henry, the physical therapist, says to me, his hands hovering just a few inches from me, waiting.

I look up to see his blindingly hopeful grin pouring positive energy out at me. I snort and white-knuckle the support bar, struggling to put just my body weight on both of my legs, my *good* leg even giving out a few times, so that I fall against him over and over again.

With a fractured femur, I should've been up weeks ago trying to regain my strength and range of motion, but I was a little too comatose for that.

My leg completely crumples just as Dr. Benefield walks in with an empty wheelchair.

"Just in time for the show, Doc," I call to her, pushing the hair out of my eyes.

"That's enough for today," she says as Henry helps her get me safely from the support bars into the wheelchair. I'm drenched in sweat.

She pushes me out of the PT room and down the hall, my entire body completely drained. I can't wait to get back in bed, and that terrifies me. I don't want to be that guy again, the one who couldn't drag himself out into the world. It feels like I'm starting all over.

I have to distract myself.

"When's the last time you pushed a wheelchair?" I tease her, craning my neck to look at Dr. Benefield. "Don't you have, like, people to do this?"

"Ha ha," she says, shaking her head at me. "I wanted to talk to you."

She wheels me into my room, parking the wheelchair by the window. I see her glance over at the iPad on my bed, the screen still on, lit up with a photo of me, Kimberly, and Sam at one of our home games. The three of us are smiling at the camera, arms wrapped around one another.

"Mind if I get nosy?" she asks, reaching out to scoop it up.

I shrug, waving her on.

She flips through the camera roll, looking at the pictures I scoured last night and this morning.

"Looking through old memories?" she asks.

I shake my head. "Looking for Marley."

I zoomed in on every background. Every person in the stands. Every passerby. But I didn't find her.

"You said my brain was making sense of things I saw, so I thought maybe I'd seen her somewhere."

Dr. Benefield presses a button and the screen goes dark. She reaches out, putting it on my nightstand. "Did you find anything?"

"I didn't make her up." I blow past her question, trying to figure out a way to make her see. To get her to help me. "I swear."

"That's what I wanted to talk to you about," Dr. Benefield says, taking a step toward me. "I've asked someone—"

She's cut off by a knock on the door, and a doctor I've never seen before sticks his head in. She motions for him to come in, continuing what she was saying. "Kyle, this is Dr. Ronson. He's a psychiatrist."

My hopes plummet.

"So you *do* think I'm crazy."

She leans down, looking me directly in the eye. "I think you're sad," she says. "You've been through a lot."

Well, yeah. Of course I'm sad. I've lost an entire year. An entire year and a whole new life I was just starting to live, and more than all that, *the girl I love more than I've ever loved anyone.*

And no one will believe it.

"Just tell him what you told me. Okay? He can help you work through what you've experienced."

She gives my arm a sympathetic pat and leaves as Dr. Ronson slides a chair over to sit next to me by the window.

"Kyle," he says with an annoying amount of pep. He offers his hand to me, and I shake it. Either his grip is super firm or I'm just that weak.

"So," he says, pushing his glasses up farther on his nose, his eyes narrowing as he studies me. "How've you been?"

I fight the urge to roll my eyes and glance out the window as the two of us begin to talk. I'm annoyed but so desperate for answers it doesn't take much to open the floodgates.

Just like I did with Sam and Dr. Benefield, I tell him the story. Our story. Every moment leading up to now.

And just like them, he slowly starts trying to poke holes in it.

"Did she ever say anything that didn't make sense? Did anyone?"

"I don't know," I say, frustrated. I push back at him, determined. "Everything made sense, I—"

"Or did you *make* it make sense?" he asks, talking over me. "That's what we're talking about here, Kyle. Did your mind take what you were hearing out here and turn it into a dream in there?"

He points at my head, like he knows everything.

"I could *see* her. *Feel* her," I say. I could never make up that feeling. "I could even *smell* her. She smelled sweet, like orange blossoms, or jasmine, or . . ."

He pushes open the window, and a sweet scent drifts in from the outside, making my stomach drop another flight.

"Honeysuckle," he says, finishing my sentence for me. He nods to the other side. "It grows wild all over the courtyard. The scent is very similar to jasmine. Or orange blossoms."

"But . . ."

I try to cover up my disappointment, turning my gaze to a giant oak tree, the sunlight streaming through its branches. I think of Marley at the park, the sunlight trickling onto her face, her hazel eyes shining up at me.

"I'm sorry," he says, staring at me. "The fact is that some people wake up with memories that never happened. Our unconscious brains process outside stimuli in ways that sometimes translate into—"

"Dreams," I say, cutting him off. "Yeah. I get it."

31

My мом wheels ме through the courtyard after breakfast while I continue my scroll through all of the "Marley" Facebook profiles within a two-hundred-mile radius. No matter what search filters I've tried so far, I've gotten nowhere.

I try to think of new filters I can add to the search. I pore over my memories for mentions of her last name but still come up empty.

Her school? I brace my fingers eagerly over the touch keyboard, but my brain has nowhere to direct them. An entire year, and I never asked her about that? Not once?

I can practically hear Dr. Ronson already: *Does that make* sense, *Kyle?*

Dick.

The more I think about it, the more it actually does make sense that I don't know these things. I think about all the times that Sam told me how much I was making things about me. My stupid freaking selfishness. We spent so much time talking about me when Marley and I were together, there must have been a hundred things I forgot to ask her.

It just means I wasn't paying attention to anyone but myself.

Just a usual day in Kyle's world.

My eyes blur as I turn back to the profiles, searching for her features, her familiar smile, frustration slowly getting the better of me.

I shut off the iPad with a sigh. I mean, who even uses Facebook anymore besides my mom and her friends? It's no surprise I haven't found her on there. Sam deactivated his last year.

Instagram. I need to try Instagram.

I look around at the sprawling trees and shrubbery and gardens taking up the entire center of the hospital grounds. There are brightly colored flowers everywhere, framing the small plants and wrapping around the roots of the trees.

I freeze when my eyes land on a patch of pink Stargazers, identical to those sprouting around Laura's grave. The warm breeze brings with it the sweet smell of the honeysuckle growing around the oak tree, and my stomach twists as Dr. Ronson's face pops into my head.

The wheelchair slows as we near a huge fountain at the center. I reach out to lightly touch the stone, little sprays of mist floating toward me from the frothing water.

A blossom falls slowly into my lap, and I pick it up, staring at it. When I look up, I see cherry trees lining the path, blowing softly in the wind. For a moment I remember the identical soft pink petals blowing around Marley, her eyes fixed on mine that day at the park.

I'd do anything to get back to that moment. A moment that everyone and everything is trying to get me to question.

I crush the blossom in my fist; then my head falls into my hands, a single flower somehow bringing with it a tiny wave of doubt. And that scares the shit out of me.

"What is it?" my mom asks.

"Do you think it's true?" I ask, throwing it onto the ground. "Do you think Marley is really gone?"

My mom stops pushing the wheelchair and kneels in front of me, her face serious. Just like it is every time I've brought up Marley. "She's not gone, honey. She was never here."

She's so sure about it. So matter-of-fact.

I stare back at her. I need to make her understand.

"What if you woke up tomorrow and I was gone and everyone told you I never even existed?" I ask quietly. "Would you stop loving me, Mom?"

I see her falter, her hand finding the armrest of my wheelchair, just the thought of it overwhelming her. Tears fill her eyes, and her fingers grab ahold of my arm and squeeze, almost like she's checking I'm really here.

"I can't either," I whisper.

When my mom leaves later that afternoon, I grab my iPad from my bedside table, but I somehow can't bring myself to scroll through

Instagram, the images of all the different Marleys. I know in my gut that she doesn't have one. I mean, she refused to write on the computer, opting to handwrite in a notebook instead. There's no way she has an Instagram.

So what am I supposed to do? How am I supposed to find her?

"Can I come in?"

I look up to see Kimberly standing in the doorway, her arm sling-free, a small blue brace wrapped around her wrist. Her blue eyes lock into mine. The fire is gone, replaced with some sense of understanding. She's looking at me like she's reading me better than I can.

"Sam told me," she says. "About your other life."

Your other life. The words cut me like daggers. I try to contain it, to keep my shit together. But the tears come spilling out, no matter how hard I fight them.

She hurries over, wrapping her arms around me. "It's okay," she says, holding me while I sob. "It's gonna be okay."

She doesn't force me to talk. She just sits with me, quietly letting me calm down enough to fall asleep. I find relief only in the darkness behind my eyelids. For a glimmering moment, nothing hurts. Nothing is upside down. Nothing *is*.

When I wake up a few hours later, I feel a warm body next to me.

I know it's Kim. But I squeeze my eyes shut and pretend it's Marley.

"I know you're awake," Kim says, poking me in the side, her finger landing right on a protruding rib, a side effect of my liquid coma diet.

I sigh. "That's what they keep telling me."

There's a knock on the door, and we quickly turn our heads to find Sam's big frame filling the doorway.

"Hey," she says, not moving her arms from around me, and somehow I feel guilty. But unfortunately, a hospital bed is only so big, and if I move, I'll topple off onto the tile floor.

"Right," Sam says, looking between the two of us and clearing his throat. "Okay. Good. I'm gonna . . ."

His voice trails off and he turns on his heel, heading back down the hallway. We watch him go, his footsteps fading into the distance.

I think of the tulips.

"What's up with him?" she asks, confused.

"You . . . should go after him," I say, studying her face.

She looks over at me. "Why?"

"I think you know why." So much has felt off since I woke up, but this part of the dream world and the real world feels the same.

I push myself up, running a hand over my face, the dynamic between the three of us feeling clearer since I woke up from whatever world I was in, since I spent an entire year forced to grapple with a life without her. And I don't want to lose her again. Not like that. But I also can't hold her back.

Not anymore.

If Sam is her Marley, he's real and he's here. He understands her when she's angry and sad. He's the person she can be completely herself with.

"Do you think people should settle?" I ask her. "Even if it's not what they want?"

She lets out a long sigh and throws her legs over the bed, standing up to pace the room. I watch as she pulls her hair into a messy bun, ready to resume our fight. "I never said I was settling. I'm sorry about the night of the accident—"

"I'm not," I say, cutting her off.

She stops and looks at me.

"When I thought you were dead, all I had left were the last words you said to me. I replayed those words over and over."

"Kyle, listen. I—"

"Let me finish. I need to say this, okay?"

She nods and reaches behind her to find the chair, slowly sitting down.

"That night, I wasn't ready to hear you because . . . I was afraid you were right." I glance up to see her eyes are wide with surprise. She was *definitely* not expecting this. But I'm not the same Kyle I was. "To turn around and not see you there . . . I thought that was the worst nightmare imaginable. But . . . to turn around and know that *there was no you anymore*, anywhere?" I let out a ragged breath, remembering that pain. That year I spent thinking she was dead. "Fuck, Kim. That blew up my whole world."

She doesn't say anything, her hands tightly gripping the wooden arms of the chair.

"But I still had your words. I finally *listened* to them. And I learned to stand on my own. I learned who I was and who I *wanted* to be," I say, thinking of Marley. The internship. Journalism classes. "I learned who I *am*. Without you."

She's stunned into silence. That never happens. I keep going, finally saying the words I needed to say but was never able to find.

"We settled, Kim. You and me. And we weren't happy."

She opens her mouth. Once. Twice. Struggling to find words. Finally they come. "Who are you, and what have you done with Kyle Lafferty?"

"Oh, that guy?" I give her a small smile. "He was a selfish kid, so I left his ass in the dust. Then I grew up. Or—I'm growing up," I say as she wipes tears from her cheeks. "Well, I'm trying to," I admit.

She stands and gives me a long, uncertain look, unsure of where we go from here.

I reach out. "Come here." She hurries into my arms, and I hold her close, her tears falling onto my shirt. "You're my best friend, Kim. I want you to be so happy," I tell her. "*At Berkeley*. Go find what you love. Find *someone* you love. Find that person you can't live without. He's out there."

The person I can't live without. I think of Marley. How it felt to hold my entire world in my arms. How it feels to have it ripped away from me.

"Yeah, right," Kim says with a tearful laugh as she pulls away. She quickly grabs a tissue and blows her nose.

"Hell, go on a date with Sam—"

The words are barely out of my mouth before she slugs me with her sling-free arm.

"You're stupid," she says, acting like I've just said the craziest thing.

I grab on to the bed rail, smiling at her as I catch myself. I see it, though. In her eyes. That *thought.* That glimmer of a possibility.

"Don't settle again, okay?" I say after I right myself. "Ever. And I won't either."

She nods, agreeing, and we shake on it. "Deal."

I take a deep, determined breath as her hand slides out of mine.

For the first time since I woke up, I feel a little closer to peace. Because I will not settle.

I won't give up until I have Marley in my arms again.

32

I'm back in my house.

My house, but *not*. The world I live in now is leaking in more and more every time I close my eyes. It's weird, even scary how much my dreams are changing.

"Kyle."

I follow the sound of the voice down a hallway, the walls crumbling around me as I fight to get to her, peeling paint giving way to the pale walls of the hospital, the standard-issue TV, the big window in the corner.

I finally find her at the kitchen table. I can see her, but ... barely.

I squint, straining, the colors so dull.

"Everything's going to change now, isn't it?" she asks, her voice the same as I remember it. Sadder now.

I try with everything in me to get closer to her, to hold her again, but my feet won't move. My legs strain, fighting to take even a single step in her direction. I look down to see my feet are enclosed in grass and mud, the cherry blossoms from the pond sprinkled around my ankles.

The second I look back up at her, I jolt back into my hospital room, my sheets twisted tightly around my body, sweat beaded across my forehead, and the loss consumes me again.

Her voice still echoes around in my head as I grip the support bars in the physical therapy room a few hours later. I put a guarded amount of weight onto my leg, carefully taking one step and then another. My only break from my tireless googling the past two days has been going down to see Henry every afternoon, the grueling leg exercises he puts me through an attempt at distracting myself from everything.

But no matter how hard I try today to focus on my legs, on getting them stronger, I can't escape the dream I had last night.

Every day the world around me gets less hazy, but that means every day she feels farther and farther away, that dream I lived in for a year crumbling, cracking, showing its holes every time I go to sleep.

"I wish I could do that for you," a voice says.

I come to a shaky stop and look up to see Sam. Even my good leg feels about as strong as a toothpick, yet somehow Sam looks worse.

"You would, wouldn't you?" I ask him. "You'd go through this for me if you could."

Sam rolls his eyes like that's an idiotic question, but he nods. "Of course, dude. You'd do the same for me."

I swallow, wobbling, and Henry takes notice. He grabs on to my forearms, giving me some extra support.

"Let's take a quick break, okay?" he says as he helps me into my wheelchair, leaving the two of us alone for a bit.

I'm trying not to live in my dreams, but I think of the day at the cemetery. There's truth in that conversation, even if we never had it. So maybe we have to have it now.

"I've been a shitty friend to you," I say.

Sam quickly shakes his head. "No—"

"You said it yourself. Kim's tried to break up with me seven times since the ninth grade," I say, looking up at him. "You paid close attention. Why?"

"Uh," Sam says, frowning, his eyes narrowing as he looks back at me. "I don't remember saying that."

Right. Off to a great start.

"Well, either way, it's true. You helped me see her perspective, and you helped her see mine," I cover. "Every time, Sam, you helped me win her back."

I think about yesterday, how he left when he saw us together. "And now you're trying to do it again. Why?"

Sam looks away, shrugging.

"Because you're a good friend. Too good," I say, flexing my skinny leg. "I've realized a lot of things. And even though I was asleep, a lot of what my brain was processing was real. There's a reason Kimberly and I could never quite get it right."

Sam looks annoyed at me, but I press on.

"This isn't about Marley. Or me. It's about *you*, Sam. Things haven't been about you for a long time. If you love her like I think you do, tell her how you feel."

Sam swats at my water bottle as I go to drink it. "Come on, dude. This is fucked up. She's going to Berkeley and she wants to have some space," he says. "Besides, you're right out of a coma and you two just broke up."

She told him we broke up. That *has* to count for something.

I take another swig, carefully staying out of swatting distance this time. "She wanted space from *me*. She talked to *you*. She's still here now. Don't you want her to know?"

"Whether or not you're right doesn't matter. You can't control everything," he says to me, his face serious. "You gotta let people be their own person, you know? Just like you gotta be yours. Whether you're with Kim or Marley or nobody. You can't *make* someone choose you."

A long moment passes, and eventually I launch the water bottle at him, my throwing arm still intact post-coma. "That was wise as hell," I say to him as he catches the water bottle, smirking.

"You know I'm the brains of this team, dude." He laughs as he mimics tucking the water bottle under his arm and running, dodging playfully around my chair.

The jokes, the no-bullshit talks. Things finally feel right between us. Like they did back in the dream world.

"You want to get some pizza?" he asks, nodding toward the

double doors out of here. "I hear the cafeteria makes a mean pepperoni."

I snort. "Is that even a question?"

I'm already unlocking the wheels of my wheelchair, knowing full well the cafeteria's pepperoni pizza is terrible, but I need a prison break right now.

In two seconds, Sam grabs the handles and we bust through the doors into the hallway, flying out of the PT room before Henry can even realize I'm gone.

33

She's here.

I know it immediately even though I can't see her. I chase her shadow down a hallway of my house, the paint peeling even more than last time, but she's always just a little bit out of reach, her hair disappearing around corners, her hand slipping through my grasp.

"I told you I wasn't meant to be this happy," her voice says from right next to me, but when I turn quickly to look at her, I jerk awake instead.

I sit up, gasping for air, my eyes scanning the room automatically for some trace of her that everything and everyone tells me I won't find.

My head falls back against the pillow, and I rub my hands over my face, taking in a long, deep breath.

When I inhale, there's . . . her smell. Orange blossoms. Or . . . I roll my eyes. *Honeysuckle.*

I lift my head toward the window and breathe in again, but no scent comes. It fades just as quickly as it came.

Groaning, I roll over and pull my blanket up over my head.

That's when the scent of orange blossoms and honeysuckle overpowers me, like it's stitched into the blanket. I breathe deeper and I know it's not coming from the garden. It never was.

It's *Marley's* smell.

Somehow, she was here. She was actually here.

I flick on the light, grab my crutches, and struggle to climb out of bed. Once I right myself, I limp over to the open window, gazing outside, the early-morning light casting a warm glow on all of the plants in the courtyard.

Looking out, I see yellow Doris Day roses, the color jumping out at me. Smiling, I picture Marley, the yellow dress she wore that last night we had together.

"You're yellow," I say, still able to feel the fabric underneath my fingers. "And Laura loved . . ." I notice the Stargazers, planted just across the path from the Doris Days, the pink and yellow next to each other.

If Dr. Ronson were here, he'd say that this was tangible proof that I made that up too.

But I get a chill.

Because I realize what a complete idiot I've been. I hobble as quickly as I can over to my bed, grabbing my iPad and opening up Google. I type in "Marley + Laura + accident," and results materialize before my eyes.

* * *

Sam finds me surrounded by sticky notes, all of them different Marleys, their geographic location in miles written next to their names.

"What's going on here?" he asks warily, picking up two of the sticky notes and reading them. "Marla and Laurie, accident, eighty-eight miles? Marley, Laura, accident, 1,911 miles? Dude, I thought—"

I hold up another one, showing it to him. "Marley, Lara, seven miles."

He stares at me, blinking, not understanding what I'm saying.

"This has to be her," I say, telling him about her smell on my blanket this morning, the flowers, and the epiphany I had. I guide him through all my research, explaining to him how I'd spent the day googling combinations of the words "Marley," "Laura," and "car accident," articles from all across the country suddenly at my fingertips.

After that it was all about efficiency. GPSing the city the accident happened in, giving the first paragraph a scan for names, and then on to the next one.

By the end, there was a sea of colored papers in front of me. And I'd narrowed it down to this.

A single yellow Post-it. The key I've been looking for.

"*Seven* miles away, dude. Plus, the story matches." I swipe through to the article on my iPad, reading for him. "'Lara, fourteen, was killed on impact by a speeding vehicle on Glendale Street yesterday afternoon.'" I look up at Sam and we both grimace, those horrific words feeling odd next to so much excitement.

"Sam, that's almost exactly what happened to Marley's sister. *Seven miles* away from here. It all adds up," I say as I eagerly reach out for the Post-it. "I told you she was real. Now I just have to get over there."

He doesn't say anything for a whole minute; then finally he shakes his head. "No."

"What do you mean, no?" I ask him, shaking the Post-it note in front of him. "I found her."

"No, you haven't," he says, grabbing the Post-it from my hand. "Even if she were the 'right' Marley, she doesn't know you. You were asleep. Forget it, man. I'm not helping you terrorize some poor girl."

I grab it back from him. "You don't have to do anything. You just have to drive me over there." I'm not going to be released for another few weeks at least because Dr. Benefield is still monitoring my brain activity, and this is definitely not something that can wait. I told Marley I would never leave her and now she's going to think I have. I can't put her through that. Not a single day more.

"How do you even know where she lives?" he asks, incredulous.

I hold out my iPad to him, showing him the GPS directions from here to the address I found with the help of the article. There was a quote from Lara's dad, Greg Ellis, about the accident.

While I couldn't find anything online about a Marley Ellis, I found plenty about Greg. Including his address.

We can be there in under twenty minutes.

"Google is scary," he says, shaking his head.

"Sam," I say, serious. "I need to see her. See if she remembers me."

"Remembers you? From where? All those nights she doused herself in jasmine perfume, snuck into your hospital room, and rubbed herself all over your blanket?"

I throw down one of my crutches and snatch the iPad back from him. "Screw you, then. Don't help."

He stalks to the door, and I know I have one last Hail Mary.

And I'm an awful person for using it, but I'm desperate.

"You owe me."

Sam spins around, confused. "What?"

"When I said I heard you talking to me . . . I heard *everything* you said, Sam. Everything." I watch as his face pales, his eyes widening as he realizes what I'm talking about.

"You owe me. For that missed tackle. For my shoulder. For my career—"

Sam holds up his hands, shaking his head. I've hit the mark. "Hold on—I'm sorry—"

"Then prove it!" I say as I raise the Post-it note. "Help me. All I'm asking is that you believe me, Sam. It's her. I *know* it's her."

His dark eyebrows pull together as he thinks, his eyes turning to the iPad, glowing on the bed. "I know I owe you, and I've really tried to be the best friend I could be," he says softly. "I wasn't always able to do that. I shouldn't have let you be blindsided by Kimberly's acceptance to Berkeley. I should have told you how I felt about Kim, even if I was never going to do anything about it. I should have helped you find something outside of football and us to focus on." He runs his fingers through his hair, swallowing. "And you're right—I should have blocked that linebacker. I should have *protected you*, and I've been beating myself up about it ever since."

He looks up, his eyes locking with mine. "But I didn't. And I've learned my lesson. I know how to be a *real* friend now. Not just a good friend."

He'll help me. The guilt I feel for playing that card on Sam is swallowed whole by relief. I grab the iPad, scooping up my crutch from the floor. "Great. Grab my wallet," I say as I nod to the table in front of him. "Let's go—"

"No," Sam says, the single word stopping me in my tracks, his voice firm. "Here's me protecting you. The right way." He takes a deep breath and points to the iPad, at the address still on the screen. "That girl doesn't know you, Kyle. She is not Marley. There *is* no Marley. So get over your dream life and start living your real one. *This* one."

He turns and walks out the door, closing it loudly behind him. I look down at the address, at the pile of sticky notes forming a thin layer across my bed.

It looks completely crazy.

But the only thing crazier would be giving up on her.

34

I squeeze my eyes shut, pretending to be asleep as I wait for the night nurse to leave. I pop one eye open to see her reaching up to flick off the lights, her features disappearing into darkness as I hold my breath, waiting. The second the door clicks shut behind her, I'm on the move.

I call an Uber, placing the pin a safe distance outside the entrance to the hospital, before throwing my legs over the side of my bed and standing, my bad leg almost buckling under the weight.

Taking a deep breath, I steady myself, grab my crutches for support, and hobble over to the cabinet. The black duffel bag my mom brought is sitting at the bottom, and I pull out a pair of Nike shorts and a T-shirt. I slide them on as quickly as I can, which is not quick at all, my leg struggling to comprehend the urgency of this entire operation.

I peer into the hallway, looking in both directions.

Nine o'clock, right after my vitals were checked, the perfect time to strike. The top of the hour brings with it an empty nurses' station, ideal for me to hobble from my room to the exit without getting caught.

I breathe a sigh of relief as the glass doors of the hospital slide shut behind me, my breakout nearly complete.

Where's my Uber?

I stare anxiously at the hospital entrance, my eyes flicking from the main road to the door and back again, praying for John in a red Prius to pull onto the drive before I get dragged back to my room. I try to keep my cool as I wait, but the thought of seeing Marley in just a few minutes makes my heart hammer in my chest. Will she be angry? Will she trust me again? What has this been like for her? Somehow I just know she'll be the one to understand all of this.

There's a flash of headlights, and the Prius glides to a stop in front of me. I yank open the door and quickly slide inside. My head is fuzzy and my leg is throbbing, but I've been through a hell of a lot worse.

We drive and I watch the time tick down on the GPS, the space between me and Marley shortening by the second. The road flies by underneath us, the yellow dividing lines in the center pulling me closer and closer to her.

Soon we're turning onto Glendale Street, slowing to a stop in front of a modest white house at the corner, a big tree standing in the front lawn. An uneasy feeling swims into my stomach as I look at the wilted flower bushes lining the porch, the overgrown lawn.

This is . . . not quite what I pictured.

I glance down at my phone to see it's almost nine thirty.

Is it too late? Will she answer the door?

"You want me to wait?" the driver asks, and I hesitate just one more second.

Then I shake my head. Marley's inside. I've got no reason to leave. I struggle out onto the sidewalk and pause as the car disappears into the distance.

Every step I take, I get more nervous, the pain in my leg growing by the second, my heart hammering in my chest.

Soon only the door stands between us. I lean on my crutches, staring at it.

A ceramic duck statue is perched on top of the welcome sign. A sign on a sign. It spurs me on.

I reach out slowly, and after a long moment my finger presses the doorbell. One sharp peal sounds and I quickly pull my hand away.

I hold my breath, listening, until I hear the sound of footsteps coming closer. A wave of dizziness passes over me, but I fight through it. The lock slowly turns; then the handle twists and the door opens.

I'm so expecting to see her that it's hard for me to fully process the stocky, middle-aged guy with a thick beard standing in front of me.

His curiosity turns to a frown when he looks at me.

"Yes?"

"Hi," I say, clearing my throat. "Um, is Marley home?"

He sizes me up. "How do you know my daughter?"

Just like that my doubt evaporates and relief plunges through me. I knew it.

"Sir, I'm—" I start to say, stopping short when a young girl I've never seen before peeks around her dad's shoulder, her eyes wide as she stares at me.

She can't be more than ten.

"Marley," the man says to her, nodding to me. "Do you know this guy?"

Her small, round eyes meet mine, and her fear kicks me in the teeth. She's just some poor kid. But how can this be? I thought all the signs pointed to this Marley. This house.

The girl shakes her head, but I'm already stumbling back, trying to get the hell out of here, seeing the cracks in the article that I ignored in my excitement.

Lara, not Laura. Her sister, but not a single mention of twins. Hit at *night* instead of the morning. I just thought maybe my coma brain had gotten some of the details wrong.

"I'm sorry," I manage to get out. "Wrong house."

I turn as quickly as I can, desperately struggling to get down the front steps, my vision tunneling. As if this isn't already bad enough, one of my crutches slips halfway down. I lose my footing and hit the ground *hard*, the wind knocked out of me as my body sprawls across the front yard.

Gasping, I fight to catch my breath as the dad trots down the steps after me.

"Why are you here?" he calls out, voice angry.

I grab my crutches. I have to get back on my feet, but my entire body is screaming. "I got the wrong house. I'm sorry." I grunt and hoist myself up.

I hear him call over his shoulder to his daughter a firm "Get inside, Marley." Just hearing her name is enough to practically knock me over again, but I hobble forward.

I make it to a streetlight by the road, collapsing against it. Looking back, I see the dad watching me from the porch, glaring, so I keep fighting, stumbling to the curb at the end of the block.

I slide onto it, under the glow of the streetlight, my vision blurring.

It wasn't her. If she's out there, this was my shot. None of the others made any sense.

Which means she's not here.

And she never was.

I pull my hands away from my face when I hear Kim's car pull up. She stops right in front of me. Sam's in the passenger seat, a worried look on his face.

They came the second I called, just like they always have.

Both of them hop out and help me off the curb, getting me safely into the front seat, my body too exhausted to do it on my own.

The three of us sit in silence, Sam's arms resting on the center console, his eyes downcast.

I feel like a complete idiot. "You were right. I should have listened to you."

He gives a sad shake of his head and lets out a long exhale. "I should have come with you."

"No," I say, defeated. "You knew it wasn't going to be her."

"Which is exactly why I should've been here," he says, frustrated with himself even though *I'm* the one to blame for all of this.

"You're here now," I say, my voice cracking. I reach for Kimberly's hand, but she pushes mine away, pulling me into a tight, bone-crushing hug instead.

She's stronger than most of the guys from the football team even with one arm in a brace.

"I don't know what I'd do without you guys," I say, my eyes meeting Sam's over her shoulder.

Sam leans over the seat to wrap his arms around both of us, tears running down all of our faces.

We pull apart and I rub my eyes, trying to get myself back together. "I'm sorry for all this."

Kim gives me a sad smile, all of the weirdness since I woke up completely erased. She reaches out to squeeze my hand. "I'm sorry you lost your Marley," she says, meaning it. "I know how you love, Kyle, and if you love her like this, then . . ."

"I'm so fucked," I say, the three of us laughing through our tears.

Then my laugh gives way, and I just sob.

Because Marley isn't real.

35

The next morning, Dr. Benefield checks my IV line while my mom stands in the corner with her arms crossed. Both of them are decidedly not psyched about my nighttime escape. After checking my leg and shining a light into my eyes, she lets out a long sigh.

"What you did last night was really, really stupid. You could have seriously damaged your leg again," she says as she hangs a small bag of morphine and attaches it to my IV, clearly disappointed that I'm back on it.

"I don't need that," I say, and her hand freezes in midair.

"Kyle, just take the medicine," my mom says. "You were in so much pain last night, you could barely speak."

I ignore her, keeping my eyes on Dr. Benefield.

"You sure?" she asks, arching an eyebrow. "You're not impressing anyone here by playing it tough. Although, maybe the pain will keep you out of trouble."

I try to return the smile, but it comes up flat. "I'm done chasing dreams."

She gives my hand a small squeeze. "No pain, then?"

"Not that kind." I shake my head.

A flash of sympathy crosses her face, and she removes the bag.

"Okay," she says, pointing to the call button. "If you change your mind, just—"

"I won't," I say, cutting her off. After a year of living in a dream, it's time to know what is real.

She nods, studying me for a moment before she leaves. I curl up in bed, turning away from my mom, this feeling of loss so overwhelmingly familiar. Because what comes to mind isn't the big-deal days, where we went to the Winter Festival or celebrated Halloween night. It's all the small, inconsequential moments I took for granted. Feeding the ducks popcorn together, or watching her make one of her bouquets, or going on walks with her and Georgia. Things I thought we'd do a hundred times more.

All gone.

The next afternoon, I finally find the strength to get out of bed. To face the world. My mom wheels me down the hall to the courtyard, where the warm sun is making the water around the fountain shimmer.

"I'm going to go grab a snack real quick," she says, nodding to the outdoor café, perched just on the other side of the courtyard. "You want anything?"

I shake my head and give her a small smile. "I won't make a break for it. Don't worry."

She gives my shoulder a squeeze and heads down the path, disappearing from view.

I look around at the cherry trees. The honeysuckle. The yellow and pink flowers, their petals intermixing along the path.

She was never real, but everything I see reminds me of her.

How's that for screwed?

I see Sam making his way toward me, his hands shoved in his pockets as he unknowingly crushes the petals underneath his feet.

"You okay?" he asks as he comes closer.

I nod and pull my eyes away from the smooshed petals. "Yeah. You?"

He nods and sits down next to me on the bench, both of us falling into silence. Sam finally breaks it. "Kim wants to come by later, if you're up for company."

"Will you be coming with her?" I ask, nudging him. "Like *with* her?"

Sam shifts uncomfortably, rubbing at the back of his neck. "You know, man, it hasn't been as long out here as it was in your coma world," he says, giving me a small smile. "We're going to feel things out. Maybe see how we feel when she gets back home for fall break. So leave it for now."

"That's not a no," I say with a grin.

Sam chuckles. "You're right. That's not a no." He pauses and sizes me up. "What about you? What's next?"

I take a deep breath, looking up at the cherry trees, the sunlight trickling through the branches. "I have no idea," I say, watching the petals slowly fall, my eyes meeting my mom's as she walks back from the café, coffee in one hand, biscotti in the other.

I let the wave of grief wash over me, trying not to let it take me under.

I was able to move on once, and it was the hardest thing I ever had to do. But this feels a million times worse. I understand now what Sam meant that day on the field.

I would never *let her go.*

I still love her. I'll never be able to stop. So what the hell do I do with that?

That night, when my eyes open, I *know* I'm dreaming again. Georgia's tiny face is nuzzling mine, covering my cheeks with kisses.

I smile sadly and reach out to pet her. This may be a dream, but that doesn't make it feel any less real. And I don't care, because it's exactly where I want to be.

I'd rather live forever in this dream than live out there without Marley.

I look past Georgia, my eyes registering the rest of the room.

Yellow.

Everywhere.

The bedding, the lampshades, even the ceiling fixtures. The walls are covered in the same yellow Doris Day roses that are in the courtyard.

Then I see her.

Marley.

She stands at the edge of the bed, wearing a long yellow dress, her brown hair hanging over one shoulder. I stare at her, her face clear for the first time since the first dream, as if now that I've stopped looking for her everywhere, my brain can finally let her in. I can see her freckles, the traces of green in her eyes, the deep pink of her down-turned lips. And it's like I forgot just how beautiful she is. *How* could I forget that?

I open my arms, and she climbs into them, curling up against me.

I know it's not happening, but I can *feel* her body pressed up against mine, as real as it always used to seem.

"I can't let you go," I whisper to her, smelling the warm jasmine of her hair. No, not jasmine. Honeysuckle. From the courtyard.

She looks up at me, her face sad. There was so much I wanted to ask her in all the other dreams, but none of it matters now. I just want to hold her for as long as I can.

I don't see her lips move, but I can hear her whispered voice echoing around the yellow room we are in.

"He was awake now. Living two different lives. One with her . . ."

The door to the yellow room creaks open, and sitting on the other side is my hospital room, a scene from earlier today right before my eyes. Me, Kimberly, and Sam, laughing while we eat off-brand M&M'S and Swedish Fish that Kim bought at the gift shop in the hospital lobby.

". . . and one with them," her voice continues.

I stare at myself through the door, my figure freezing suddenly and turning to look directly at me. My lips move, but Marley's voice comes out.

"Don't let go."

Never.

I pull her close to me, holding her tighter as rain begins to fall all around us, drenching the yellow lampshades, the Doris Day wallpaper starting to peel off the wall. The only thing that stays dry is us and the bed we're lying on, Marley safe in my arms.

The sheets of water get closer and closer, closing in on us. I fight to keep my eyes open, to keep myself there just a few minutes longer. But eventually my brain takes over, and even though I don't want to, I wake up back in my real hospital room, where it's still the middle of the night. Arms empty. Alone.

Water splatters loudly against my window, startling me.

It stops abruptly only to start again a couple of seconds later. On and off, over and over, the sound filling the room.

Sprinklers. In the courtyard.

I roll over to my other side, turning quickly away from the window, my leg screaming out in pain. Frustrated, I roll onto my back, but I can't get comfortable on this hard-as-hell hospital mattress.

I turn my head to look outside, watching as the sprinkler noisily batters the glass again. My eyes find a small snail crawling slowly across the window. I watch it fight its way along.

I want to tell it to just sit there and wait it out. There's no use in the struggle. But suddenly, without warning, it's plucked from the glass by a pair of fingers that disappear from view just as quickly as they came.

Huh?

I look closer, realizing there's someone outside in the court-yard. Pushing myself out of bed, I grab my crutches and shuffle to the window. A girl in dark clothes on the other side of the glass is moving up and down the courtyard, plucking snails out of the way of the sprinkler and moving them to safety.

I smile sadly to myself, watching as she looks around, finding another and moving it over to one of the benches, setting it carefully down on the wood.

I freeze as she turns, the glowing lamplight illuminating her face.

Marley.

My heart speeds into triple time, my stomach going molten as it flips over itself. I squeeze my eyes shut, trying to wake myself up. To pull myself out of this cruel second dream. But when I open them, she's still there.

This is real.

Before I can process what I'm doing, I'm booking it out of my room and flying down the hallway. I almost make it to the door before a nurse slides in front of me, blocking my way.

"Where do you think you're going this time?" she asks me, crossing her arms. "Are you determined to rebreak your leg? No more evening excursions for you."

I try to get past her, desperately shuffling right and left, but she's too quick for a guy on crutches with only one working leg.

"Goddammit . . . ," I say, frustrated. I need to get out into that courtyard. I have to get to her before I lose her again. She's here. There's no fog. No clashing of my dreams with reality.

"Really?" the nurse says, plucking a crutch out from under my arm.

I wobble, grabbing ahold of the wall and bracing myself, but it's obvious I'm not getting any farther like this.

"See you guys in a few," a nurse in a pair of blue scrubs says to the ladies at the station, oblivious to our standoff. She walks past us. "They've got me in Cardiology the rest of this week."

I glance to the side at her, my eyes widening when I see her eyes, her long brown hair, the wrinkle in her forehead, all of it triggering a memory. Her face peering down at me as I woke up, her voice calling out into the hallway for Dr. Benefield.

The features just like Marley's, only older. Long brown hair, rose-petal lips, warm hazel eyes, but hers crinkle at the corners.

I watch her go through the double doors.

And then . . . I remember.

She was the nurse who checked my vitals the night I broke out of the hospital. The nurse who wheeled me down to my first physical therapy appointment.

I've been too distracted searching for Marley to pay attention to everything around me.

"Holy shit," I say aloud, and the nurse blocking my way glares at me.

I give her an apologetic smile, and she grants me the crutch back, steering me to my room. I hurry to the window. I get there just in time to see the woman in blue scrubs call out to Marley, leading her away and out of the courtyard. It's her mother. It's got to be.

My mind is exploding.

I stagger to the bed, sinking down on it. "Holy. Shit." She's real. Marley is *real*.

I grab my phone off my nightstand, quickly starting a text to Sam, but the words won't come out right no matter what I try to say. So instead I scroll through my recent calls and press Kimberly's number.

I rip the phone away from my ear and quickly disconnect after the first ring.

No. Not yet. I have to be 100 percent sure this time.

Cardiology. The nurse said she'd been in Cardiology this week. And if she's in Cardiology this week, maybe that means Marley will be too.

I flop back on my bed and stare up at the ceiling, a smile breaking out on my lips.

36

The next evening, I check my hair quickly in the bathroom mirror as I wash my hands. I see that one stubborn, unruly strand of hair, but I don't even try to smooth it down. Marley never seemed to mind it.

My face is still gaunt, though, from the accident and the weeks lying in a coma. Will she recognize me? A pasty complexion is probably the least of my worries on *that* front.

Grabbing my crutches, I brace myself, flicking the light out and heading into the hallway. I peer at the empty nurses' desk before working my way down the hall, hiding behind doors and around corners as I move toward the sign that says CARDIOLOGY in big black letters.

Pushing inside, I quietly look around for her.

Doctors, nurses, orderlies, all of them distracted by the clipboards in their hands and the monitoring of their patients. No Marley, though. I try one waiting room and then another, stepping through the second door to find the seats are all empty. She's nowhere to be found.

The only thing there is a book lying open, facedown on one of the green chairs. I walk over and pick it up, studying the intricate, flowery cover before flipping through a few pages.

It's a love story, two people hell-bent on ending up together. And it starts with "Once upon a time . . ."

I go to put it down, but something about the cover is familiar. Images from the night of the accident pop into my head. The fluorescent lights flashing as I'm wheeled down the hallway, my eyes flicking down to see a doctor carrying a child, tears streaming down the little boy's face. An elderly woman dragging a green oxygen tank behind her. *A girl with long brown hair reading a book.* This book.

I look over to the door, and that's when I come face-to-face with those same hazel eyes from that night. The ones I've been dreaming of for weeks.

But this time they're real.

It's her.

Marley.

"It's you," I say, taking her in and moving toward her as quick as my crutches will let me. "I didn't make you up."

Something about her looks different. She's paler. Thinner. Dark circles ring her eyes, dulling the usually vibrant color to almost brown. Her shoulders are hunched, bent forward, like she's shielding something she doesn't want anyone to see.

And on top of all that, she's dressed head to toe in all dark colors, from the charcoal gray of her hoodie to her scuffed black shoes.

There's not a single trace of yellow. What's happened?

"Marley," I say, reaching out. "It's me. Kyle."

When I move toward her, though, she hurries from the room, disappearing around the corner. I adjust my crutches under my arms to follow her, but when I get out to the hall, I can't tell which way she went. She's gone.

I freeze when I see her mom at the end of the hall, and I know I have to call it and get back to my room, so I crutch out of Cardiology and back through my wing of the hospital. When I get there, I collapse onto my bed and let out a long exhale.

I saw her. She saw *me*. She's real . . . but she ran. My stomach sinks for the thousandth time. That can't be a good thing. To have a girl literally run away from you.

Now that I can place her from before my coma, does that mean my brain just created a whole persona for her?

Do I even know her?

Does she know me?

Exactly twenty-four hours later, I limp back to the same Cardiology waiting room, hoping she'll be there again. I round the corner to see her sitting in one of the green leather chairs.

It's still as shocking as it was two days ago. To see her after I gave her up. To see her looking so different.

Her long hair hangs around her face, and she's focused on

a book open in her lap. In the chair next to her sits a book bag, unzipped.

She must feel my presence because her head snaps up, and when she sees me, she flinches. I take a small step toward her, but she shakes her head, jumping up and darting into the bathroom, the door slamming shut behind her.

"Marley!" I call to her. "You know me."

But then I hesitate. "Don't you?"

Slowly, I approach the bathroom door, knocking lightly and resting my forehead against the wood.

"I don't want to scare you. I'm sorry if I did. I just need to know if you're the Marley I think you are, or if I just saw your face and then made up everything else about you." Actually hearing myself say it sounds even crazier than I expected.

I stop talking and hold my breath, hoping that doesn't sound stalkerish. When she doesn't say anything, I continue. "Just please can you tell me if you know me? Tell me if you're . . . you."

I wait for an answer, but minutes pass and it doesn't come.

I think of the girl at the house. The wrong Marley and how scared she looked. I'm doing it again. I'm an idiot for thinking she actually knows me and that I actually know *her*. I mean, I was asleep the whole time.

Why is it I never considered that if she was real, she wouldn't love me?

"I'm sorry. I—shit." I take a step away from the door, shaking my head. "I'm sorry. I'm leaving now."

I curse at myself. When the hell am I going to learn? In my

rush to get out of there, the bottom of my left crutch tangles on something, and as I struggle to right myself, there's a loud *thud* behind me. I look down to see the strap of her book bag wrapped around the crutch, her bag lying open on the floor.

Great. Now she'll think I was going through her stuff.

I grab for it, picking up a few loose pencils that have tumbled out onto the floor.

But as I slip them back inside, I see the corner of a bright-yellow notebook.

I glance back at the closed door, before carefully picking it up. On the front, handwritten in familiar neat calligraphy, is her name: *Marley Phelps.*

"You do have a last name," I murmur. *Take that, Sam.*

Before I can think better of it, I flip to a random page, my eyes widening when I see what's written on it.

It's the story of the two of us at Halloween, all of it exactly the same as it happened. Or how I dreamed it, I guess. My zombie football player costume, me tossing the entire bowl of candy to the kids, her hands reaching up to unclip her shell.

I keep searching, seeing tiny glimpses as I skim, memories I had. The Winter Festival, getting Georgia, eating hot dogs by the pond.

All of it right here.

I'm shaking. If this was all in my head, how does she know?

My eyes land on a single word. "Storyteller." I think about our conversation that day at the park. When she told me the best part about telling stories.

The audience. Without an audience, a storyteller is just talking to the air, but when someone's listening . . .

Someone was listening. *I* was listening.

Quickly, I close the notebook and put it away, but as I do, a feather falls out of the back and drifts slowly onto the floor.

A *duck* feather.

I hold it up to the light, smiling. It's her. I *do* know her.

And she knows me. At least some part of her does, even though we've never actually met.

Gently, I place the feather on top of the notebook and reach into my pocket to pull out a cherry blossom petal I plucked off a flower in the courtyard today. I slide it over the feather, hoping she sees it.

Hoping it means something to her, too.

37

I wait impatiently outside the double doors of the hospital, scanning the parking lot for Kimberly. I check my watch for the millionth time, groaning, hoping she won't be too late. Now is so not the moment for us to be operating on Kim Standard Time.

It's almost 7:10. She's going to miss it.

Finally, under the parking lot lights, I see her blond head bobbing its way around the parked cars.

I frantically wave her over, looking like a madman.

She jogs the rest of the way, her face half-puzzled, half-amused. "What? What's the big secret?"

I grab her hand, pulling her around the corner and behind one of the huge stone pillars outside the hospital entrance.

"Kyle—"

I put a finger over my mouth and nod toward the door. She

peeks around the pillar. I stare over her shoulder, holding my breath. Less than a minute later, Marley and her mom, Nurse Catherine, come out of the lobby, walking in the direction of the parking lot.

"What—"

"Shh."

Catherine turns, motioning to Marley, who is lagging a few steps behind her. "Marley? Hurry up, baby."

Kim's eyes widen, and she grabs ahold of my arm, squeezing it in a vise grip. "Oh my *God*," she whispers, excited. Now she's the one practically flailing.

I grin at her like I just won the lottery.

"How long have you known?" Kimberly asks the second we get back to my room.

"Three days. I wanted to be sure. And . . ." I grab my iPad and turn it around to face her. "All the things I was telling you guys about her are true. Look."

"Back up—slow down—hold on—*stop*," she says as she tries to regain any sense of chill.

"The accident I told you about? It was real. I didn't pay attention to this one because it was halfway across the country, but here it is." I hold up the Post-it that reads *1,911 miles away* and hand her the iPad with the newspaper article about Laura's death. Once I found out Marley's last name, all of the pieces fell into place. I did some more googling and was even able to find a photo of Laura and Marley smiling, one wearing pink, the other wearing yellow.

Kim skims the article, her smile wide until she gets to the very end. Then her face grows serious. Quietly, she shuts the iPad off and puts it down on my bed. She's thinking hard about something. Finally she says, "Why are you telling *me*? Why not Sam?"

"Because you were right," I say, giving her a small smile. "About everything."

I get up and limp over to my closet. I dig around in the bag from my mom until my fingers wrap around a dented blue jewelry box.

I sit down on the bed next to her and hold it out to her. She opens it, and her eyes widen when she sees the charm bracelet inside, a tiny Berkeley charm I ordered last week on Etsy taking the place of the UCLA one.

"Kyle, I—"

"Kim, you're still my best friend," I say. "And now I need your help, because . . . you know me better than anyone. Even Sam."

Her lips quiver and she puts it on, then throws her arms around me, the bracelet jingling noisily. Laughing, I hug her back, adding, "*And* because you know how crazy I get when it comes to love. I need you to keep my feet on the ground."

She snorts, nodding. "Boy, do I."

We pull apart, and she wipes the stray tears that have fallen from her eyes, giving me a determined nod. "Okay, then. What's the plan?"

I head into the gift shop the next evening after Mom leaves to grab a snack, stopping short when I see Marley with her back to me, staring at the wall of candy bars. Her hands are shoved into the pockets of her black hoodie as she decides, like she isn't going to just get a Kit Kat.

I hesitate, looking from her to the premade bouquets in the window, and an idea pops into my head.

I pull a few different flowers out, pausing when I see a yellow duck stuffed animal sitting on a shelf next to the greeting cards. It's just like the one Marley won at the Winter Festival, sans Santa outfit. The one from her story.

I grab it and follow her up to the cashier, a Kit Kat clutched in her hand. I smile. I do know her.

Gently, I lay a daisy on the counter in front of her. Her back stiffens as she looks down at it.

"A daisy. I *hope* you remember what it means," I say. She doesn't turn around to look at me. She doesn't say anything. But her gaze stays fixed on the white petals.

"Your words, Marley, gave me a *new life*," I say as I lay down a thin cherry blossom branch on the counter. I follow it up with a hydrangea, just like she gave to me.

"Words that you wrote for me. Told me. Words that I'm *grateful* for."

She still doesn't turn around, so I keep trying, placing a single peony on top of the small pile forming. "I would feel so *fortunate* if you said them again, Marley. Now. While I'm awake. Please?"

Then I lay down the yellow rose, the final flower. Her favorite flower. "Please talk to me. Like you did before."

She looks away, her brown hair covering her face, a barrier

between us. So, because I have nothing else to lose at this point, I try one more thing.

I softly place the stuffed duck on top of the pile, my last chance, the buzzer beater.

"Pretty sure it likes popcorn."

I hold my breath as she reaches out to pick up the duck, a chord struck. She studies it while I wait, hoping she'll say something.

But she puts the duck down, grabs her candy bar, and leaves without a word. I watch her go, the glass doors sliding shut behind her. *Damn it.*

"You know, you're supposed to just get one of the premade arrangements. Not mix and match," the unamused clerk says from behind the counter.

I grab a bag of chips, putting two dollars down on the counter. I want to tell him it's because they mean different things, but instead I just mumble an apology, knowing the only person who would give a shit about that just walked out the door.

"You can't control everything," Kim says to me the next morning over FaceTime. She's packing up her room, getting ready for Berkeley, the charm bracelet on her wrist. She eyes me knowingly through the screen. "It's different for her than it is for you, Kyle. A lot different."

I sigh. I know she's right. It was different for Marley. She was telling a story to a guy in a coma. A story she never expected me to hear.

But would she have made it up for me, made up a whole life for the both of us, if she didn't wish in some way it could be real?

"You can't convince her she lived something she didn't. She's clearly dealing with shit. You know what that's like."

"So, what do I even do?" I don't know where to go from here.

Kim shrugs. "You have to learn how to talk to *this* Marley."

I flop back hard against my pillows.

How do I do that when *this* Marley doesn't talk at all?

38

Crutching around in the courtyard a little after noon a few days later, I find Marley in the outdoor café. Kim spent the better part of the morning snooping around the hospital, trying to get more information. On a break to get an iced coffee, she spotted Marley and tipped me off to her location.

Now that I'm here, though, I have no clue what to do.

I glance over at Marley to see her head is buried in a book, her hair covering her face. I watch her for a moment, the way she's sitting reminding me of those small moments when she'd speak of Laura. When the sad stories she refused to tell would cast a shadow over her.

I scan the menu, stopping when I see they sell iced tea, another idea coming into my head. Like this moment was meant to be.

A way to talk to this Marley. I can *write* it.

I make my oddly specific request and snag a pen from the cashier, scrawling on the back of the receipt, *Marley. You thought I wouldn't hear you, but I did. I heard your stories, the fairy tales. I lived one—with you. I know you don't share those memories, but you were my whole world while I was asleep. I miss hearing you talk. Please talk to me again. When you're ready, I'll be here.*

I head over and put the glass of tea down in front of her, the note just next to it, her eyes darting up. "Iced green tea, no sugar, fresh mint. Your favorite summer drink."

I look at the seat next to her, but I don't sit. I remember in the dream world how hesitant she was. I don't want to come on too strong.

I hobble over to a table a few feet away and slide into one of the chairs, pulling out my phone and pretending to look at it.

At first she doesn't read the note.

She doesn't even lift her head from her book, her fingers drawing circles on the page in front of her.

But then, out of the corner of my eye, I see her hand stop abruptly, frozen over a single spot, her eyes now fixed on my messy handwriting.

She closes her book and gets up, and I try desperately to refocus my attention on my Instagram feed, but it's no use. I can't help it.

I glance up to see she's looking at me. Her eyes hold mine for the first time out of the coma, and I see something in them debating. I hold my breath, but instead of coming over, she turns and walks out of the outdoor café and back into the hospital, her book tucked under her arm.

I stare at the untouched mint iced tea, the sweat from the glass bleeding onto the note, the ink blurring as the words all run together.

Sighing, I text Kim she can meet me at the outdoor café now, and a few minutes later she appears, sliding into the seat across from me, wearing a pair of dark sunglasses, an iced coffee still clutched in her hand.

"All right," she says, her business face on. She's taking her role in this very seriously, darting around the hospital like a secret agent. "It took a minute to find someone who even knew who the hell I was talking about, but I finally got a nurse to talk to me on her way out on shift change. She stays here when her mother works," she says, pulling out a color-coded schedule and pushing her sunglasses up on her forehead.

"How did you get that . . . ?"

Kim peers around, eyeing a table next to us suspiciously, still in full recon mode. "Don't ask," she says, scanning the sheet and pointing at a blue block labeled CATHERINE PHELPS. "Anyway, her mom works twelve-hour shifts Monday, Tuesday, and Friday through Sunday. They let Marley hang around because she keeps to herself. She reads a lot. Takes a walk around the hospital grounds every day before she has lunch, alone, by the fountain."

She shrugs and slides the schedule across the table to me.

I fold it up and shove it in my pocket, more than a little impressed at how much Kim found out, but she's not done.

"The weirdest thing, though? You're not the only one she won't talk to. She doesn't talk at all. So I'm not sure you actually can break through to her."

But I know I can. Because I did before. She might not talk to anyone else, but at some point she talked to me. I just have to figure it out, but I can't explain that to Kim right now.

Kim leans back in her chair and takes a long sip of her iced coffee, thoughtful. "I wonder why, though? Who refuses to talk when they can?"

I think about Marley's hair covering her face, her arms crossed tightly over her chest as she walked away, holding every part of her in, like a snail.

"Someone who's hiding from life."

39

She doesn't come see me.

Two days go by, and then three. Dr. Benefield says we can start talking about discharge soon. The most recent scans on my brain came back normal, and the bones in my leg are healing much better now that I'm not lying unconscious 24/7. My mom is pretty thrilled, but I can't help feeling nervous.

I'm afraid she won't come in time.

On the fourth day, I head down to the physical therapy room alone to distract myself, slowly working my way through a list of strength exercises Henry gave me to do whenever I feel up for it.

I pause at the top on my seventh straight leg raise as my mind drifts to Marley at the outdoor café. I can still see the debating look in her eyes after she read my note.

Maybe I can do something like that again. . . .

No. I shake my head and sit up. I told her to come when she's ready to talk to me. If she hasn't come yet, it means she isn't ready. Or . . . maybe it means everyone was right.

I fight back against the sinking feeling in my chest, reaching out to grab ahold of a rail and pull myself back up onto my feet.

Maybe she's *not* my Marley after all.

I move to do a standing calf stretch, stopping short when I look up through the glass door into the hallway to see . . .

Marley. Watching me.

Her eyes widen and she turns, darting out of sight.

Or *maybe she is.*

I try to hurry after her, but my leg slows me down so much she's long gone by the time I get out into the hallway.

Dr. Benefield may have let me lose the crutches, but I would probably still get smoked by a turtle.

I head back upstairs to the Cardiology wing, the elevator moving frustratingly slowly. When the doors slide open, I limp my way over to the waiting room I once found her in, my heart hammering noisily in my chest.

Only it's empty. Not a single trace of her backpack or her yellow notebook or the book she was reading a few days ago. Nothing.

I let out a long exhale and plop into one of the chairs.

I sit there for a long moment, listening to the hum of the TV across the room, the sound of a nurse's squeaking shoes moving down the hallway.

She was watching me.

She didn't say anything, but she was there. Standing in the

doorway of the physical therapy room. If she thought I was crazy, she never would've come looking for me. Right?

Sighing, I head back to my room and collapse onto my bed, my leg aching from all this running around. I look over as water loudly batters the window, then cuts off completely in the next second. It reappears a moment later.

The sprinklers in the courtyard. Where I saw her the first time. I'm up and moving before the spray returns.

I limp as fast as I can down the long hallway and slip quietly through the exit door when I see the nurse on duty caught up in a conversation down the hall. The late-summer air feels warm and sticky. Humid. The sweet aroma of the flowers lining the path fills the air.

The daylight is fading, and lampposts have flicked on, giving off a warm yellow glow, so much softer than the fluorescent lights of the hospital.

I zero in on a figure with long hair plucking snails out from under drenched greenery and moving them onto a stone ledge. I hesitate before cautiously walking over, smiling as I see the look of concentration on her face. It feels like déjà vu. A memory come to life.

"I remember the first time I saw you do this," I say. She doesn't look up. "It rained on us at our spot by the pond, and on the way to the car, you stopped to pick up every snail on the path. You were afraid someone would step on them."

She just keeps picking them up and moving them, over and over again, as if she can't hear me.

"That was one of the first moments I knew I was in trouble," I say, remembering how she had all the patience in the world to get each and every snail. "I'd never met anyone quite like you before, Marley. I still haven't."

I keep trying. "You said once that you like talking around me. So . . . *talk* to me. It can be about anything. Just talk to me."

She carefully moves the next snail out of harm's way, but as she does, I see the pink sapphire necklace around her neck, the jewel glimmering in the dim light. I almost forget where I am as understanding hits me.

Laura.

Is that why she isn't talking to me, too? Maybe . . . maybe *this* Marley is still hurting.

I open my mouth to say something, but I don't want to push too far. That Marley had to be ready on her own. This Marley does too.

So, not knowing what else to do, I bend over and pick up a snail, moving it out of harm's way while I just stay with her in the silence. Waiting. Hoping she'll talk to me when she's ready.

40

Marley's MOM has off on Wednesdays and Thursdays, so I try to fill my time until Friday with as many distractions as possible.

I go to breakfast in the mornings with my mom before she goes to work, and physical therapy in the afternoons to work on my leg strength, then right into spending my evenings with Kim and Sam until it's time to close my eyes again.

On the bright side, her mom having off gives me two whole days to plan my final attempt at breaking down the wall between me and Marley.

Thursday night, Kim and Sam come over with pizza, and the three of us half watch a rerun of *Parks and Recreation*. I'm staring at my laptop, Sam is staring at Kim, and Kim is . . . I look up when she nudges my knee, quickly slamming my laptop shut in surprise.

Jumpy much?

I laugh at my overreaction and send her a quick grin before turning my attention back to the TV and acting like I haven't already seen the "Li'l Sebastian" episode eight times. From my periphery, I see her narrow her eyes at me.

She *definitely* knows I'm up to something, but she won't ask me about it with Sam here.

It feels weird not to have told him yet, but after the incident two weeks ago, I didn't want to jump the gun and tell him anything too soon in case it all turns out to be another disappointment.

I smile to myself, watching the two of them try not to look at each other.

I remember one of my first couple of times at the park with Marley. The way we kept glancing at each other, some unstoppable force moving between us. I can still see her shy smile when we caught eyes, even for just a second.

I reach out, my fingers drumming impatiently on my laptop.

"Well," Kim says when the episode ends, dusting the pizza crumbs off her leggings. "We better get going."

She gives Sam a sweet smile. "Want to walk me to my car?"

I've never seen that dude move faster. Not even in a championship game. He's on his feet and ready to go in under a quarter of a second flat.

"See you guys later," I say, quickly throwing open my laptop the second the door clicks shut.

Luckily, my cart hasn't timed out yet. I click through the prompts and place my order, a green checkmark appearing on my screen.

This is it. My last hope.

＊ ＊ ＊

Three days later, I sit down on a bench in the garden a little before lunchtime, watching the petals of the cherry tree tumble slowly down to the ground. A slight puff of mist wafts over my face from the fountain, and when I look over, my eyes land on a familiar silhouette, sitting on the ledge, long brown hair falling around her face as she looks at her reflection in the water.

Marley. Here to eat her lunch by the fountain, right on time.

I stand and walk carefully over, looking down to see my face reflected next to hers, just like it was that day at the pond.

She closes her eyes and ducks her head, and I wonder if it's seeing us side by side that is freaking her out. It feels a little surreal to me, too.

"I just have one more thing to say, and then if you want me to, I'll walk away," I say, watching as tiny droplets ripple across the water. "I'm trying . . . not to be such a control freak anymore. So if it's what you want, I'll leave you alone. I promise."

I take a deep breath, collecting myself, and start in on the words I've finally found. I don't know if they're the right ones, but they're mine. "Of all the sleeping people you could have talked to in that hospital, you chose me," I say. "I have to believe it was for a reason. The same reason that I couldn't help but hear you, Marley."

I turn to look at her, taking in her profile. The freckles on her nose. The circles around her eyes, the bright hazel I remember, still tired, dulled. I want to take this weight from her, but she has to give it to me. I know that now. "We were meant to find each other. And now here we are. Together, but . . . not."

I think of the two of us tumbling onto the grass at the park, the kite drifting away. Of our kiss under the mistletoe at the Winter Festival, Marley's cheeks a deep, rosy red from the cold. How it felt to just hold her hand, her fingers enclosed safely in mine.

"There was a place where I loved you, a place you built with your words, and the happiness we shared was as real as anything here in the real world," I say, my heart beating unsteadily in my chest. "We knew each other there. Because we talked to each other. We told each other everything. And I fell in love with you—the heart of you. The you in your stories. That Marley—you couldn't have just made her up. I'm ready to start our story over, at the very beginning, if you'll just give me a chance to make you happy."

I notice tears welling up in her eyes, see her breathing through it, fighting them off.

I want to know what's going on in her head, why she's fighting so hard. Why she's hiding.

She takes a deep breath, her chest rising and falling.

Finally she whispers a single word.

"No."

I'm so ecstatic just to hear her voice again that I almost don't register the meaning. Then my lungs collapse in on themselves, that one word pushing all the air out of me.

"I can't," she adds, her voice scratchy, barely audible. "I can't be happy."

Her words from that last night come back to me all at once.

We were never meant to be this happy.

"Why not?" I ask, trying to keep my voice steady, as if my whole world isn't riding on this moment.

"If you really know me," she says, still staring at her reflection, "then you know why not."

"Laura."

The thing that pulls her away from me each time she gets close.

"I understand how hard her loss must be, believe me, but, Marley—"

"She died because of me!" she says, her voice cracking. "I saw that car. I saw it and I couldn't move. I didn't save her. I didn't even *try*." She sucks in a long breath, continuing. "Laura would have saved me. She would have . . ."

She stops and fights the tears back again.

"Then wouldn't Laura save you now?" I ask her, leaning closer, desperate to make her see. "Wouldn't she tell you to be happy—"

"I don't get to be happy. I don't get to cry and feel bad about Laura, because I'm the reason she can't feel *anything*," she says, frustrated, heartbroken. "So I can't love you, Kyle. I won't."

Those words bounce around inside my head. *I can't love you, Kyle. I won't.* She said my name like she's said it a thousand times before, like she *knows* me. Like . . . she already loves me. Because how can she say she *won't* love me if she doesn't already want to?

That's when I realize that her fingers are clenched tightly around mine. The feeling is so familiar to me that I don't even know when she grabbed me. I just know that her hand is in mine.

I turn my palm up, twine my fingers with hers, and I silently plead with the universe to let this work. Please, please, please let this work.

"I traveled many roads to find this lost treasure, this piece of me," I say softly.

She looks up, startled, as I reach into my pocket.

"But it was you who found it and returned it to me," I say as I hold up my hand, palm up between us, fingers closed around something. "Now I wish to give it to you."

Marley looks from my hand up to my face, questioning. She looks down again as I slowly unfurl my fingers.

Nestled there in the center is one perfect snow-white pearl.

I hear Marley's sharp intake of breath as I lift her hand and gently place the pearl in her palm. It's too much. Her lip quivers, and the dam breaks. Tears she's held in for years finally rush out. I wrap my arms around her as her shoulders heave, and she buries her face into my chest.

I sit there, holding her, letting her cry. I keep her safe while she feels the pain she's never let herself feel.

After, we sit under the cherry blossom tree, her eyes still red and puffy.

She plucks little flowers from between the strands of grass, dozens of tiny blooms littering the ground around us.

"I don't know what to do now," she says as her hair falls in front of her face, still shielding her in some small way from me and everyone else.

My hand brushes lightly against hers, that magnetic pull between us suddenly alive again. Somehow stronger than it's ever been. "We'll figure it out as we go," I say, her hazel eyes shifting up to meet mine. "I've waited all this time for you. The slower we take it, the longer it lasts."

I reach up to tuck a yellow Doris Day behind her ear. "And I'm okay with that."

The smallest trace of a shy smile lets me know she's okay with that too.

41

The next evening we meet up in the Cardiology waiting room, and Marley hands over her yellow notebook of stories.

It's so cool to see the story that she wrote for us, a world that I actually lived in for an entire year, here on paper. I see the places my brain filled in the gaps, building, making real memories from every one of her sentences.

I tell her about those moments. How I thought Kim had died in the accident. How I almost lost my mind trying to cook my mom's béarnaise sauce. How I got into a fight with Sam at one of our Saturday touch football games.

I laugh as I read a few paragraphs about a time we fed the ducks at the pond, a big brown-and-white one almost taking my finger off while Marley laughed in amusement. I look over at her sitting on the opposite side of the couch from me, taking in the small smile on her face. The same girl I fell in love with.

Real.

I study the dark circles around her eyes, the curtain of hair hiding her from the rest of the world. Her sadness is heavier now than it was in my dream because she lets me see it all. She doesn't hide behind her words, writing about the person she so desperately wants to be. Sometimes the darkness completely overtakes her, but I can see the Marley I know hiding just inside the shadows, fighting her way out.

I grew in the dream world. But I think she did too.

"This duck that almost bit my finger off . . . it was the same one that chased me that one time, wasn't it?"

Marley's lips tug up at the corners. "He didn't stop until you gave him the rest of your popcorn." Her leg lightly brushes against mine as she shifts her position, my heart skipping a beat. "That duck was always my favorite."

"Of course it was." I laugh, nudging her.

"Did you write it all down?" I ask, pointing to the page in front of me. "Everything you said to me?"

She nods, her finger lightly tracing the top of the notebook. "I tried to. Sometimes I would just start talking and the story would come flowing out. I didn't even have time to write it."

"What did you say about the first time we met?" I ask, flipping back to the beginning, thinking about the moment. I've been so busy jumping around looking for certain memories, I didn't even start on the first page. "He looked like a complete wreck? Garbage on two legs?"

Marley laughs and shakes her head, the look in her hazel

eyes making me melt. "I definitely didn't say that."

I smile to myself as I turn my attention back to her notebook, her words jumping off the page at me.

She saw him and she knew. She knew that he would understand.

The next day, I scroll slowly through another page of rescue dogs, trying my best to focus on the floofy Alaskan malamute or the stocky bulldog, but Marley's arm resting up against mine is all I can think about.

That and the fact that we're shoulder to shoulder in my tiny hospital bed, her face *literally* inches from mine. I force the thought out of my head.

We're taking things slow. Pull it together, Lafferty.

I stop my scrolling, pointing to a silver Yorkie rescue.

Marley sits up and grabs the iPad, her eyes widening as she flips through the photos. "Oh my God. It's her. It's Georgia!"

And sure enough, it is her. Down to the markings on her paws. "You like her?" I ask, looking over her shoulder at the page.

"Oh." She stops, leaning back, deflating like a balloon. I catch sight of a red box in the corner of the photo. ADOPTED. "Someone already got her."

"Oh well," I say, shrugging at the letdown. "Maybe she'll go to a good home."

Marley rolls her eyes at me, just like she would have before, and . . . it feels like we were never apart. Suddenly the electricity crackles between us, exactly how I remember. I can feel the both of us leaning forward ever so slightly.

She hesitates, tentatively reaching up to brush my hair back, lightly touching my scar, her fingertips gentle as they linger on my cheek, my mouth, tracing my lips, her touch familiar and new all at the same time.

I hold my breath as she leans farther in, our lips *almost* touching, when the door swings wide open.

"Oh shit, sorry," Kim says from the doorway.

Marley and I quickly jump apart. "Early," I say, letting out a groan. "You're early."

I look from Kim to Marley, her alarmed gaze turning to shock when she sees what Kim's holding. The silver Yorkie from the animal rescue website is cradled in Kim's arms. The second the pup sees Marley, she starts yipping like crazy.

She looks just like her picture, only cuter, a tiny yellow bow tied around her neck.

I'd spent the entire afternoon trying to get it just right before Kim nudged me out of the way, declaring she hadn't done cheerleading for ten years to stand by when somebody butchers a bow.

"Oh man, I ruined it, didn't I? Shit. I'm so sorry," Kim says as she quickly closes the door before we can get in trouble, the puppy letting out a tiny bark. "Hey, Marley, I'm—"

"Georgia," Marley whispers.

"Well, okay. Yeah," Kim says, taken aback. She pauses, squinting as she fully processes that's not her name. "I mean—no . . ."

I roll my eyes, shaking my head at her. In all the years I've known her, I've never seen her so nervous.

It's kind of sweet, to be honest.

I smile and motion to the dog, and she comes to, collecting herself.

She turns to look at Marley, taking her in. "I'm Kimberly," she says, clarifying that her name is not, in fact, Georgia.

Marley smiles shyly, pushing her hair behind her ear. "I know." She looks between the two of us anxiously.

And Kim, still not knowing what to do, looks back over at me. So I point to the Yorkie puppy, loudly whispering, "Give it to her."

"Oh, right! Yeah." She holds up the dog. "She's for you."

Marley looks over at me, her hazel eyes filled with wonder.

Kim puts Georgia down on the bed, the tiny puppy clamoring over Marley's legs to get to her. Marley sniffs, wiping away a tear.

"Oh man," Kim says, super bummed. "That was a terrible surprise. I really botched it. I'm so sorry—"

Suddenly Marley's hand reaches past me, taking Kim's. "It's perfect," she says as Georgia tumbles into her lap, all wiggles and puppy kisses. "Thank you."

Kim lets out a long sigh, finally relaxing. She smiles and looks down at Marley's hand in hers. "I'm happy to finally meet you."

"I'm happy . . . that you're alive," Marley says awkwardly.

There's a long beat, and then Kim and I absolutely lose it, tears streaming down our faces as we laugh. Bashful, Marley joins in after a pause, and little Georgia, not wanting to be left out, lets out a *"Yip!"*

I wrap my arms around Marley, so in love. I'm not ever going to let her go again.

Suddenly there's a knock at the door, and we all look up to see my mom and Sam, frozen in the doorway, both with absolutely no idea what they just walked in on.

I feel Marley fidget, pulling away from me, her eyes wary. This is a lot of people, all at one time. She starts to stand up, but I put a hand lightly on her arm, calming her.

"It's okay," I whisper. Her eyes meet mine, the tension slowly ebbing. She settles down and looks over at my mom and Sam, but stays quiet.

"Mom, Sam," I say, a thousand-watt grin on my face. "Meet Marley."

You'd think I just told them exactly what goes down in Area 51. They stand there, staring, for ten whole seconds. Then my mom squeals, running to the bed.

I hold out my arms, trying to stop her, but it's no use. She throws her arms around Marley, who looks helplessly over at me, then at Kim, who shrugs in a way that says, *Deal with it, girl.*

Then, unexpectedly, Marley's arms wrap around her, too.

I look over at Sam, still collecting himself in the doorway. He ruefully shakes his head at me, giving me one of his lopsided smiles. "You really are the luckiest son of a bitch—"

"Sam!" my mom says, pulling away from Marley to scold him.

He flinches. "Sorry, Mrs. L."

My mom stares him down for a long moment, then . . . Marley begins to laugh. It's infectious, working its way around the room until we're all doubled over, a new memory forming, real and wonderful.

42

Early the next morning, I look through my phone at the pictures I took yesterday. Georgia being cute as hell, running around all of us in the courtyard. Sam and Kim laughing as they sit at the edge of the fountain. And finally a picture of just Marley, the only one I have. A yellow rose is tucked behind her ear, little Georgia snoozing in her lap.

She isn't quite smiling, but she's beautiful.

There's a quiet knock on my door, and I look up as it opens, surprised to see Marley's mom standing in the doorway, not wearing a pair of scrubs. She gives me a long look before finally clearing her throat and speaking. "She told me what you did."

My eyes flick to the calendar pinned to the wall under my TV, and I see it's a Wednesday. She's supposed to have off today.

Uh-oh.

She walks to my bed, her eyebrows jutting down in the same way Marley's do when she's upset.

"I'm sorry," I say, sitting up. "I—"

"She *told* me," she says, her voice breaking. "It's been years . . . To hear her voice again . . . Thank you."

She hugs me, and I feel a wave of relief that she isn't here to tell me she is deathly allergic to dogs or to stay away from Marley with my dream nonsense. Mostly, though, I'm happy that Marley spoke to her. "Uh," I say as she pulls away, wiping her tears. "Does that mean you're not mad about the dog?"

She laughs, shaking her head. "It'd be pretty hard to be mad about something that cute."

An hour later, the whole crew comes over, my mom, Kimberly, and Sam crashing into my room, bringing bagels from the shop near school. They sprawl out across every available inch of space, and it's still not enough. Sam ducks out of the room, rolling back in a few seconds later on an unused office chair from the nurses' station.

I'm just starting to dig into my everything bagel with cream cheese when there's a knock on the door and Dr. Benefield strolls in. "Perfect. The gang's all here," she says, pushing her glasses up onto her head. "How do you feel about giving us back that bed? We can get you out of here in the next couple of days."

I nearly break my neck nodding yes.

I glance to the side to see Kim practically bouncing from happiness. I'm nervous she's excited enough to bust out an entire floor routine right here, right now.

"Wonderful! First things first, we need to plan a dinner. With Marley," my mom says, already making plans. "And I'll try to settle down. I won't, you know, be myself. I don't want to be too much too soon—"

I stop her, shaking my head. "Be yourself, Mom. You're great."

She gives me a big hug, kissing my head, just under the scar. Her face grows somber. "I'm sorry I didn't believe you."

I grin at her, shrugging. "I probably wouldn't have believed me either."

My mom turns to Kimberly, beaming at her. "And *you*, you little sneak."

"Smuggling a puppy into a hospital is pretty badass," Sam says proudly, freezing when Dr. Benefield raises her eyebrows in surprise.

"I'm not going to ask," she says as she turns her attention back to me, a knowing smile on her face. "It's all anyone's talking about this morning," she says, nodding toward the door. "I guess dreams do come true."

I smile back at her. They really do.

43

The next day, Sam swings by in the afternoon, and the two of us stroll through the courtyard. His normally long strides are only a little bit cut short by my limp as the two of us slowly make our way toward the oak tree.

I pause, snapping a picture of the yellow Doris Days, adding in a HELLO before sending it over to Marley.

"Oh my God, dude, you've got it so bad."

I grin at him, shrugging. "I do. Don't you?"

But Sam doesn't take the bait. Instead he pretends to hold up a phone, mimicking my selfie face.

I shove him playfully as my cell phone buzzes noisily in my back pocket. I grab it, accepting the call, fending off Sam while he tries to get to the phone.

"Hello. Hi. Hey," I say as I wrestle him away. "What are you doing?"

"I'm at the park," Marley says, her voice coming in softly through the speaker. "Playing with Georgia."

"Can I see?" I ask, elbowing Sam again before he can say something stupid into the phone.

"Uh . . . ," she says, hesitating.

"It's okay. You don't have to—"

"No, it's fine," she says, and the call switches to FaceTime, her face appearing in front of the tall trees and grass of the park. She went to the cemetery to talk to Laura this morning and she seems to be holding it together. I study her face as she tucks her hair behind her ear.

It looks like it went well. I want to ask her about it, but . . .

Sam.

His head pops into the frame and he grins at her, waving. I shove him out of the way, smiling. "Ignore Sam," I say as Sam pouts, peering at the screen, comfortably out of view. "What's she doing? Lemme see."

Marley flips the camera to show a few kids playing with Georgia in the grass by the park path, the tiny pup chasing after a tennis ball that's way too big for her mouth.

"They're so sweet," Marley says offscreen as one of the kids scoops it up and they begin to play monkey in the middle. Georgia's tongue lolls out as she zooms back and forth between them.

"Look at her go," I say, realizing how much I missed that little ball of energy. "Are you there by yourself?"

The camera turns and her face reappears, her hazel-green eyes glowing in the afternoon sun. "Mom's here with me. She's feeding the ducks," she says, a small knowing look passing between us. "Popcorn," we say at the same time.

"Speaking of moms," I say, casually segueing into it. "Just something for you to start thinking about. No rush, of course," I quickly clarify. I'm still not quite sure what's too much too soon. "My mom really wants to have dinner with you and . . ."

I stop, watching as she looks quickly offscreen, her eyes widening in horror, but not over the dinner prospect.

"Georgia!" she says, and the phone drops from her face. I see for a fraction of a second the ball bouncing toward the road on the other side of the path and Georgia bolting after it. Marley sprints after her.

"Marley! What're you doing?" I yell, the scenery blurring around her legs, the phone still in her hand as she runs.

A familiar icy panic courses through my veins.

Then, abruptly, the motion stops and the camera swings up to show Marley at the edge of the path, the street behind her, Georgia tucked safely in her arms. "I got her. We almost lost our girl—"

But behind her, I see the ball in the middle of the road and a little kid running toward it.

"Joey, look out!" a voice screams from somewhere out of view.

Marley's head whips around to look behind her at the little boy. Her eyes turn back to me for a fraction of a second, the look in them filling me with dread.

I know exactly what she's going to do before she does it.

"No!" I shout, trying to stop her. "Mar—"

The phone falls from her hands, and the screen fills completely with green as it tumbles into the grass. I hear the squeal of tires, then the sound of screams from the kids.

"Marley!" I scream, feeling helpless. "Marley!"

I hobble back inside as quickly as I can, hating this slow fucking leg. Sam's already run ahead of me. As soon as I get inside, I'm forced into a wheelchair. Sam leans over me, right in my face. "Stop yelling, Kyle." Am I yelling? My throat feels hoarse. Dry. Yes, I'm definitely yelling. But I can't stop. Marley needs help. I need to get help. I fight the hands that keep me in the chair, but before I can push myself up again, I feel the prick of a needle and everything goes dark.

44

I jolt awake in my hospital bed, still screaming her name. "No!
Marley—"

Hands grab on to my arms, and I look up to see Kimberly, my
mom, Sam, all of them blocking my path.

"Kyle," Kimberly says, trying to stop me from getting out of
bed, but I slip out of her grip, struggling to walk, my leg aching.
"Hold on. Wait. *Kyle.*"

I have to get to her. I have to get to Marley. No more waiting.
Not again.

I slide past Kim as my mom runs to the door, calling for help.
Sam kicks a chair out of my way a split second before I crash into
it. I've almost made it into the hallway when a nurse steps inside,
blocking my way, a syringe in her hand.

"Do I need to sedate you again?" she asks.

"Where is she?" I ask, frantically spinning around to look at all of them, my eyes meeting theirs one by one. "Where is she? Where . . . ?"

This can't be happening again.

I'm steered into a chair and Kimberly kneels in front of me, grabbing ahold of my hand.

"Stop."

I stare at her earnest expression, angry. Why is everyone telling me to wait? Why are they here with me when we should all be with her?

"I need you to listen to me."

I fight the impulse to run, zeroing in on her blue eyes, trying to collect myself. I nod impatiently for her to continue.

"She saved the kid. She saved him and she's alive, but . . ."

"We don't know for how long," a voice says from the door. I whip my head around to see Dr. Benefield, her face serious, a scrub cap in one of her hands. Our eyes meet, and she nods toward the hallway. "Come with me."

I follow after her, everything a blur. The bright lights, the white tile, and the pale walls all morphing together. I hear Kim's and Sam's and my mom's footsteps trailing closely behind us.

She stops short at a door, looking back at me before she reaches out and slowly opens it.

I step inside, afraid to look. Afraid to see Marley hurt. Dying.

Her mom sits at her bedside, her eyes fixed to the heart rate monitor, like she's personally keeping it going with pure willpower. The steady *beep, beep, beep* is the only sound in the entire room.

I swallow, forcing myself to look from Catherine to the bed, my legs feeling like they're going to give out. She looks so small. Battered. I clench my jaw as my eyes trace every bruise and scrape on her body, working their way up to the bandage wrapped around her head, her eyes tightly shut.

"I'm sorry," I manage to get out, her mom turning her head to look at me. *Georgia.* "It was my fault—"

Catherine shakes her head, grabbing my hand. "No. None of that. That's how we got here," she says, giving my fingers a tight squeeze. "Don't do that to yourself."

Her gaze slides from my face to the monitor, focusing on the steady thumping in Marley's chest.

"She's going to wake up, right?" I ask, taking a step toward the bed, afraid to hear the answer.

"It's up to her," Dr. Benefield says from behind me. "She should already be awake."

What? Then why isn't she?

I look over at her, confusion painted on my face.

"She hit her head, but the bleed was light and the scans don't show any sign of massive trauma," Dr. Benefield says, pushing her glasses up onto her head, her eyes sad. "She should be waking up, but it seems she doesn't want to."

Catherine begins to sob next to me, her hand pulling away from mine to cover her face.

"Sometimes the choice to live or die is up to us," Dr. Benefield says, looking from me to the bed. "Marley's not fighting."

The choice to live or die. I see the dark shadows under her eyes, her words ringing loudly in my head.

She died because of me.

I don't get to be happy.

Laura.

But I also hear the other voices. The things I heard while I was asleep that made me keep fighting, that pulled me through.

Don't let go.

Always forward. Never back.

I take a step toward her, knowing I sure as hell won't let Marley go this easily. This is not how her story ends. It can't be.

I take her hand. Her fingers feel cool in mine, limp, like she's already gone.

"I won't let you leave me," I whisper. "I told you no more sad stories. That goes both ways, you know." I try to joke, but my laugh comes out as a garbled choking sound. I squeeze my hand tighter around hers, trying to warm those cold fingers.

How did she do this? What did she . . . ? Ah. Yes. I hear her words that first day at the cemetery.

I lean close, my lips against her ear.

"Once upon a time there was a girl who was sad and alone."

An electric jolt zings through me. Maybe, just maybe, I can do this. Maybe I can make her hear me. Believe me.

"She told stories. Happy stories," I say as I imagine that worn yellow notebook full of her writing, not knowing where the fairy tales ended and our memories began. It doesn't matter, though. It was all real to me, every page a part of my life with her.

I won't give up until I get it back, get *her* back, and I know that starts *here.*

"But for herself she only told the same sad story, over and over again."

Marley hasn't moved. No flutter of lids, no twitch of fingers, nothing. Instead, I take my cue from the steady beeping of the monitor, urging me to continue.

"Until she met a boy. They found each other when they thought their stories were at an end. But they started writing a new one, and for the first time in a long time, the girl allowed her story to be a happy one. Her story with him. And he promised her . . . he would never let her go."

Another tingle of electricity skitters along my forehead, right down the length of my scar. Her fingers give the barest twitch in mine—or is that wishful thinking?

I think of the man in the moon, the wishes the girl made for her love. So I close my eyes and let the story carry me to her, to the girl I know is waiting for me, lost somewhere in a story that is ours and ours alone.

Suddenly, behind my closed lids, I see the ducks quacking loudly at my feet, waddling down the path to perch under the cherry tree with its falling petals. I look around. It's *our* world, Marley's and mine, but it holds a different hue now, as if covered by a dark-blue gauze. The air is ominous, heavy. My heart thumps in my chest. This doesn't feel right. This isn't our story, not the one we were building together.

Where is Marley? I need to find her. Now.

I run up the path that will take me to the cemetery. That's where I'll find her, at Laura's grave, where we first met.

I see a field of pink Stargazers in the distance, the sight pushing me forward. I haul ass, some part of me knowing that I can't really run this fast, not with my leg, but here, in this world, I am whole. My legs churn, faster now, as they carry me toward that sea of endless pink, extending far past the boundaries of Laura's plot.

"Marley!" I race headlong into the wild wave of Stargazers.

I push aside the flowers, searching. She's not here. But . . . she has to be. It's the only place she would go.

I keep charging through the pink lilies, calling frantically for Marley, until suddenly I burst out the other side of the flower field. *Where am I?* It's darker here, grayer, a thick, roiling mist clinging to the ground. It's the cemetery, but . . . different.

That's when I spot it, that bare gravestone, lonely and desolate, pronouncing that one aching word: GOODBYE.

God, I remember this grave. It broke my heart when I saw it, so much so that I placed a single flower upon its stone. I blink, unsure if my eyes are playing tricks on me.

That flower is still there, exactly where I left it.

I move closer to pick it up. Sorrow settles on me like a dark cloud. Almost instantly I'm filled with it, the raw emptiness of loss as I stare at the flower.

Then I hear it. A sniffle. A tiny broken cry. Marley.

She's hunched over. Her back is resting against the single word inscribed on the stone.

GOODBYE.

Realization floods me. This isn't just any sad gravestone. It's *Marley's* gravestone. Every time we walked by it, smiling and laughing, it was right here, *waiting* for her. *Taunting* her. And I had no idea.

No! I drop to my knees in front of her, determined to make her hear me.

"Not like this, Marley," I tell her. "This is not your fate. This is not the end of your story."

My arms reach for her, but she pulls away.

"Just leave me alone."

"No. I won't. You invited me into the most secret places inside of you, and, Marley, this is not it. This place, this *you*, is a lie. I know the real you. It doesn't look like this."

As I speak, the world around us seems to listen, to take up the story I'm telling. The sky fights off the dark, growing lighter above us. Green explodes from the ground beneath our feet, rich verdant grass that sweeps past us to cover the whole cemetery. Flowers sprout and bloom. Our world again.

"*This* is our story, Marley. This is where you belong. In our place, the one we built together," I say, so sure I'm getting through to her.

I pull her close, and for a moment she leans her sweet head against me, her jasmine scent tickling my nose. *Yes.*

Then she says softly, brokenly, "I wasn't meant for that world."

What? I cup my hand under her chin, pull her face up to mine, and say the words that I know to be truer than any others: "You were meant for *me*. Come back with me. Let me show you where our story can go. . . ."

Images appear around us like snapshots:

A college graduation, Marley throwing her cap and grinning wildly.

Me and Marley running down the aisle, the train of her wedding gown trailing behind us.

Marley at a book signing, a line of excited kids waiting to meet her.

Us in a baby's room. Marley rocking our newborn daughter to sleep.

More images flash and pop. Kids growing up. Birthday parties. Backyard barbecues. School plays. Football games.

Marley's eyes take them all in, hope in her gaze. *Hope.* I can work with that.

"Those are memories just waiting to be made," I promise her. "You created that dark place because you think it's what you deserve. It's not, Marley. You deserve a good life. A happy life. I promise to try every day to give that to you, to build that *with* you, together."

I lean in, leaving just a breath of space between us. Will she close the gap? It's up to her. I shut my eyes and wait, hoping and praying that she's heard me. That's when I feel her lips on mine. Relief makes me weak.

I kiss her back, then open my eyes, surprised to find she's crying, tears rolling down her cheeks.

"Marley? What's—"

A light rises behind me. I feel its warmth through my shirt as it washes over Marley's face. She stares into the light, a sob escaping her lips.

Dread creeps up the back of my neck as I turn to see what Marley sees.

There, standing right in front of that vast field of Stargazer lilies, is Laura.

She's backlit by some otherworldly light, standing in a glowing circle, like the sun during an eclipse. She raises her hand as if reaching for something. With a sinking feeling, I know exactly what she's reaching for.

Marley.

Marley pulls herself from my arms.

"No. Marley, no. Don't do this," I beg, the breath leaving my lungs in a plea. "Please, Marley. Stay."

She looks up at me, the green in her eyes lighting up the hazel like fireworks. I stare, trying to memorize her face, her eyes, because I'm so afraid this is the last time I'm going to see her.

She knows what I'm thinking. Her fingers trace my scar, my brow, my cheek, and come to rest against my lips.

"I love you, Kyle Lafferty," she whispers fervently. "I will love you forever. Our story will live on forever."

She presses her lips to mine, then says, "But I need to do this."

She pulls away from me again.

"No!" I try to run after her, but my feet won't obey. I watch helplessly as she walks toward Laura.

"Marley, stop. You *don't* have to do this. Stay with me! Marley!"

My words come out in harsh, broken sobs. She gets closer to Laura and takes her outstretched hand. I want to close my eyes so I don't have to see her go, but I can't. If this is my last moment with her, I want my eyes to be open. I want to see it.

Marley looks back at me, tears flowing from her eyes, as if she can hear my heart breaking. But then she looks to Laura, who wraps an arm around her waist.

Marley, my Marley, gives me one last smile . . . then follows Laura into the lilies.

"No!" The cry that comes from my throat sounds inhuman.

My shout echoes around me until it becomes the sound of the beeping hospital monitor. I'm there, at Marley's bedside, my hand around hers. I look at everyone, all of them waiting desperately for some good news, but I have none to give.

"She's not . . . she's not coming back."

"No." Catherine hurries to the bed, runs her hands along Marley's face. "Marley, baby. You wake up right now."

But the girl in the bed doesn't move.

Kimberly covers her mouth and presses her head against Sam's shoulder, both of them looking at me with so much pity and love that I have to turn away.

I feel Mom's hand on my shoulder, offering me any strength she can lend me.

And the monitor *beeps . . . beeps . . . beeeeeeeeps. . . .*

Flatline.

Catherine's anguished scream rips through us all, the sound finding a home in the shattered remnants of my heart.

Marley. Gone.

Dr. Benefield shoves us all away from the bed as she starts to call the code blue. But . . . she hesitates. Catherine yells, "Do something! You have to—"

Dr. Benefield holds up her hand in a gesture so sure and confident that we all freeze. She nods toward the bed, toward Marley's hand . . .

. . . where the fingertip monitor now lies in Marley's palm, her fingers closing around it as we watch in disbelief. My eyes fly to her face, afraid to hope.

Then her lids flutter and open, those beautiful hazel eyes searching for and finding mine.

"I had to say goodbye. To Laura."

My knees buckle and I collapse onto her bed.

Catherine smothers her face with kisses. Marley gives her a long look. "I'm back, Mom. I'm back."

Everyone in the room loses it. Even Dr. Benefield. The tough doctor turns away to wipe her eyes. I would laugh if I had any room inside me to feel anything but relief and gratitude.

Marley turns to me, and I memorize all of those features I was afraid I'd never see again. She takes my hand. "I had to say goodbye to my life with Laura . . . before I could start my life with you."

Her life with me. No words have ever been sweeter. I kiss her cheeks, her nose, each tiny freckle precious to me. The soft jasmine scent of her skin makes me dizzy. *She's here. She's really here.* My lips move lower to hover over hers, and just before they meet, I thank every higher being that ever lit up the sky for this second chance.

Marley closes the distance and kisses me. It's the world's most perfect kiss.

"Thank you," I whisper. "Thank you for not letting go."

Her fingers flutter in my hair, down the back of my neck, as she says, "Thank you for our story."

"Our story. What happens next, then?" I tease her, still unable to process my own joy.

She looks at me like I've just asked the dumbest question ever. "We live happily ever after," she answers. "Obviously."

I laugh. "Just like one of your fairy tales?" I ask.

She smiles that sweet, shy smile that I love so much and brushes her lips against my ear as she whispers, "Yes. Just like that."

Her lips pull me in again, and I'm overwhelmed by everything that's happened, from the shriek of twisting metal to the look in Marley's hazel eyes the first time I told her I loved her. My breath catches in my throat, knowing this won't be the last time I see that look. We'll have a million more moments like this one, an entire story to live together.

Starting now.

A Note from Mikki

I was told once to stop believing in fairy tales. I was told that only dreamers keep their heads in the clouds and their eyes on the stars. I was told that true love was only for books and movies, that life would teach me that none of these things exist in the real world.

They could not have been more wrong.

My belief in fairy tales and true love sustains me; it keeps me alive in a world that doesn't always welcome dreamers, and while my feet never leave the ground, my gaze is forever on the sky above and the universe beyond.

Like most of my stories, *All This Time* came to me from a place deep inside myself, a place I inhabit when I'm living in my heart instead of my head. It's a place of magic and dreams and wild illusions, where my stories come alive and my characters talk to me in voices clear and bright.

This place, this inner world, is my reality. It's where I belong and it's where I thrive. In this place, I've known my Marley; I've loved my Marley. I've loved Kyle. I've met Will and Stella, Poe and Barb. I've loved them, too. So much. I've known true love and true heartache. These are the things that make life worth living, the things that make stories worth telling.

The choice to fashion *All This Time* into a kind of fairy tale was an easy one. Like Marley tells Kyle, we live our lives telling stories, creating them as we go. Sometimes these stories are small, everyday moments: folding laundry with our parents, feeding popcorn to ducks beside a tranquil pond.

Sometimes the stories are so big they consume our imaginations and our hearts: The Man in the Moon who smiles down upon the girl who wishes for love. A boy who meets his true love in a coma and wakes with a mission to find that girl and live happily ever after.

I believe in all these things. The Man in the Moon? He's up there. I know he is. The thought that two people can connect in a world made of stories and dreams and somehow find their soul mate? It can happen. I'm sure of it. These ideas, these notions, are as true to me as the green grass, the blue sky, and the air we breathe.

Call me crazy. Call me delusional. Call me a dreamer. I'm okay with that. I'm just thankful that you've chosen to meet me here, in my world, and have allowed me to share my stories with you, because I will always believe in fairy tales. I will always believe in true love. Just try and stop me.

Acknowledgments

As writers, we start with an idea—a seed. We plant that seed into the fertile soil of our imaginations. We warm it with the sunshine of commitment and water it with love and patience. Then we let it sprout and grow, cheering as it blossoms into its own unique being.

What's not always acknowledged are the army of gardeners and gatekeepers who stand ready to wrangle weeds and shoo away pests until the flower is in full bloom and ready to be shared.

To Liz Parker, my kick-ass agent and primary hand-holder. Thank you for battling the elements on my behalf. The wind and the rain could've easily twisted themselves into one hell of a tornado and uprooted all of our hard work. Thank you for bearing the brunt of the frenzy.

To Alexa Pastor, our trusted editor. Thank you for pruning, trimming, and shaping the foliage. Without your guiding hand, this garden wouldn't have evolved into the beautiful landscape it has become. Thank you!

Rachael! Rachael, Rachael, Rachael. Thank you for once again digging into the dirt with me. Lugging water and shoveling shit is hard work. I'm so glad I didn't have to do it alone. Thank you for beautifully adapting another of my screenplays into book form. Love you, lady. I really do.

To Scott Whitehead, my expert attorney, who kept the brambles of business at bay so I could focus solely on the art. Thank you for always having my back.

To my "movie" team: David Boxerbaum, Adam Kolbrenner, Sara Nestor, and all of the Verve, Lit, and MWF folks. You guys got this ball rolling years ago when you signed this green, unknown writer. Thank you, thank you, thank you for your faith and belief. I love you all.

And last but never, never least . . . to Tobias Iaconis. You are the Great Oak that shelters every garden we build. Under your protective branches, I know that I am always safe to plant and play and dream to my heart's content, because you've got me covered. Ampersand forever—&&&.

—Mikki

·· (··

Thank you, first and foremost, to my editor, Alexa Pastor, who got this team from start to finish, through rain and ice and hellfire. I am continually in awe of you! May you celebrate with a platter of pizza rolls.

To Mikki, for trusting me with *All This Time*, which has been so very close to your heart for so long. This is your story. Thanks for letting me live in it for a while.

I am beyond grateful to Justin Chanda, Julia McCarthy, and the rest of the incredible team at Simon & Schuster. I feel extremely fortunate to be able to work with such an amazing group of people.

Huge thanks to Rachel Ekstrom Courage and my agent, Emily van Beek, at Folio Literary, for all the time and care you put into me and my writing.

Also to Siobhan Vivian, for the advice, for the guidance, and for Writing Youth Literature 1 (& 2!) at the University of Pittsburgh.

To my ride-or-die, Lianna Rana, and to Ed, Judy, Mike, Luke, and Aimee, for family dinners, games of Dominion, and vacations smack in the middle of a deadline.

I am especially grateful to my mom, who has always supported me in everything I do. I love you.

And finally, to Alyson Derrick, for making happily ever after everything a girl could dream of.

—Rachael